RELEASE

ALY MARTINEZ

RELEASE

PROLOGUE

Thea

TWELVE YEARS, EIGHT MONTHS, THREE WEEKS, FOUR DAYS, twelve hours, and thirty-seven minutes.

That was how long it had been since my heart took a single beat without a searing pain piercing through my chest.

That was how long it had been since my future exploded, leaving me on my knees, lost in the wreckage.

That was how long he'd been *gone*.

I lifted my gaze from my watch as Nora's car slowed to a stop at the guard station. The corrections officer took our driver's licenses, and Nora prattled off all the usual answers about why we were there. It was the same old song and dance. One I knew well after…

Twelve years, eight months, three weeks, four days, twelve hours, and thirty-*eight* minutes.

He pressed a button to lift the metal arm and we drove around the corner to the second guard station. That was where my familiarity of the process ended.

I'd never been allowed through the second gate, despite the fact that I'd spent two hours every other week sitting in my car in the parking lot. This time was different though. Nora wasn't there for a visit. And I wasn't there to warm the chill in my veins knowing he was somewhere nearby.

1

"Breathe," Nora ordered after the guard had instructed her to follow the road around to the side of the building.

I couldn't breathe though. I could barely keep my heart beating. Vital functions were no longer involuntary but rather an arduous task that made every inhale feel like I was pushing a boulder up a mountain.

He was in there. My Ramsey, the boy who had branded my soul in ways time could never heal.

Tears flooded my vision as I imagined the seventeen-year-old with chocolate-brown eyes and shaggy hair. Ramsey didn't look like that anymore though. He was almost thirty now, but I still dreamed of him as the tall, lanky boy who had once held me in his arms and loved me with his entire being.

For us, love was the original four-letter word.

I was in fifth grade the first time we heard, "Ramsey and Thea sitting in a tree K-I-S-S-I-N-G." We were told first comes love, then marriage, then a baby in a baby carriage. No one mentioned that *love* would also be the most devastating emotion we would ever experience.

As I got older, I heard people preach that *love is patient* and *love is kind.* And I could have jumped on that train if the Bible verse didn't also contain the biggest lie of all: Love never fails.

For Ramsey, it did.

Love failed him.

I failed him.

The entire fucking world failed him.

Love was a curse. Make no mistake about it.

But Ramsey was *my* curse. And there was nothing that could change that. Not even twelve years, eight months, three weeks, four days, twelve hours, and forty, no…forty-one minutes.

RELEASE

Since the judge had banged his gavel, I'd been counting down every excruciating minute leading up to that very moment. Now that it had finally arrived, I was utterly terrified. The what-ifs of our reunion ricocheted in my head like a symphony of nightmares I couldn't escape.

I had faith though. What Ramsey and I shared was not a light switch that could be turned on or off at will. Our bond was sewn into the very fabric of our lives. Without Ramsey Stewart, there was no Thea Hull. That wasn't because of some twisted codependent obsession.

I didn't *need* him in order to breathe.

I didn't *need* him in order to smile.

I didn't *need* him in order to be happy.

But under those parameters, I didn't exactly *need* my left arm, either.

I *wanted* him beside me every morning as the first ray of the sun warmed my skin.

I *wanted* his contagious laugh echoing in my car as we drove out to the hayfield—sometimes to make out, sometimes to sit in unbelievably comfortable silence together.

I *wanted* to travel the world with him before settling down to have a family the way we had always planned.

Bits and pieces of Ramsey were intertwined in everything I'd ever wanted in life. He was my family. My best friend. The yin to my yang. The heart to my beat. But in the years since he'd been locked away, everything had been on hold. I'd grown up. Gone to college. Started my own business. But nothing was ever the same without having him there to experience it with me.

That wasn't the way it was supposed to have happened.

We were supposed to get out of Clovert, travel the world hand in hand.

Instead, we'd been forced to wait twelve years, eight months, three weeks, four days, twelve hours, and forty-two minutes to start our lives together.

My stomach rolled and my hands shook with a unique mixture of grief, guilt, and pure exhilaration. Over the years, I'd labeled it as the Ramsey Stewart trifecta. For too long, it had devoured me each time someone mentioned his name. And for a small town in Georgia with nothing better to do, people loved to mention his name.

They'd heard what had happened. They talked. They judged. They made up lies.

But I knew the truth because I knew Ramsey better than anyone else.

Nora and I lived a quiet life together. We'd bought a house about half an hour away from our old neighborhood. She was a proud first grade teacher, and I'd opened a successful internet travel agency in the small space next door to my father's barbershop. We were two independent women, neither of whom needed a roommate. But since the day we'd lost half of our hearts, Nora Stewart had never left my side.

I pretended it was because she'd lost her big brother and needed someone to lean on, but I knew she was there to take care of me. I told her almost every day that she didn't have to. She ignored me. Just like her brother would have.

A puzzle of tan buildings surrounded by chain link fences and barbwire came into view as we made our way up the hill.

He was in there.

Oh, God, he was in there.

"Thea, stop. You're making me nervous here," Nora said, pulling into a parking spot in the virtually empty lot.

"I can't stop. He's coming home."

"I know," she whispered, shooting me a smile that looked so much like his that it caused a sharp pain in my chest. "It's almost over."

It wasn't though. He was being released three years and some change early and would have to spend the next thirty-six months strictly adhering to the conditions of his parole.

But he'd be free.

And he could come home.

And he could be mine again. Twelve years, eight months, three weeks, four days, twelve hours, and forty-three minutes, and he could finally be mine again.

"What time is it?" I asked Nora, physically unable to drag my eyes off the chain link gates.

"Twelve thirty."

God, how was I ever going to get through another thirty minutes of torture? I was exhausted and my entire body ached, but I was so damn close to pressing play on my life again. After pulling the visor down, I busied my trembling hands by smoothing my long, brown hair. I'd done the best I could with concealer to hide the bags under my pale-green eyes. It was a lost cause. Sleep had been a fruitless effort in the weeks since I'd found out he was coming home.

Nora let out a sigh. "Listen. I want you to be prepared for—"

"Don't say it," I clipped, closing the visor.

Her brown eyes sparkled in the midday sun. "You don't understand. He's changed. *A lot.*"

"We all have." I was far from the sixteen-year-old tomboy he'd once dated.

Hell, he was probably going to have a heart attack when he saw me in the navy-blue maxi dress I'd chosen simply because it hugged all the right curves. Though, curves or not, the way I looked had never mattered to Ramsey before, and I didn't suspect now would be any different.

"You need to be realistic here," Nora warned.

I turned in my seat to give her my full attention. "I am being realistic."

"Thea—"

"Don't. Not today. I don't need a lecture right now about how we're not teenagers anymore. I get it, okay? Things have changed." I tapped my finger over my heart. "But not in here. In here, nothing will *ever* change. So please. Give it a rest and let me have today."

Her face got soft. "I just want you to be happy."

I smiled and, for the first time in as long as I could remember, it breached the numbness and warmed my skin. "I know, and this is easily the best day of my *entire* life. We can be nervous. We can be excited. But no more worrying. I'm going to be fine. We're all going to be fine from here on out."

She smiled, entirely unconvinced, but she loved me enough not to argue.

This wasn't the end of a fantasy where we lived happily ever after. It was going to be a hard transition for all of us. When Ramsey had been locked up, Nora had been fourteen, I'd been sixteen, and he'd been seventeen. Back then, we'd been invincible for no other reason than we'd had each other. But for the last decade, we'd been forging our own paths. Ones I was desperate to finally merge back together.

With Ramsey back, time could finally start again. No more countdowns. No more hollow seconds passing without him. No more hiding under our tree, crying and pleading for the boy who had stolen my heart to suddenly appear.

No. Those days were gone.

In mere minutes, a *man* I no longer knew—but had never stopped loving—was going to emerge from between the chain link gates. I'd never been more ready for anything in my entire life.

I stared down at my watch, the minutes passing with the agonizing speed of millenniums. while Nora fidgeted beside me. We didn't talk. There were no words left to say.

Sometime between thirty minutes and five hundred years later, movement caught our attention.

And then time officially stopped.

I could live forever and I'd never forget the moment when those gates opened, revealing the most gorgeous man I would ever see. That had more to do with the fact that it was Ramsey than the way he actually looked.

He was taller than I remembered. Clean shaven, and his hair was short. With a garbage bag thrown over his shoulder, lean muscles showed beneath his plain white tee. The lanky legs that had once carried me on his back anywhere I wanted to go were stretching the thighs of the jeans I'd helped Nora shop for a week earlier. But none of that, not one damn part of that, was why my lungs seized and my throat closed.

He was smiling—a pure and genuine Ramsey Stewart special edition I had missed every single day for over twelve years. A sob tore from my chest as I slapped a hand over my mouth and stared at him.

Not in cuffs.

Not in a prison jumpsuit.

Not locked behind bars.

My Ramsey was finally free.

Nora climbed out of the car first, tears already falling from her eyes. And at the sight, her brother's smile grew tenfold.

His full lips moved in the pattern of, *Hey you* as she jogged toward him. The second he got close enough, she jumped into his arms. He laughed, holding her to his chest, her feet dangling off the ground. It was hard not to be jealous.

Sucking in a sharp breath, I collected myself and gave them a moment for their private reunion. Seeing him with her, grinning with so much pride and adoration—it made my nerves momentarily calm. The longing only grew. When I couldn't force myself to wait any longer, I threw my door open and climbed out.

It took him several beats to notice me, but like I'd been hooked up to a set of jumper cables, I felt the shock down to the core of my soul when his dark gaze landed on mine. His back shot straight and surprise robbed me of his smile. His jaw got hard, and a mixture of agony, shock, and fury mingled in his handsome features. This was more than likely what he had dubbed the Thea Hull trifecta.

"What the hell," he rumbled in a raspy voice I would have recognized anywhere.

That fool. It was as if he'd really thought I wasn't going to show up on the day he was *finally* released.

Nothing could have kept me away.

Not his first and only letter from prison lying to me that he didn't love me anymore and urging me to move on.

Not twelve freaking years of him ignoring all of my correspondence and blocking me from visiting.

Not the overwhelming hatred I felt for him because he'd ruined us in ways he'd sworn he never would.

Not even because he'd turned his back on me when I'd needed him the most.

Yet there I was twelve years, eight months, three weeks,

four days, thirteen hours, and thirteen minutes later, waiting for him just like I'd promised.

Because unlike him, I knew how to keep my word.

So yeah. I was pissed off at Ramsey Stewart with the fiery passion of a woman who had spent over a decade trapped in hell. But as he dropped his bag, turned on a toe, and tried to get back inside the gates, I finally got to say the words that had been devouring me from the inside out for the better part of my life.

"I fucking love you too, asshole!"

ONE

Thea

Eighteen years earlier...

FIFTY-ONE...NO, FIFTY-TWO MINUTES. THAT'S HOW LONG it had been.

I should have been crying. Fat, ugly tears should have been rolling down my face. I should have been lost in a sea of grief. Instead, I couldn't stop staring at my watch. It was the digital kind with the date and time. The one that counted individual seconds as they passed, never to return again. My mother had ordered that watch for me a few weeks earlier because it had a little button on the side that made it a stopwatch. She'd said it was so I could time myself as I raced around the neighborhood on my bike. It wasn't like I had any friends to compete with. I was a girl who hated dresses, dolls, and gossipy, hair-flipping girls. I was also a *girl*—therefore I wasn't cool enough to hang out with any of the boys.

But with everything that had happened over the last few months, I didn't mind riding alone. I liked the peace and absence of despair that had been hovering in my house like a cloud of smoke suffocating us all.

Fifty-three minutes. Almost an hour.

Was she still there? Had the funeral home picked up her

body yet? Was my father going to force me to wear a dress to her funeral? Would my bratty cousins come in from out of town? Was my life ever going to be *normal* again?

Fifty-four minutes.

I crossed my legs at the ankle and leaned back against the tree. This should have been easier. She'd been sick for so long. We'd spent months preparing for this day. Or at least my father had. I'd spent months pretending it wasn't happening. And now that it had, I was hiding under a tree in the freshly mowed hayfield behind our neighborhood, wishing like hell that I had prepared too.

Fifty-five minutes.

The numbers kept changing. The seconds created minutes she would never experience. The minutes—

"All right, I gotta know what you're staring at," a boy said from somewhere nearby.

My head shot up but only an empty field stared back at me.

"Hello?" I called out.

"Is that one of those watches that has games on it and stuff? This kid Kevin at my old school had one. He played Tetris on it during math class. The game was stupid to begin with, but the screen was like an inch, so it made it even more stupid. He was a dumbass, so I guess it made sense."

I leaned around the tree, trying to figure out where the voice was coming from. It was possible I was suffering from some kind of hallucination. I'd seen that happen in the movies when someone was experiencing an emotional trauma. But why had my mind conjured a boy's voice instead of my mother's? And why the hell was he talking about Tetris and some random kid named Kevin?

"Where are you?" I asked.

"Up here."

Craning my head back, I found him perched—heels to butt—on a tree branch. His arms were over his head, clinging to a thin branch that looked like it was hoping for an excuse to snap, but his dark gaze was locked on me.

He flashed me a wide grin and extended a small red-and-green package toward me, forgetting—or ignoring—that he had to be at least fifteen feet in the air. "You want some gum?"

"What the…" I breathed as I took him in. I didn't recognize him from school, but he looked like he was around my age, maybe a year or two older.

His jeans were faded, and his sneakers had seen better days. There wasn't a name brand or logo in sight, though there weren't many kids in our area, myself included, who could afford more than discount or secondhand clothes.

However, the real mystery at the moment wasn't *who* he was, but rather *how* he had gotten up there.

The tree had been stripped of its branches halfway to the top to allow the tractors to pass beneath it. I knew bears that couldn't have made that climb. Okay, well, I didn't *know* them. We didn't really have bears in Clovert, Georgia. But I'd seen videos of bears on TV.

I stood, brushing the dirt off my cutoff shorts. "What are you doing up there?"

He shook the gum at me one last time in a silent offer before shrugging. Precariously balancing, he released the branch above his head long enough to unwrap a piece and shove it into his mouth then tuck the pack inside his back pocket.

He smacked his lips as he answered, "Just hanging out."

"In a tree?"

"I'm not sure if you've dragged your attention away from Tetris long enough to notice, but it's hot as Hades today. I swear this was the only shade I could find." His shaggy, brown hair, which curled at the tips, fell over his forehead. With a subtle twitch of his chin, he shifted it out of his eyes.

"Have you been up there this whole time?" I accused more than asked. I'd been sitting under that tree for… I looked at my watch.

Fifty-eight minutes.

Well, less the three minutes it took for me to sprint over there after the hospice nurse had announced that my mother "had passed." The word *passed* implied that there was somewhere else she was going. When in reality, the cancer had finally devoured her from the inside out until her lungs filled with fluid and she'd drown lying in bed.

Fifty-nine minutes.

"It wasn't like I was spying on you or anything," he defended. "I was going to say something earlier, but then I got curious about what the heck you were doing."

What was I doing? Hiding? Avoiding? Clinging to the theory that ignorance was bliss? Knowing she was dead was one thing. After I'd listened for days to her gasp and gurgle, it was honestly a relief. But seeing them wheel her out of our house on a stretcher much like the first time she'd collapsed after chemo had been more than I could take. This time, there was no hope left to cling to. When she left that day, she was never coming back.

I just had to wait. Soon, it would be over. Soon, her hospital bed in our living room would be empty for the first time in three months. Soon, she would be *gone*.

Only then would I go home.

"How did you get up there?" I asked.

"I climbed."

"Wow, okay. Awesome. Thanks for the details."

"What kind of details do you need with that?"

"Uh, maybe *how* you did it. There are no branches."

He grinned again—big, toothy, and smacking his gum. "I know, right? I didn't think I was going to be able to do it at first. It took me a solid twenty minutes of scrambling before I remembered I was wearing a belt."

I blinked at him like he was an idiot because I was starting to think maybe he was. Who the heck smiled that much anyway? Not me. At least, not anymore.

"What the heck does a belt have to do with anything?"

"Have you ever seen one of those lumberjack competitions on TV? They use this belt thing to hook their way up. I didn't think it was going to work without the spiky shoes. But here I am."

Another grin.

Another chew.

Another head twitch to keep his hair out of his eyes.

"Any plans on how you're going to get down?"

He shrugged. "None yet. You got any ideas?"

Considering I *still* couldn't wrap my mind around how he had gotten up there, it was safe to say I had no flipping idea how he was going to get down. Not to mention, I wasn't sure I should help him figure it out. What kind of creeper hid in a tree and watched a person at the bottom for... I looked at my watch.

Sixty minutes. One hour.

I could finally stop counting the minutes and move on to counting the hours. Those were longer. There were only twenty-four in a day and I could sleep through at least eight of them. Then there would be days. Months. Years. Before I knew it, I'd barely remember her at all.

Those were the days I longed for. I loved my mother. I didn't want her to be dead. I just wanted to stop hurting.

One hour and one minute.

I wondered if my dad had noticed I'd taken off yet or if he was still doubled over her bed, holding her as if he could bring her back. Secretly, I was glad he couldn't.

"Oh, good. You're thinking," he prodded when I didn't reply.

I should have left. Leaving the peeping Tom hung out to dry. But where would I have gone? My mother was dead, my father was destroyed, and the world kept turning as people continued on with their lives as if nothing had happened at all. Well, everyone except for that boy in the tree. Because, in a different way, he was just as stuck as I was.

"Well, I've got a few ideas. Though most of them are about how you shouldn't spy on people or trespass on private property."

His thick eyebrows shot up. "Trespassing? Are you kidding me? There's no fence or signs or anything. It's a dang tree in the middle of an empty field."

"Yeah. A field owned by the Wynns."

"Oh, please. The Wynns don't care if I climb their tree."

"You have no idea who they are, do you?"

"Of course, I do." His grin had faded into something that I assumed was supposed to be a scowl, but his face was too gentle to pack any heat.

"So, what are their names then?"

"Psh." He cut his gaze off to the side. "George and…um, Betty. Duh."

"Errr!" I made the sound of an obnoxious buzzer. "Wrong! It's Mason and Lacey."

He gave me back his chocolaty-brown eyes. "Well, those are their nicknames. Everybody knows their real names are George and Betty Lynn."

"Wynn," I corrected.

His voice rose, but the sides of his mouth hiked into a wide smile. "That's what I said!"

I rolled my eyes. "Whatever. You're probably safe. Mason only carries his gun out to the field on Sundays. Oh, wait, that's today."

"Shut up. That's not true."

"You sure about that?"

Panic hit his face, and if I'd been able to feel anything over the ache in my chest, I would have laughed. Mason Wynn would have built a playground around that tree if the neighborhood kids asked for it. He didn't care if people were hanging out in his field. But Tree Boy didn't need to know that.

"Back up. I'm coming down."

Using my hand to shield the sun from my eyes, I watched as he swept his leg, trying and failing to make purchase on the bark with the tip of his toe. He crouched lower and tried again. Then again. And then one last time before he rose to his full height.

"Crap. You gotta help me get down. If I get shot my first week in town, my dad will ground me for the rest of my life."

"Just to be clear, you're more worried about being grounded than you are getting shot?"

"Grounded means I have to sit in my room with nothing but stupid books. Not all of us are lucky enough to have a Tetris watch. Now back up. I'm gonna jump."

"You can't jump from up there. You'll break your leg."

"Then I'll break my leg. What do you care?"

That was a really good question. I didn't even know his name. God knew I had more than enough other stuff to care about without adding him to my list. If he wanted to launch himself from a tree, who was I to stop him?

Turns out, it wasn't *his* leg I should have been worried about.

No sooner than I took a step away, he shoved off the branch. He hit the ground with two feet and then sprang forward like he'd landed on a trampoline. Horror showed on his face as he crashed into me. Our bodies tangled, and pain exploded in *my* leg as it buckled under our combined weight, sending us both down to the grass.

"Oh, shit!" he exclaimed, pushing off me faster than I'd ever seen a person move. "Are you okay?"

I wasn't. Not in any way, shape, or form.

My mother was dead.

My father was destroyed.

And my leg was broken.

Of course it was. Because when I'd assumed that day couldn't possibly get any worse, God had clearly seen that as a personal challenge rather than a plea for help.

A silent scream exploded in my head and agony unlike anything I'd ever felt before radiated through my body. My ankle was on fire. That was the only explanation. Wails tore from my throat as I rolled to the side, holding my knee for fear of tracing the pain any lower.

"I'm sorry. I'm sorry... I'm, oh God!" he yelled, scrambling away from me. He punctuated it with a gag and then that boy— that *damn boy* who had once been stuck in a tree, spying on me as I mourned—dry-heaved, spitting out his gum, his eyes glued to my ankle. "Your...your...foot. It's... Oh God. Please tell me you have a fake leg."

"Don't just stand there, you idiot!"

He drew in a deep breath and fought back another gag. "Where do you live? I'll run and get your mom."

My mom.

My *mom*.

The stabbing in my chest was almost strong enough to eclipse the pain in my ankle.

"She died," I croaked.

"What?"

"She's dead!" I screamed, the words shredding me as they came back in an echo. "You can't get my mom. Nobody can get my mom!"

His voice shook as he asked, "What about your dad?"

I screwed my eyes shut.

I'd had the perfect parents. High school sweethearts. Married by eighteen. Had me at twenty-five. They didn't argue or bicker. They were the type of weirdos who left love notes hidden around the house and danced in the kitchen when they thought I was in bed. They loved each other so completely that it blinded to them to the world outside of their relationship. As far as I knew, they'd never spent a night apart.

That night they would though. That night and all the nights to come, they would never be together again.

My mother had been the heart and soul of our family. Without her, my father wasn't going to be able to survive. He'd breathe. He'd wake up every morning. He might even smile once in a while. But without her, his life was over. And then where did that leave me?

Alone. So utterly alone.

But judging by the boy's face and the fact that my leg was in so much pain that my vision was starting to tunnel, even my poor broken father could help me more than this kid.

"His name is...Joe and we live at three-one-nine Leaning Oak Drive," I panted. "Go past the big ditch to the..."

"I know where it is. I'll be right back. Don't move, okay?"

I listened to his feet crunching in the grass as he sprinted away, and then I lay there staring up at the sky, wishing it would swallow me up.

Mentally. Physically. Emotionally. Everything hurt.

But through it all, I never cried.

What was the point?

TWO

Thea

FOUR DAYS, THREE PINS IN MY ANKLE, ONE SURGERY, AND A neon-yellow cast later, I went to my mother's funeral in a wheelchair. I cringed while listening to my father's constant whimpers and sniffles. He didn't look at me or ask if I was okay. He didn't seem to care that I was *ten* and had lost my one and only *mother*. He'd lost his wife—his one and only love.

Anger and resentment brewed inside me, swirling into a wicked rage. I sat in my wheelchair, listening to the preacher talk about how my mother was now looking down on us from the arms of Christ, and I couldn't stop wishing that it had been my father instead.

I wished he'd gotten cancer.

I wished he'd spent three months wasting away.

I wished we were at his stupid funeral instead of hers.

I looked at him, tears streaming down his cheeks, his gaze anchored to her coffin like he could somehow see through it. Only then did I realize he probably wished I were the one dead instead too.

I just wanted to go home. It was supposed to be over. Her hospital bed and monitoring equipment had been removed from our living room. The rental company had picked it up not long after she'd died. Our home had returned to its warm and welcoming façade, filled with smiling pictures and bright-colored art. The handrail in the hall bathroom my father had installed when she was still mobile enough to get around was the only proof left that my mother had been ill at all.

But the memories of those nights, listening to her struggling for survival, would stay with me forever.

The ladies from the neighborhood brought us dinner every day for a week. Dad had no appetite, and we eventually ran out of room in the fridge. Sometimes I'd throw it away. Sometimes I'd freeze it. But I'd never be able to eat spaghetti again without tasting the stale, putrid flavor of my mother's death.

The desserts were pretty great though, and since I couldn't escape The House of Despair due to my bum leg, I spent the last week of my miserable summer vacation sitting in front of the window with a spoon in my hand and whatever chocolaty delight had been delivered that day in my lap.

That was when I saw him.

The boy from the tree.

It was the first time I'd seen him since my father had carried me out of the Wynns' hayfield. That boy had followed us to the car, saying he was sorry with every step. I had been too concerned with my foot facing the wrong direction to entertain any kind of apology—or plan my revenge.

Right then, however, he was outside my house, riding his bike with a little girl who looked so much like him that it was impossible she wasn't his sister. He was wearing the same faded jeans. Same worn-out shoes. Same shaggy hair. More than likely the same obnoxious personality too. He was having a grand old time, while I was stuck inside, downing half of a chocolate pie, with my worthless leg in a cast, requiring help just to go to the bathroom.

And it was All. His. *Fault.*

Nothing, not even the two cups of sugar I'd consumed, was enough to sweeten that kind of bitterness.

"Hey!" I yelled, pounding my fist on the glass.

The boy abruptly stopped his bike at the end of my driveway, almost causing his sister to run into the back of him.

"Get out of here!" I shouted, making a shooing motion with my spoon and dropping chocolate all over my shirt. "Go home! Nobody wants you here!"

I assumed he couldn't hear me because the jerk did a head twitch to get his hair out of his eyes and then shot me a grin as he chewed a mouthful of gum and waved. Using his best charades skills, he inquired about my ankle. At least that's what I thought he was doing as he hopped around one foot, pointing at his leg.

I wanted to kick it out from under him.

"You look like an idiot!" I yelled.

He gave me two thumbs-up and a huge smile. He had spied on me, broken my leg on the same day my mother died, and ruined the rest of my summer, and now he was giving me a thumbs-up. He could take that thumb and shove it up his—

"Thea?" my dad called as he walked into the room.

I jumped, nearly knocking the rest of my pie onto the floor. He hadn't been back to work at the barbershop since she'd died. And short of my doctor's appointments, he hadn't been out of his room much since the funeral.

"Hey," I replied, taking in his pajama pants and mismatched T-shirt hanging off his thin frame. He'd lost so much weight in such a short time.

Nine days to be exact. I hadn't yet switched to weeks to count the length of time she'd been gone. But there was no time like the present.

She'd been dead for a week. Over a week actually.

No. No. I liked counting in days better. More precise and torturous. Like the seconds on my watch.

I peered up at him as he walked to the window. The scruff on his face had grown out enough to be considered a beard, and he reeked of sweat and filth—or maybe it was tears and grief. I couldn't be sure. Regardless, it was terrifying. When she'd been alive, it was rare I'd see him in anything other than pressed slacks and a white button-down. He was always clean shaven, and his hair was meticulously styled. That was the way my mom liked him. So that was how he'd dressed.

I swallowed hard, wondering if he was going to die too. Could people really die of a broken heart? I wasn't exactly his biggest fan at the moment, but he was the only parent I had left. Watching one die had been enough.

"Is everything okay? I heard you yelling," he said.

"Um, yeah. It's fine. That kid who broke my leg is outside. That's all."

"Ramsey?"

Ramsey? What a stupid name. And that assessment came from a girl named Althea Floye Hull, but somehow his was still worse.

"How do you know his name?" I asked.

"His family moved in two doors down a couple weeks ago." My zombie father lifted his hand in a wave, and I glanced out the window in time to see *Ramsey* return it. With that, my dad ran out of energy for the day and headed straight back to his bedroom, muttering, "Nice kid. You should get out of the house and see if he wants to ride bikes with you."

I gritted my teeth, biting back a dozen words I wasn't allowed to say. "Yeah. I'll get right on that."

The door closed behind him without another word spoken.

For three days.

THREE

Thea

"**D**ANG IT, COME ON," I MUMBLED, STRUGGLING TO SHARPEN my pencil while balancing on my crutches.

I wasn't supposed to be using them yet. The doctor had told me to wait three weeks to make sure my ankle had healed enough in case I accidentally put weight on it. I was beyond done with the wheelchair thing though. Limping and hobbling had to be better than sitting around all the time.

Getting on and off the bus that morning had been a nightmare. I don't even know how my dad had expected me to get to school in my wheelchair. Not that we'd really discussed it. He didn't talk much anymore.

He nodded.

He hummed in acknowledgement.

He sometimes smiled when he thought it was socially required.

But he was a shell of the man I'd grown up with.

It had been fifteen days since she died, and while he'd returned to work, he was only going through the motions.

Just as I'd feared the day she died, I was on my own.

The class chattered behind me as they worked on the obligatory first-day-of-school get-to-know-your-neighbor assignment. I didn't need to get to know Josh Caskey. I'd known and hated him since we were both in diapers.

"Thea," Mrs. Young called.

I pivoted on one foot to face her, and then my life as I knew it changed all over again.

My breath caught in my throat when I saw Ramsey, the freaking leg-breaking spy, standing beside her. Fifth grade and he was already taller than the teacher. He had a hand shoved into his pocket, and the ends of his hair tangled with his long lashes with every blink.

There were a lot of rules at school. Sit down. Be quiet. No running in the halls. But secretly we all knew only one was enforced.

No gum.

Yet there he stood, chewing away as he shot me a smile and a wave.

I didn't return his greeting, and that only had a tiny bit to do with me needing two hands to balance.

I begrudgingly tore my gaze away from my archnemesis and replied, "Yes, ma'am."

The teacher grinned. "I heard you and Mr. Stewart know each other."

"Then somebody lied to you."

Ramsey cocked his head to the side. "How'd you get that cast then, gimpy?"

Judging by the smile twitching his lips, he was teasing me.

Judging by the inferno brewing inside me, he was standing entirely too close to a ticking time bomb.

Cocking *my* head to the side, I retorted, "An idiot fell out of a tree."

His dark eyes twinkled in the florescent lighting. "Hang on now. Did he *fall* or did he jump *after* he told you to back up?"

I glared at him with everything I had. "I *did* back up."

He returned my glare, smiling the entire time. "Obviously not far enough."

"It would have been far enough if you could stick a landing."

He shrugged. "Never claimed to be a gymnast."

"Funny, you never claimed you weren't an idiot, either."

"Figured that went without saying."

"Well, you figured wrong, *idiot*."

Mrs. Young stepped between the two of us. "Okay, okay. Enough with the name calling. Ramsey, since you're new, Thea will be your official Clovert Elementary tour guide. And, Thea, since you will be needing help getting to and from the bus over the next few months, Ramsey will be your personal book bag carrier. You two think you can do that for me without someone else breaking a limb?"

"Yes, ma'am," Ramsey answered immediately, though he'd tucked his gum under his tongue before he'd spoken.

Both of their expectant gazes landed on me.

I would have rather been listening to one of Josh Caskey's riveting stories about skinning deer and killing squirrels than this crap. But much like the rest of my life, it was going to happen whether I wanted it to or not. "Do I have a choice?"

She shook her head. "Not really."

I flashed Ramsey a tight and entirely fake smile. "Fine. I'll do it. But no promises on the broken limbs."

He let out a loud laugh as if I'd told a joke rather than threatened his life. And worst of all, it was a laugh that made me want to laugh too.

I glowered.

And of course, he bulged his eyes at me, grinning like a fool and mocking my glower.

God, this was going to suck.

"Okay, you two. Get to know each other. And be nice." Mrs. Young walked away and started helping Josh move his stuff to the free desk across the room.

Oh, goodie, this arrangement came with the added torture of being deskmates too.

"Great. Now we're stuck together," I mumbled.

"Oh, I'm not stuck. I asked for you."

My long, brown hair whipped the side of my face as I cranked my head around to look at him. "You what?"

He took the pencil from my hand and gave the arm of the pencil sharpener a whirl. "You're the only person I know here."

"Stop saying that. I don't know you."

He tested the tip of the lead on his finger. Finding it un-worthy, he guided it back into the sharpener. "Okay, fine. I'll put it this way. I know your name is Thea Hull. Your dad's Joe. Your mom just died. You live two houses down from me. You like to hide *under* the Wynns' tree. I just so happen to like to hide *up* it. And you're always mad about something. That's more than I know about any other person in this school, short of my little sis-ter, Nora. So yeah, when the teacher asked if I wanted a helper, I asked for you."

I hated that he knew that much about me. I hated that *any-one* knew that much about me. This time last year, I'd been a no-body. Just the way I liked it. Then my mother had gotten sick and word traveled fast through our small town. From teachers to students, pity shone on all of their faces. And now that she was dead, the attention was suffocating. I was so dang sick of the sympathetic hugs and awkward stares. If one more person told me they were sorry for my loss, I was going to lose my ever-loving mind.

I couldn't escape the overwhelming density of sadness in my

own house, but for Pete's sake, I had really been hoping school would be different.

Clearly, I'd been wrong.

Only, right then, as Ramsey shot me a crooked smile that made me debate the merits of dropping out of school in the fifth grade, I realized there wasn't an ounce of pity anywhere on his stupid—yet kinda cute—face.

For that alone, I decided I wouldn't use my crutch to push his chair out from under him when he sat down.

"I'm not always mad about *something*. I'm always mad at *you*."

"Me? What did I do?"

I pointedly flashed my gaze from my cast to him and back again. "Are you kidding right now?"

"Oh, come on. How long are you going to hold that against me? It was an accident. I said I was sorry."

"An accident is running into my bike or knocking over my milk at lunch. Not shattering my ankle. Did you know the doctor said I might walk with a limp for the rest of my life?"

"Then we should probably start thinking about your new nickname now to get ahead of the competition in high school. I think Gimpy has a ring to it."

My mouth fell open. He had not just said that to me. He had not—

"No wait. What about Ol' Peg Leg." He lifted his finger in the air. "Oh, oh, oh! I know. What was the name of that pirate? Captain Jack…" His eyes flashed wide, and his lips stretched so wide that it was a wonder they didn't swallow his face. "*Sparrow*."

It was really unfortunate that I was wearing my favorite white tank top that day, because my head was about to explode all over that classroom.

Leaning in close, I dropped my voice to a whisper. "Listen up, *Ramsey*. One of these days, I'm going to get this cast off. I may look small, but I'm quiet, and I'm fast, and I know where you live. You call me Gimpy, Peg Leg, or the name of any pirate who ever lived and I will tie you up, bury you in the ditch by the old mill, and then help people search for you across town. Got it?"

That should have been the end of it. Ya know, if I'd been talking to a sane individual with a healthy respect for his own life. But not this kid. Not freaking Ramsey Stewart.

He aimed his smile at his shoes and rocked onto his toes. "Jeez, Thea. Are you flirting with me? I'm not really looking for a girlfriend, but you seem cool, I guess."

Oh, yes. He'd said that. The ultimate comeback for a ten-year-old. The implication that I liked him when in fact I hated him with the wrath of a thousand daggers—or however the saying went.

I had no other choice than to retreat, collect my thoughts, find a tree, jump out of it, and maybe that time I'd break *his* leg.

"Okay, everyone. Find your seats. It's time to get started," Mrs. Young called out.

Ramsey handed my pencil back and swept his hand out in front of him in a grand gesture for me to go first. I rolled my eyes as I started the grueling journey through the crowded classroom on a set of crutches.

Swear to God, I almost choked on the pheromones wafting off hair-twirling Tiffany Martin and her lip-gloss-loving girl gang as they drank in the new kid in class. But if Ramsey noticed them at all, he never let on. He walked beside me, grinning like the fool he so obviously was.

Mrs. Young started reviewing the class rules as I got settled at my desk and I paid attention for no other reason than to avoid his scrutinizing gaze. When she got to the one about candy and gum, I leveled him with a hard stare. He laughed, not even trying to hide it.

I got busy on the stack of work the teacher had left on the corner of our desks while Ramsey scribbled stick figure pirates. Not that I was watching out of the corner of my eye or anything. I was on my third math worksheet and Ramsey had made it up to a cannon and stick men walking the plank when he whispered, "Hey, Sparrow."

I clenched my teeth and cut my gaze at him. "What?"

Mischief danced in his eyes as he boldly blew a bubble. "Since we're partners and all, you think I can play Tetris on your watch?"

Tetris. The idiot wanted to play Tetris on my Timex.

How was this happening?

I closed my eyes and dreamed of better days.

Two weeks, twenty-one hours, and six minutes to be exact.

I'd never forget the hollowness I felt that first day as I made my way to the bus with my book bag awkwardly weighing me down. By the time three o'clock had rolled around, I'd been ready to collapse. My leg was killing me, my armpits were on fire from the crutches chafing them, and my arms were shaking from the constant struggle to hold myself up in order to keep my leg and my armpits from hurting worse.

Going home to an empty house was going to hurt the most.

A year ago, my mom had been waiting for me, my special first-day-of-school treat of M&M Rice Krispies Treats on a plate and a proud smile on her face.

This year would be different. Forever would be different.

Ramsey had spent the day talking to me. No, seriously, the kid never stopped talking.

Or smiling.

Or chewing gum.

Or breathing.

It was overwhelming. And because it was Ramsey, it was infuriating too. I'd ignored him as best I could, but there was no avoiding him.

Just before lunch, I'd been called to the counselor's office. I'd never been so excited to get away from a person in my life, even if it did mean discussing my feelings since my mother's death. As I left, Ramsey waved, his arm over his head, his hand looking like it had taken up a secondary career as a windshield wiper. It was as if he'd thought I was leaving for good and not a half hour.

It had only been a day, but being his only friend had to end. And fast.

"Move," I barked at Tiffany Martin as she waited at the door to the bus, desperately waiting to catch Ramsey's attention.

I'd all but sprinted out of the class before he'd had the chance to finish packing his bag. Regardless of what Mrs. Young thought, I didn't need help.

"Excuse me?" she snapped back.

"I said, *move.*"

Her pink lips curled with attitude. "What is your problem?"

"Move," he rumbled as he stepped up behind me.

I rolled my eyes at his knight-in-shining-armor routine.

"Oh, hey, Ramsey," she purred.

Rolling my shoulders forward, I faked a gag.

"Hey, Tiffany," he replied absently, too busy yanking my left crutch from under me to give her his eyes.

"What are you doing?" I snapped, falling to the side.

He caught me with a hand on my bicep and slid my book bag off my arm. Then he repeated the process on the other side. "There," he said with a satisfied smirk as he slung it over his free shoulder. "Maybe next time you can wait on me instead of trying to break a world record for speed."

I righted my crutches and shot him a fiery glare. "Maybe next time you can keep your dang hands to yourself."

"Maybe." He shrugged. "Maybe not."

If looks could kill, Ramsey would have been on his ninth life for the day. Fortunately for him, and really unfortunately for me, he was wearing a force field that made him immune to my rage.

I hated him, but I wished I knew where to get one of those force fields too.

By the time I performed the herculean task of climbing the three steps with Ramsey trying to help my efforts by shoving me from behind, the bus was full, leaving only one seat open—the dreaded bench of Loserville directly behind the driver. And because I had clearly insulted God at some point over my short ten years, it was the same day Mrs. Perkins decided to give us assigned bus seats for the rest of the *year*.

Ramsey had been wrong. Five days a week on the bus *and* at school—we were absolutely stuck together.

And it was, without question, the single best thing that happened to me that year—maybe even ever.

FOUR

Thea

I T TOOK A WHILE FOR ME TO REALIZE HOW IMPORTANT Ramsey was to me. Honestly, for about a month, I just thought he found it entertaining to annoy me.

Every day, he asked me if I wanted to get my wheelchair and ride around the neighborhood with him. Or go to the Wynns' tree. Or go to the gas station and get a pack of gum.

My answer was always no.

His response as I snatched my backpack and slammed my front door in his face was always, "Aw, man, come on, Thea. Don't be so lame."

He never let the rejection dissuade him. The very next day, he'd be back at it again. He'd laugh and try to chat with me in class, introducing me as *Sparrow* to people he'd just met but I'd known my entire freaking life. I hated the nickname, but I was too numb to do anything about it.

Most of the time, I ignored him altogether, pretending that a ghost was carrying my book bag instead of the school's new heartthrob. I never said thank you or upheld my end of the bargain of showing him around school, but he didn't seem to care.

He also didn't seem to care that pretty much everyone in class hated the miserable Thea Hull. The few people I'd hung out with or played with during recess in the past wanted nothing to do with me. It wasn't like I was a lot of fun anymore. I honestly wouldn't have blamed Ramsey if he'd hated me too. God knew I hated myself.

My dad was still a zombie who worked long hours. I suspected that it was in an attempt to steer clear of my mom's memories as much as possible, but it was hard not to take it personally.

On good days, I took a bath and wore clean clothes to school, stared into space during class and didn't get caught. I'd come home, eat whatever microwave dinner my dad had bought that week, and spend the rest of my night watching TV until I passed out on the couch.

On bad days, I wore the same clothes from the day before, got sent to the counselor's office for not paying attention, came home, locked myself in my room, and stared at the ceiling until sleep devoured me.

My grades crashed, and despite three requests from Mrs. Young for a parent-teacher conference, my father never replied.

I was relieved he didn't care about my grades.

I was heartbroken he didn't care about *me*.

But through it all—the bad, the worse, and the sometimes stinky—Ramsey was always there. Why, I had no idea. But for a girl who essentially lived alone in a house she shared with her father, *there* was the biggest gift of all.

"So then, Josh, was all like, 'Watch this,' and kicked the dog in the stomach." Ramsey let out a loud laugh and dropped his head against the back of the bus seat.

My mouth gaped open. "Why are you laughing? That isn't even close to funny, you idiot."

"Then you obviously didn't see Josh's face when the dog whipped around and bit the crap out of his leg. It was like one of those cop shows where the dog latches on and starts shaking back and forth." He chomped his teeth, pretending he was going to bite my shoulder.

I put a palm in his face and shoved his head away. "Good. Josh deserved it."

"I thought his mom was going to have a heart attack. She came flying out of the car, screaming about rabies and begging for someone to call nine-one-one knowing good and dang well she was the only one who had a cell phone. I'm telling you what, rich people are crazy. My leg would have to fall off before my dad would call an ambulance."

The bus doors opened as we arrived at our stop. We waited for all the other kids to get off before I started the production of getting to my feet. Ramsey got off the bus first, but he stood at the bottom, waiting for me. Like pretty much everything else in our relationship, I'd found this habit extremely obnoxious. Until a few days earlier, when I'd fallen. He'd caught me before I'd face planted on the road and it had taken every bit of the manners my mother had taught me to mutter a quiet thank-you.

You should have seen the smile on that boy's face.

I knew Ramsey. With as much as he talked, it was hard not to. But with two reluctant and mundane words of gratitude, it was as though I'd offered him a brick of gold. It was sad.

He was a nice kid who deserved far more than my misplaced wrath. Though, back then, I hadn't realized that it was misplaced, so I'd ignored the pang of guilt in my gut as I'd hurried up the driveway. Thankfully, Ramsey hadn't harped on my gratitude as he'd handed me my backpack and I'd slammed the door in his face.

Yeah, fine. I felt guilty about that too. But what the heck was I supposed to do? Shove the wrappers and TV trays out of the way and invite him in for a drink? In a glass I would have had to wash first since Lord knew when the last time the dishes had been done. Oh wait, I knew exactly how long because I'd never stopped counting.

One month, two weeks, four days, three hours, and twenty-nine minutes.

"Did they figure out whose dog it was?" I asked as both of my crutches landed safely on the ground.

Once he was sure I was steady, Ramsey backed out of my way. "Yep. Mine."

"What? You don't have a dog."

"How do you know? You been spying on me, Thea?"

The side of his mouth hiked adorably—I mean, annoyingly. Totally annoying.

"Psh, yeah right. That's your job. I'm not that bored," I lied. I was actually bored out of my freaking mind. I still had six more weeks until my cast came off. And just the thought of spending those days locked inside The House of Despair made me panic anytime I thought about it.

"Yeah, right," he mumbled, clearing the hair from his eyes with one of those twitches that had long since become involuntary.

We started toward my house, and as usual, Ramsey walked in the grass so I could have the sidewalk to myself.

"So if it was your dog, how'd it get to the school soccer field?"

"Well, I only said he was my dog now. Not that he was my dog at the time. Animal control showed up, but it took off into the woods. The dog bit Josh Caskey. He deserved a medal of honor, not the gas chamber. So yesterday, while you were being *lame* hiding out in your house, I grabbed some meat and rode my bike out there to find him. Poor thing was scared to death.

But nothing bologna couldn't cure. You wanna come over and see him?"

I don't know what happened. Maybe it was the old adage that time healed all wounds. Or maybe it was that I'd always wanted a dog but my mom had been allergic. Whatever it was, for the first time in as long as I could remember, a spark of excitement ignited inside me.

It was small.

But I felt it, and after months of pain spiraling like a tornado inside me, I was willing to do whatever I had to do to hold on to it. Even if that meant voluntarily spending time with Ramsey.

"Yeah," I replied.

His smile nearly blinded me. "Yeah?"

I nodded, and he wasted not a single second with further conversation. At a dead sprint, he ran straight to his small, brick ranch, our book bags bouncing on his shoulders.

A little girl filled Ramsey's empty spot beside me as I continued to hobble down the sidewalk.

God, she looked so much like him that it was almost scary. But where Ramsey was tall and rugged, Nora was petite and beautiful. She didn't wear dresses or lip gloss, but there was something inherently feminine about her even in dirty jeans and scuffed sneakers. She was two years younger than we were, but wherever Ramsey went, she was usually only a few steps away. This included when he'd built a shoddy ramp out of two concrete bricks and a piece of plywood about as sturdy as a spider's web. She'd gotten one jump off that thing before it'd broken and caused her to crash, skin her elbows, and pop her chain. She'd cried and cried as Ramsey tried to fix her bike. But even from my vantage point of the living room window, I'd known that it was a lost cause.

I was all too aware that not having a bike sucked. So that night, after everyone had gone inside, I hopped over, nearly breaking my neck twice to leave my bike on their front porch. I made sure to leave a note that read *loaner* taped to the handle bars. It was going to be months before I could ride again. Someone should get some use out of it.

Ramsey tried to thank me seven hundred times the next day. I'd snapped at him to shut up.

He'd smiled.

I'd hit him with my crutch.

And then he'd started talking about something dumb and I'd gone right back to ignoring him.

Business as usual.

I'd seen Nora countless times, but in all the weeks Ramsey had been making my ears bleed with his motor mouth, she'd never spoken to me. Until then.

"What was that about?" she asked, her eyes glued to her brother's back as he raced to their house.

I glanced around to make sure she was actually talking to me before I replied, "Ramsey's going to show me the dog he got yesterday."

Just like her freaking brother, her whole face lit. "Bologna? He's so cute."

"He named the dog Bologna?"

"Yep. I tried to get him to name it Oscar like Oscar Mayer, but he said no. Besides, he's brown, weird, and nobody wanted him, so I guess Bologna kinda fits." She giggled musically, and for a moment, I was jealous that she still had the ability to laugh.

I'd long since lost mine.

When we got to their driveway, Ramsey came running out with a dog that came up to his knees on a leash. Well, it looked like a leash. When he reached Nora and me, I realized it was one of his father's belts looped around the dog's neck.

Nora had been right; the dog was brown and weird. His snout was short like maybe he had some kind of bulldog in his bloodlines, but his legs were long, and his ears stood on end. It was as if the day he'd been created, God had been cleaning the spare parts off his workbench. He was easily the ugliest dog I had ever seen. But that was exactly what made him so dang cute.

"Bologna, meet Sparrow. Sparrow, meet Bologna."

"Don't call me Sparrow. And don't call him Bologna. That's a terrible name." I eased myself down to sit on the curb.

"What would you name him, then?"

I studied the dog for a second. Crap. Bologna did suit him. "Whatever. He's your dog. Name him whatever you want."

The dog inched toward me. I didn't know much about animals, but the tuck of his tail between his legs couldn't have been a good sign.

"You sure he's not going to bite my face off like he did Josh?"

Ramsey sat beside me. "Nah. He prefers legs and good news yours is already covered in plaster. I think you're safe."

I shot him a scowl that only made his perma-grin spread, and if I was being totally honest, it made the warmth in my chest spread as well.

"Here," he said, pulling a wad of lunch meat from his pocket. "Feed him this and you'll be his new best friend."

"First gum and now meat. What else do you keep in those pockets?"

He laughed. "Depends on the day. Play your cards right and I might smuggle you candy into class tomorrow."

"Oh goodie, bologna-flavored Skittles. I can't wait." I tore off a piece of the meat and offered it toward the dog.

Sure enough his tail started wagging immediately. He was a gentle guy, nibbling rather than snatching the treat from my hand. Ramsey eventually dropped the belt, convinced he wasn't going to run off. The dog sat there patiently until every morsel of the meat was gone. And when he was absolutely positive Ramsey wasn't going to produce any more, he flopped down between us and put his head in my lap.

His hair was coarse and scratchy against my skin, but I pet him for at least a half hour.

And for a solid half hour, I didn't think about my mother.

Or my leg.

Or my father.

Or my broken heart hanging by a thread inside my chest.

I just sat there. Ignoring my watch, petting the dog, and pretending everything was okay.

At some point, Nora got bored of her brother's ramblings—a sentiment I shared the majority of the time—and went inside. In the miracle of all miracles, Ramsey didn't transfer his rampant need to hear his own voice to me. I could feel him watching me out of the corner of his eye, but he didn't say a word for a long while.

Cars sped by and kids rode bikes past us, attempting to strike up conversation with Ramsey, but he simply lifted his hand in a wave that served as both a greeting and a dismissal.

Together, we sat on that curb as the entire world carried on around us, but for the first time in months, the loneliness wasn't killing me.

Because he was there.

Ramsey was *always* there.

"He's adorable," I finally whispered, opening what would surely be the floodgates to a conversation.

"You look happy," Ramsey said, giving the dog's back a scratch. "You're pretty when you smile."

My head snapped up almost as quickly as my cheeks heated. It felt amazing. All of it. The dog. The fact that Ramsey thought I was pretty. The fact that I did still have facial muscles that would allow me to smile.

But I was ten, claiming to be miserable, and the boy that I told myself I hated had just called me pretty. I couldn't let that one slide.

I punched him in the shoulder. "What the heck is wrong with you?"

Bologna curiously lifted his head, and stupid, stupid beautiful Ramsey just grinned.

Feigning innocence, he laughed, "What?"

"Don't tell me I'm pretty!"

"Why not? You are."

"Stop saying that."

"Fine. You're a troll. Happy now?"

I punched him again. "I'm not a troll!"

He fell over to the side, laughing. And if that wasn't annoying enough, Bologna moved out of my lap to lick his face.

I patted my lap and Bologna came back to me, settling at my side. Ignoring his owner, I scratched between his ears and imagined kicking Josh Caskey in the stomach for what he'd done to that sweet puppy.

"I was just trying to say something nice, ya know. You don't have to get all mad about it."

"I'm not mad."

He rubbed his shoulder. "You could have fooled me. You always seem to be so cranky."

"I'm not cranky," I mumbled, keeping my gaze locked on Bologna.

He bumped me with his shoulder and I swear I felt a chill down my spine. "Well, not right now you're not. But usually—"

"I'm not cranky," I snapped.

"Right. Of course not. *Totally* not cranky." He pushed to his feet and a blast of dread nearly knocked me over.

Not yet. Don't go. Please don't make me go home.

"I need to go in and get Nora something to eat." He grabbed the belt and looped it around Bologna's neck.

"Yeah. Okay. I should go anyway." *The empty house might get worried or something,* I added in my head.

In true Ramsey fashion, he helped me to my feet. I acted like I didn't need him, all the while trying to think of an excuse to make him stay.

In the end, I came up with nothing. "See ya later."

"Listen, if you happen to hear of anyone who wants a dog let me know. My dad won't let me keep Bologna. He said I'm the only wild animal he can afford to feed. I had to hide him in my closet last night, I'm not sure—"

"I'll take him!" I yelled so loud and so fast that it startled him. I swallowed hard and then lowered my voice in a poor attempt to keep it cool. "I mean… I guess I could take him."

"You sure your dad won't mind?"

"That would require him to notice I exist, so yeah, I'm pretty sure it will be fine."

Ramsey's eyebrows popped up his forehead and I regretted the overshare immediately. "Thea—"

Nope. Nope. Nope. I was not talking about my crappy life. Not with Ramsey. Not with anyone. "So anyway, if you're sure you want to get rid of him, I'd be happy to take him off your hands. Though I can't promise I'll keep the name Bologna. Poor dog already got kicked, the least I can do is give him a decent name."

His forehead crinkled. "What are you going to name him then?"

We both looked down at the dog.

"I don't know," I mumbled. "Nora suggested Oscar. That's pretty cute, don't ya think?"

He passed me the end of the belt. "Yeah, that one's not too bad. Her first choice was Sir Hairy Barkington though."

When my eyes got wide, Ramsey immediately realized his mistake.

"Oh my God, don't you dare name him that."

My lips broke into a smile. "Why not? It's cute."

"You know what? I changed my mind. You can't have him." He lunged for the belt, missing it when I pulled Sir Hairy to my other side.

"Ramsey, stop!" I laughed, hopping on one foot.

"No way. Naming a dog Sir Hairy Barkington is animal abuse. I won't allow it." He once again made a dive for the make-shift leash, but I managed to spin away from him. "Thea, I'm serious," he said, laughing the entire time.

And I laughed too. Real. Genuine. Rejuvenating.

For those minutes as he tried to get the belt back from me, with Sir Hairy barking and wagging his tail as we played, I didn't have to pretend that everything was okay.

My mother was still dead.

My father was still broken.

But I was laughing with the boy next door. For a few brief moments, it didn't feel like I was going to suffocate anymore.

I didn't know it then, but that day, Ramsey Stewart saved my life.

And six years later, I'd repay him by ruining his.

FIVE

Thea

"**Y**OUR MOTHER IS—"

"Dead!" I screamed at the top of my lungs. "It doesn't matter if she's allergic to dogs. She doesn't matter at all anymore."

"Don't say that," my dad scolded.

I shook my head, anger vibrating inside me. "You don't matter, either. She'd hate you, ya know. If she could see you now, she'd hate you almost as much as I do."

"Shut up!" he boomed, leaning against the wall for balance. "You have no idea what the last few months have been like for me."

Okay, so I'd been wrong. My father did know I existed. Or at least he'd noticed when Sir Hairy growled at him when he came stumbling home from work drunk as a skunk. He'd yelled at me to get that damn dog out of his house.

And I'd promptly lost my mind.

Everything I'd been bottling up came spewing out of me like a broken sewer line.

All the hate.

All the pain.

All the resentment.

My father got it all.

That wasn't the first time I'd seen him drunk. But it was starting to become more and more frequent.

I got it. He was sad and miserable. I was too. But I didn't ignore him twenty-four-seven.

I didn't forget that I had a father.

I didn't abandon him when he needed me the most.

And I sure as hell wasn't going to destroy his only sliver of happiness if and when he finally pulled his head out of his ass and found one.

It had only been four hours since Ramsey gave me that dog.

Four hours since I had been reminded what it felt like to laugh again.

Four hours since I'd looked at my watch and counted the minutes since she had died.

I was desperate to hold on to that kind of emotional freedom.

With bitterness dripping out of me like venom, I leaned toward him and yelled, "I do know what it was like! I was here too, remember? Every single day. I watched her die."

"What the hell do you expect from me, Thea? She was my wife!" he roared, so unlike the soft-spoken man I'd grown up with.

"I expect you to be my father!" I roared right back. "You promised her you were going to take care of me. I heard you. You swore to her that you'd make sure I brushed my teeth every morning and ate something other than microwave dinners every night. You told her you'd help me with my homework and be home by the time I got off the bus. I heard you. You told her all of that and you *lied!*"

His voice broke as he slid down the wall. "I didn't lie. I just didn't realize how hard this would be without her."

With a heaving chest, I stared at the wet tracks streaking his hollow cheeks. I wanted to feel bad. He was a shattered man, and I was all but pouring salt in his wounds. But I couldn't stop myself. I hated him. Everything about him. But only because I couldn't make him love me the way I needed him to.

Frantically, I started knotting a long ribbon around the collar I'd braided out of hay twine for Sir Hairy as soon as I'd finished giving him a bath. "I'm keeping the dog. I don't care what you say."

Dad closed his eyes and hung his head low. "Sure. Fine. Whatever you want, Thea."

I really just wanted my family back. I'd even settle for just my father. But they were both equally impossible and therefore worthless to hope for.

"I'm taking him for a walk."

He nodded but didn't say anything else.

Story of my life.

My hands were shaking and my head was swirling when I got outside. The pink Georgia sky was striped with clouds as Sir Hairy and I made our way down the driveway.

Not surprisingly, Ramsey pulled up on his bike, skidding to a stop beside me. "Hey, where ya going?"

"Away," I mumbled, continuing past him.

Sir Hairy pulled me up short, sniffing at Ramsey's pockets. And sure enough, Ramsey pulled out a slice of cheese wrapped in plastic.

I mean seriously, what didn't the guy keep in those pockets?

"Hey bud?" Ramsey cooed, feeding him the cheese. "How's it going at the new place?"

My heart raced, and my emotions were going to overflow at any second. I didn't have time to deal with Ramsey and his never-ending chitchat.

I kept walking. "It's going great. Just. *Great.*"

"Is that why I heard all that yelling?"

My whole body locked up tight, and I stopped in the middle of the sidewalk. "Are you eavesdropping now too?"

He grinned. "No. I was riding my bike when your dad came around the corner and almost ran me over."

I bit out a silent curse. Jesus. What was wrong with him? "Um… He's not usually…" I had no idea how to finish that. *Usually* wasn't really a word that applied to my dad anymore.

He'd changed so drastically over the last few months that I wasn't sure what *usually* looked like for him at all. And the worst part was that also meant I didn't know what *usually* looked like for me, either. I'd have killed for a single day of normalcy, even if that meant listening to her die all over again.

When further explanation failed me, I skipped right to the point. "Sorry."

"No biggy. I survived. After he tripped on the sidewalk and went rolling down the driveway like a bowling ball, I helped him to the door. I left around the point you told him he didn't matter." Uncomfortable, he looked down and ruffled the dog's ears. "Figured you'd be grounded for the next twenty years after that. I was prepping to do a search-and-rescue mission for ol' Bologna here. Trust me when I say, this guy has no problems pissing in a closet if you don't take him out regularly." His dark eyes came back to mine as he reached for the leash. "Maybe I should hold on to him for a few days until you get things worked out with your dad."

Balancing on my crutches, I switched the ribbon to my hand farther away from him. "It's going to take more than a few days to get things worked out with my dad. And *Sir Hairy* is mine, so back off." I made a kissy sound, snapping the dog's attention away from Ramsey's pocket cheese. "Let's go, boy."

His tail wagged, and after stealing the last bit of cheese, he trotted after me.

Unfortunately, so did Ramsey. "Where ya going?"

"Somewhere."

"Hang on. Let me put my bike up and I'll come too."

"No."

"No? What's that supposed to mean?"

"It means I don't want you to come with me."

"Why not?" He kept following me, matching me step for step.

"Because I'm trying to get away from you."

He barked a loud laugh that echoed off the houses on our quiet street. "No, you aren't."

I made a show of speeding up. "I'm pretty sure I am."

"Then you'd be wrong." He abandoned his bike on the curb and fell into place at my side in his usual spot in the grass.

It wasn't lost on me that my dad didn't have a *usual* anymore, but Ramsey did.

I just didn't want Ramsey's usual, at least not right then.

"Go away," I grumbled, stopping at the end of the sidewalk.

There was an old dirt path that led through the woods to the Wynns' farm. It was going to be a nightmare to navigate it on my crutches, but the pressure in my chest was building by the second. I needed to get out of there fast. Maybe go sit under the Wynns' tree and hold my breath until I could convince the cruel universe to cut me some slack. I needed—

"All right, hop up," Ramsey said, appearing in front of me. He squatted with his back to me as if he expected me to jump on for a piggyback ride.

I was about to have a nervous breakdown and he was offering a piggyback ride.

Fan-freaking-tastic.

"Go. Away," I seethed.

He ignored me, backing up so he was only inches away. "Drop your crutches. We'll get 'em when we come back."

"Come back from where?"

"I don't know. I figured the tree, but we can go wherever you want."

Unable to hold it in any longer, I broke. On the one person who never deserved it.

"There is no *we*," I snarled. "Why are you so stupid? Do you have mental problems? I'm trying to get *away* from you!"

His body went stiff as he stood up straight. I couldn't see his face, but for the first time since I'd met him, I was positive he wasn't smiling.

His hands fisted at his sides as he spun on a toe to face me. "Stop calling me stupid! If I wanted insults, I'd stay at home with my dad."

"Well, maybe you should," I fired back before his words had a chance to sink in. "I bet he at least likes you."

If I hadn't been so damn mad, I would have seen his flinch and taken a second to read the pain as it flashed across his face. But I was a volcano mid-eruption and poor, sweet Ramsey was in the path of destruction.

His jaw ticked as he stared at me. "You are such an asshole! You know that? I was trying to be nice to you. That's all I've ever done. And you're always so damn mean."

"I don't want you to be nice to me. I want you to go away and leave me alone!"

"Why?" he snapped, taking a giant step toward me. "So you can go hide, feeling sorry for yourself because your mom died? Oh poor, pitiful Thea. Wah, wah, wah." He rubbed his eyes like a crying baby before slapping his hands on his thighs. "Well, you know what? I don't feel sorry for you. She died. So *fucking* what."

I loathed pity. Avoided it at all cost. But right then, from Ramsey of all people, the absence of it felt like a slap to the face. "Shut up! You don't know what you're talking about. I watched her die. Do you have any idea how hard that was?"

"Yeah!" he yelled back. "Probably a lot like watching my mom back out of the driveway knowing she was never coming back."

My chest heaved as I opened my mouth, ready to scream exactly how much I hated him, but nothing came out.

Ramsey hadn't mentioned his parents much. I'd seen his dad once in the driveway coming home from work, but I didn't spend a lot of time outside. Ramsey was always so happy that I assumed he had a decent parent. Though I might have been too preoccupied with my own emotional turmoil to notice the signs of his. Or maybe whatever this was about had just happened.

My heart shattered as understanding suddenly dawned on me.

Tragedy and crap parents weren't isolated to me.

"What happened?" I asked. It was quite possibly the first question I'd ever asked him—or at least the only one where I cared about the answer.

His chest rose and fell with heavy breaths as he shook his head. "Your mom didn't choose to leave you. She'd still be here fighting if she could. And not everyone's that lucky. Maybe you should think about that before you go around treating everyone like dog crap."

I kept my voice low and firm. "Ramsey, what *happened?*"

He cocked his head to the side and stared at me. "What do you care, Thea?"

My stomach twisted.

I hated that he thought I didn't care.

I hated that up, until that moment, *I* had thought I didn't care.

But it was Ramsey. How could I not?

"Because we're friends," I whispered.

He scoffed, but I didn't take it to heart. I deserved that.

I inched closer until the foot of my crutch was almost touching his shoe. "I'm sorry, okay? You're right. I wasn't thinking. I had a bad night and… Well, you're always there when I need you. And I think tonight you might need me."

"I don't need you," he told the ground.

I wasn't sure if he was telling the truth or not. But after everything he'd done for me, even when I hadn't wanted him to, I owed Ramsey something huge. However, when you're ten, options for payback are limited. So, dropping one crutch and balancing on my good foot, I gave him the only thing I had. The one thing I'd truly needed over the last few months.

His tall, lanky frame went solid as I wrapped my arms around his waist and pinned his arms to his sides.

"What the hell are you doing?"

"Hugging you," I mumbled into his chest.

"Yeah, I got that. But *why?*"

"Because you won't tell me what's going on, so I'm just doing it and hoping it will help."

He squirmed in my grip. "Let me go."

"Nope."

"Thea, I'm serious."

"I am too. You need a hug. I'm giving you a hug. Just accept it."

He blew out a ragged breath, but after a second, his body

sagged. "You would have punched me in the balls if I hugged you tonight."

"Probably."

"Any chance you'll let go if I tell you what happened?"

What I wanted to say was: *Absolutely not.* After the initial shock of contact had worn off, I liked hugging Ramsey. He smelled like dirt and sweat, but he was warm and comfortable, his heart playing a soothing melody in my ear.

Unfortunately, I was really curious about what had caused some Freaky Friday attitude switch between the two of us. I was the cranky friend. Not him.

"Promise you'll tell me the truth?"

He sighed. "I promise."

Reluctantly, I released him. The loss was staggering as the cool night air stole his warmth.

He backed away, but not before leaning down to retrieve my crutch. I hated when he helped me, but it was so classically Ramsey that I couldn't help but smile.

His eyes narrowed on my mouth. "Did your dad give you some booze tonight? You're acting weird."

I rolled my eyes. "Nope. That would have required him talking to me."

"Your dad sucks too, huh?"

"He's the worst."

Ramsey kept his voice low, but there was a jagged edge to it I'd never heard before. "He hit you when he drinks?"

"What? No. He just ignores me."

Ramsey hummed in acknowledgement and then squatted to pet Sir Hairy, who had long since given up on our walk and curled into a ball at our feet.

"It could always be worse," he said. "He could hate you."

"Is that what happened tonight? You get in a fight with your dad too?"

His eyes lifted to mine and for the first time I recognized the torment brewing within them. "No. Tonight he got into a fight with my mom. She left over a month ago and called to tell him she was sending over the divorce papers."

My heart stopped. "A *month* ago?"

"Yep. On Nora's birthday, she told us she was going out to get Happy Meals, took our order and everything, and then never came back."

Oh, God. Suddenly his explosion about my mother made a lot more sense.

"Ramsey, I—"

He wedged his hands inside the pockets of his jeans. "I knew something was wrong, but you should have seen Nora's face. It was like the kid had never tasted a chicken nugget in her life." His smile returned, but this wasn't the Ramsey Stewart special I'd grown accustomd to. It was a lot sad and entirely heartbreaking. "One month, two weeks, and four days later and Nora's still waiting for her to come back. I don't have the heart to tell her it's never gonna happen. She and my dad were fighting on the phone tonight about who *had* to keep us. Not who *got* to keep us. But who *had* to. From what I could gather, she's in Texas with a soldier she met online. I don't know. And I honestly don't care, either."

My.

Heart.

Stopped.

I glanced at my watch. One month, two weeks, and four days was the exact amount of time since my mother had died. Which meant…

"That day? In the tree?"

His eyes lifted to mine. "I told you I wasn't spying on you."

I rocked back as guilt plowed into me with the speed of a runaway train. Ramsey's mom might not have been dead, but we had both been at the tree that day mourning a life we would never get back. I'd spent every day since feeling utterly lost and alone, when in reality he had always been *there*, silently suffering right beside me.

"Why didn't you tell me?"

"Why *would* I tell you? You've hated me since the day we met. Calling me names. Dodging me every chance you get." His lips tipped into a genuine smile so familiar that it eased the ache inside me. "You don't even like me, Thea. So why on Earth would I tell *you* about my mom?"

His words might as well have been a rusty dagger for the way they slayed me.

I was a horrible person.

My father was probably still sitting on the floor by the door, crying after what I'd said to him. And now, Ramsey, the only person who gave a damn about me, was standing in front of me, thinking I didn't care about *him*.

I was worse than horrible. I was horrible *and* cruel *and* selfish.

"Ramsey…" I trailed off without the first clue what to say. *I'm sorry* wasn't enough. "I do like you."

He shrugged. "I know you do. I figure you would have poisoned me by now if you didn't."

I choked out a laugh. "I'm really, really sorry."

"Nah. Forget about it. I said some stuff about your mom too. And I'm sorry your dad sucks. I don't really like to talk about it, either. So if we could just, ya know, forget this happened, that'd be great."

I couldn't forget though. Not after finding out how much Ramsey and I shared. But that wasn't what he needed to hear at the moment. "Consider it forgotten."

That time when he grinned, my heart skipped a beat.

"Listen," he said, "I know we can't outrun all of this stuff and hide forever, but if you want, I'll always be around to help you try." He turned, once again offering me a ride on his back. "But maybe, in the future, you can give me a warning about the hug thing."

I didn't quite understand it yet, and I wouldn't for years to come, but in hindsight, that was the exact moment I fell in love with Ramsey Stewart.

I stood there staring at his back for several seconds. I didn't deserve him. I would never deserve him, but I'd never wanted something so much in my entire life.

"Come on. Flutter up, Sparrow. We ain't got all night."

I didn't hesitate another second before I dropped my crutches and hopped onto his back.

And because Ramsey wasn't done shining his bright light onto my dark existence, I even smiled when he took the leash from my hand and gave it a gentle tug, asking, "You're really going to make me call this dog Sir Hairy, aren't you?"

SIX

Ramsey

To explain how I fell in love with Thea Hull, I'd need to go back to the beginning. Fair warning, this is not a story of hearts, flowers, and romance. That would all come later. But in the beginning, my love for Thea was born out of death, broken hearts, and desperation.

Coincidentally, that was also how it ended.

When I was eleven years old, my life was in shambles. My family had recently been evicted from our house. The one we'd lived in since I was born. It didn't matter that the place was a piece of crap, essentially falling down around us. It was *home*. Or it had been until I got off the bus from school to find all of our belongings on the street corner.

We didn't have much. My mom had pawned anything of worth months earlier trying to keep us afloat for a while longer. But I'd never forget as long as I lived the embarrassment heating my face as Nora and I were forced to dig through the piles to gather our clothes in garbage bags. My old "friends" stood around laughing and pointing, and after that, I wasn't all that sad about moving anymore.

Maybe a fresh start was exactly what we needed.

It couldn't hurt. It wasn't like my parents could fight more than they already did. Sometimes they'd hurl insults with words.

Other times it was with fists. Starting at about the age of nine, wrestling my dad off my mom had become a monthly activity. It hadn't always been that way though.

Once upon a time, before he'd gotten his third DUI and lost his driver's license, my dad had been a truck driver. It was nice when he was on the road. My mom would cook Nora and me grilled cheese sandwiches—her specialty—and then let us watch TV way past our bedtime. We didn't have to be quiet for fear of pissing him off or tiptoe into the kitchen so he didn't hear us getting a snack. Without him around to bitch and complain, my mom would get the phone, smoke cigarettes, and talk to one of her girlfriends for hours. I still remember looking over at her each time she'd laugh, her head thrown back, her mouth open, and her short, brown hair brushing her shoulders. I relished in the sound because it wasn't one I got to hear often.

When Dad was gone, my mom was a totally different woman.

Don't get me wrong. Whether he was home or not, she was always smiling. It was how I learned what an incredible disguise a grin could be. People didn't pry about why you had bruises if you were happy. Nor did they inquire if there was enough food to feed your children or if your husband had spent all of his money on beer, video poker, and truck-stop hookers. (Yeah, my old man was a real class act.) People didn't actually ask questions at all if you were sporting a smile. It became my family's greatest defense.

Around town, we were known as an all-American, hard-working family.

Behind closed doors, Nora cried herself to sleep every night, hugging a ragged teddy bear to her chest.

Behind closed doors, my mother wrapped her battered ribs with bandages.

Behind closed doors, I lay in bed, dreaming of all the places I wanted to go when I finally escaped that hell.

I had high hopes for the small town of Clovert. It was only sixty miles away, but that was more than enough distance for me to start over. The new house was a dump on the inside, with peeling linoleum, filthy carpet, and holes in the walls, which my father promised to patch in exchange for a discounted rent. The outside didn't look so bad though.

That was exactly how I lived my life, showing the world a pretty exterior to hide the disaster on the inside.

And trust me, on the inside. I was a disaster of epic proportions. I'd failed fifth grade. Math was not my thing. Neither were science, history, English, tests, quizzes, or homework. My mom told me she'd pick up an extra shift at the restaurant to pay for me to go to summer school so I didn't have to repeat the year. My dad said he wasn't going to waste a single cent on a dumb fuck who probably wouldn't make it any further than eighth grade anyway.

I hated that man something fierce, but when he made up his mind, there was nothing that could be done to change it. And for some reason, my dad had made his mind up that I was a loser who would amount to nothing when I had still been in diapers.

Luckily, I had my mom. No matter how hard things got, she was always there with a warm smile and a kind word.

Until she wasn't.

She left on a sunny Sunday afternoon with a big purse busting at the seams thrown over her shoulder. I knew she was never coming back the minute I saw her answer a cell phone my father didn't know she had.

I'd imagined running away every night since I was old enough to dream. But in my dreams, I'd taken her and Nora with me. We were a family. The three of us against him. Forever.

In the end, my angelic mother, who I'd placed on the highest of pedestals, proved she was no better than he was.

She blew me a kiss as she backed out of the driveway.

She wasn't crying.

She wasn't frantic.

She smiled.

And then she was gone.

So there I was, eleven years old, abandoned by my mother, stuck with an abusive father, repeating fifth grade, completely overwhelmed with life, crying in a tree, belt in hand, trying to convince myself that Nora would be okay without me.

Cue Thea Hull.

The first time I saw her, she was sprinting across a hayfield. Her long, brown hair, the color of the sparrows we used to feed in my old backyard, flowed behind her as she raced to the base of the tree I was hiding in. I'd love to wax poetic about how she was the most beautiful girl I'd ever seen, because one day, she would become exactly that. But right then, she was just a girl who had interrupted me while I was on the verge of self-destructing.

Quiet and careful not to rustle the leaves, I watched her for what felt like forever. I wanted her to leave. I all but prayed for it. The last thing I needed was for her to look up and catch me with red-rimmed eyes and tear-streaked cheeks. But she just sat there, staring at her watch as if it were the most entertaining thing she'd ever seen. About the time she got comfortable and leaned back against the trunk, I realized that the good Lord my grandpa used to preach about wasn't going to deliver me a miracle. My foot was asleep and my arms were shaking from holding the branch above me. The only thing I could do was dry my eyes on my shoulders, put on my mask, and hope I never saw her again.

Of course, that was before I accidentally broke her leg.

As guilty as I felt about that, especially given that it happened on the same day her mom had died, it turned out to be a miracle in and of itself.

See, with as much as I was hiding about my life, being the new kid in school was going to be hell. Questions. Everyone was going to have questions.

Where'd you move from?

How old are you?

What's your family like?

And if I didn't answer or didn't answer convincingly enough, their curiosity would only grow. Hiding wasn't an option when dealing with nosy kids who literally had nothing better to do than figure out my life story.

That was where Thea came in. In the weeks after I'd broken her leg, no fewer than ten kids rode their bikes down our road, slowing down as they passed her house. I felt bad for her, always sitting in the window, staring at a bunch of fools who went out of their way to gawk at her pain. But if I wanted to fly under the radar, beating them senseless wasn't an option.

A few of them stopped to introduce themselves while Nora and I were outside playing. And you know what happened? Each and every one of them told me about Thea's mom. It was always a different story. Sometimes cancer. Sometimes pneumonia. Heck, one of them even told me it was a snake bite. Whatever they'd overheard or made up based on the town's rumblings, it was always told quietly and with morbid fascination.

That was when I decided that, along with my smile, Thea Hull was going to become the star of my defensive line.

With the poor, pitiful, motherless girl at my side, everyone was going to be too busy whispering about her to pay me any attention. Just the way I liked it.

For almost two months, it worked. Thea was rotten company in the beginning, but with nosy girls purring around me like alley cats in heat, having her at my side worked in my favor. By the time the curiosity about her had worn off, she'd been a viper to virtually everyone in our class. This included me more often than not, but I was slightly more inclined to forgive given that I needed her for security and all.

Yes, there was a part of me that felt bad using her like that. But she was going to be miserable whether I was hiding behind her or not. It wasn't like I was being mean to her. I stood up for her and put people in their place when I heard them talking trash behind her back. She wasn't a bad person or anything. She'd just...been through a lot. Something I more than understood. She didn't know the smile trick. I'd teach her though.

Around the six-week mark, things changed between Thea and me. Or maybe it didn't change *between us*; she was still awful, but it changed *inside me*. Every wildfire begins with a spark, and for me, that spark was when she left her bike on our front porch for Nora. I had nothing. I was fine with having nothing. But Nora was different. She'd been close to my mom and was taking it hard now that she was gone. Her smile had dimmed a little more each day until it finally vanished. I'd have done anything to make her happy again.

That bike was more than just entertainment. It was a temporary escape so she could get out of the house and do something on the days my dad was too drunk to find work as a day laborer. I couldn't fix the chain on her bike after it'd broken, and there was no way I could come up with the money to buy her a new one any time soon. I'd figure it out though; I always did. That time, Thea figured it out first. And because she'd done it for Nora, it meant more than anything she ever could have done for me.

After that, I started looking at Thea differently, and you know what? She wasn't that bad. Sure, she was a smartass, but I kind of liked that about her. Her sniper-quick comebacks made me laugh. She did call me an idiot and it got under my skin like a bag of fleas, but she didn't mean it. She was just so pissed off and bitter all the time. I couldn't blame her; deep down, I was raging too.

Thea and I were two of a kind. Lost. Broken. Forgotten. *Stuck.*

But it didn't feel like I was stuck when I was with her. She was a code I couldn't crack, but the challenge alone made me obsessed.

I wasn't positive she listened when I talked. She gave no reaction and offered me no advice. Sometimes her only acknowledgement was to hum or nod while staring off into space. But something extraordinary happened on that bus when the two of us were alone in the confines of our ugly brown bench seat cocoon.

I forgot.

For thirty minutes every morning and then thirty minutes every afternoon, I didn't have to think about my dad. Or my mom. Or how I was going to feed Nora that night. I didn't have to think about math tests or failing fifth grade—again. I didn't have to think about anything at all.

For one hour every day, I got to be eleven.

I filled Thea's ears with all things bikes, school gossip, and TV I'd watched the night before. I didn't mention that it was a bike I could never afford, that the school gossip was something I'd created to take the attention off us, or that I was only watching TV because Nora had woken me up with another nightmare. No. I didn't mention any of that. And it was hands down the most liberating hour of my entire life.

My stomach would churn every afternoon when the bus came to a stop at the end of our street, cuing my mandatory return to reality. I tried to hold on to her, begging her to come out and play, but she never took the bait.

I'd often wished we had a cool story about when our relationship transitioned from that of tolerating each other to discovering we were two halves of one soul. But the truth is Thea and I evolved much like the seasons: slow, steady, and unstoppable.

With the way we'd met, our friendship was unlikely at best. Then, after I yelled at her and told her I didn't feel sorry for her that her mother had died, I half expected it to be a *nonexistent* friendship. But in a twist of fate I'd never be able to fully explain, she hugged me.

I wasn't a virgin to human touch or anything. Nora hugged me. My mom had hugged me. But I knew down to the marrow in my bones that there was something life altering about the way Thea hugged me. And I fucking loved it.

After that, I caught her looking at me more. And not the usual scowl she shot my way when I offered her gum.

No, this was more.

She'd watch me out of the corner of her eye when we were sitting in class.

I'd feel her gaze on my back when I'd be waiting in line for my county-provided free lunch.

On the bus, she'd turn to face me as soon as she sat down.

And I noticed it every single time because I was watching her too.

Despite the unbelievably ridiculous name, Sir Hairy changed things for us too. Dogs had to pee and it gave Thea an excuse to come out of her fortress at least twice a day. And when she'd hobble out, I was always there, waiting like a junkie for a few more minutes of the emotional reprieve she provided me.

Most of the time, she'd sit on the end of the driveway while I took Sir Hairy into the woods to do his business. But occasionally, after a few minutes of pleading and heckling, I could convince her to hop onto my back and go out to the tree in the Wynns' hayfield. I loved those nights. A peace I hadn't felt in, well, *ever* would wash over me as the cool fall wind rustled the leaves. She'd sit at the trunk with her back propped up against the bark while I'd make myself comfortable in the branches.

Sometimes we'd talk. I'd tell her about my shit day and she'd tell me about hers. We'd commiserate, make sad jokes about our crappy parents, and act like our screwed-up lives were perfectly normal. And when we were together, they *were* perfectly normal. I didn't have to pretend to be someone else with Thea, because in some twisted way, I was exactly who she needed me to be.

Other times, we hung out at that tree in silence. She had the most amazing sixth sense for knowing when I needed the quiet. I wasn't so great at reading her, but she had no qualms telling me to shut it.

"Not tonight, Ramsey," she'd whisper. "Please."

No matter how bad my day had been or how much I needed to unload my burdens on someone who would understand, I'd give her those moments, because without a shadow of a doubt she would have given them to me.

Occasionally Nora would come with us. She'd trot Sir Hairy around on his leash while collecting acorns. Those were the afternoons Thea would smile. And God, did I love her smile.

Love changes a man—even when he's not yet a man at all. We were friends, but Thea was still quiet, stoic, borderline rude a lot of the time. However, in that tree, suffering alone and also together, I fell in love with her like the stars falling from the sky.

Thea made me *feel*.

It didn't take long before I was utterly addicted.

The day she got her cast off was terrifying for me. I'd been expendable to my own mother. How was I supposed to expect a ten-year-old girl I'd only known a few months to stick around? What if we weren't really friends? What if I was as useless as my father claimed? I spent the entire night pacing and panicking that I was going to lose her. She wouldn't need me to carry her book bag or give her piggyback rides anymore. I wasn't positive what she had done for fun before I'd broken her leg, but I couldn't imagine it was sitting under a tree, listening to a boy ramble about meaningless crap.

She wasn't on the bus that morning and I swear it was the loneliest I'd ever felt. My smile failed me that day as I alternated between doodling stick-figure wars and staring at the door to our classroom, anxiously waiting for her to come walking through.

Lunch passed and still no Thea.

I had friends in class, people I sat with and played pranks on, but none of them were her. By the time the final bell rang, I was ready to peel out of my skin. It was the first time I was ever in a hurry to get *home*.

Armed with nothing but her missed work for the day that I promised our teacher I'd deliver and a healthy dose of nervous rolling through my stomach, I jogged up the driveway and knocked on her door.

She was smiling when she opened it. Probably because she was happy to have her cast off, but it filled me in unimaginable ways to think that maybe, just maybe, that smile was because she was as excited to see me too.

"Hey," she said.

It had been twelve weeks since I'd met her, but I'd never felt more awkward in my life. "Hey."

She tucked a strand of long, brown hair behind her ear. "How was school?"

"Good."

She nodded. "Good."

"How was the doctor?"

She lifted the leg of her jeans, revealing a thin, pale ankle. "Good."

I nodded that time. "Good."

There was a long pause, my nightmare where she slammed the door in my face only seconds away from playing out in front of me.

I thrust the stack of papers toward her. "Here's the work you missed today."

"Thanks."

We both nodded that time.

Any other day, with any other person, that entire exchange would have been laughable. But that was the day everything would change for us—again. It's crazy to think a silly piece of plaster around her leg had dictated so much of our time to-gether. But it had. Our relationship had started with that cast, and I was scared out of my wits that it was going to end it all too.

She was smiling. That had to be a good sign.

But then again, Thea didn't smile often, so maybe this was part of her gentle letdown before she told me to take a hike.

I was losing it. All I had to do was rip off the Band-Aid and ask her if she wanted to hang out. If she said no, I'd have my answer. She was done with me. Or maybe not. Thea always said no. Okay, so all I had to do was ask her, then beg her, then harass her, and if she still said no, then I'd have my answer.

Oh God, what if she was done with me?

"Uh...why do you look like you're about to throw up?" she asked.

Because I was, in fact, about to throw up. I kept that to myself. "I don't."

"Yeah, you do. Any chance you can aim that in the grass so I don't have to clean it up later?"

"I'm not going to puke," I bit out entirely too roughly.

Her eyebrows shot up her forehead. "Jeez, somebody's in a bad mood."

I huffed and cut my gaze over her shoulder. It was now or never. My entire life hung in the balance. Or at least it felt that way. Rip off the Band-Aid. Just do it. "Listen, are we cool?"

"No."

My gaze jumped to hers. "What?"

She looked down at the papers I'd handed her. "Who brings homework for their friend when they get to skip school?" She slapped the papers against my chest. "Take that and burn it. We can tell Mrs. Young that you lost it on the way home."

The relief tore from my lungs. I didn't just smile with my mouth—it radiated through my whole body.

I shoved the papers back in her direction. "No way. *My friend* skipped school today, so I had to do all of those worksheets in class without anyone to cheat off of. The least you could have done was give me a heads-up that you weren't coming so I could sit next to Tiffany."

"Tiffany!" she exclaimed, pure Thea Hull disgust crinkling her forehead.

Yeah. We were going to be all right.

"What? She makes good grades."

She twisted her lips. "Right. You were going to sit next to her because she makes *good grades* and not because she's the only girl in the class who has boobs."

Truthfully? I had Thea. I hadn't even noticed that Tiffany had a face.

I barked a laugh, anxiety ebbing from my system, leaving the most unbelievable calm behind. "How about we stop talking about Tiffany and take your new leg out for a spin? Wanna ride bikes down to the ditch?"

She groaned. "I'm not allowed to ride my bike for two weeks while my ankle strengthens."

I leaned back and made a show of looking at her empty driveway. "Your dad at work?"

"Yeah."

I quirked an eyebrow. "Soooo, we riding or what?"

She shrugged, completely oblivious to the celebration roaring inside me. "Yeah. Give me a minute. I need to pee before we go."

I grinned impossibly wide as she turned on a toe and swung the door shut in my face.

And that was the story of how Thea became the other half of my soul. It wasn't the romantic beginning people had inscribed in wedding rings or shared with their grandkids for generations to come. But it was us, and we would later learn that finding unconditional understanding in another human being was more extraordinary and romantic than any love story.

Thea and I rode our bikes that day.

And the day after that.

And the day after that.

Little by little, she became my entire world.

Which should have been the first clue that I'd eventually lose her.

SEVEN

Thea

OVER THE NEXT YEAR, RAMSEY BECAME MY BEST FRIEND IN every sense of the word. My dad slowly started to reemerge from the depths of his depression. Though nothing ever went back to *normal*. He worked seven days a week at the barbershop, which I understood. He was the sole provider for our little family. He had to work hard. Plus, he owned the place, so he had things to do like bookkeeping, maintenance, and avoiding me. It was rare for him to be at home before dinner. I'd gotten used to the peace, quiet, and uninterrupted TV time, but it drove Ramsey crazy that I was always alone.

His solution was to never leave my side.

And my solution was to always leave the door unlocked for him.

Nora and Ramsey quickly became a fixture in my house. Without my dad around, we had free reign to do whatever we wanted. This usually consisted of eating too much junk food, arguing over what we were going to watch, and then giving up and going outside to play regardless of the weather.

Nora wasn't the athletic type, but thanks to the guy on the corner who let Ramsey mow his grass for the asinine highway robbery price of twenty bucks a month, we'd gotten her a new bike so she could tag along with us. The three of us became inseparable, but that did not mean it was all smooth sailing.

A few days before Ramsey's birthday, Nora spilled the beans that he was turning twelve rather than the eleven I'd assumed. It was stupid, but a piece of my heart broke when I found out he was keeping secrets.

Ramsey had become my everything, and it hurt to realize I wasn't his.

I probably wasn't as delicate as I should have been when I confronted him about it. My temper needed a little work in those days. He got mad, slammed the door, and stormed off.

I waited for him at our tree for several hours.

When he finally showed up, he offered me a piece of gum and then spent the next ten minutes pouring his heart out about his parents fighting, him failing fifth grade, and them being evicted.

I ached for him and Nora. How he still smiled at all, I would never understand. But I showed him no pity. Instead, I yelled at him that we were best friends and I didn't care if he had a third nipple—he was required by best friend law to tell me about it.

The little things meant a lot to Ramsey. And the way his face lit at such an obvious declaration was a little sad but a lot heartwarming. He smiled throughout the rest of that tongue lashing while I stared up at him pretending to be pissed off but secretly happier than I'd ever been.

My grades were still in the toilet because I didn't care enough to try, but knowing that Ramsey was struggling with school kicked my butt into gear. We started doing our homework together, and I stopped letting him copy the answers off my tests.

He glared at me a lot at first.

Which made me laugh.

Which made him smile.

Which made my cheeks get hot.

Which made his smile fall as he asked if I was feeling okay.

Which made me snap at him to shut up and get back to work.

Which made him laugh and started the vicious circle all over again.

When we got our final report cards in May, Ramsey had one B, three Cs, a D, and a ticket to sixth grade. We partied hard that night. Okay, fine, we sat at our tree, arguing if it was too late to change Sir Hairy's name or not. I was having some serious regrets about that one. We settled on dropping the Sir part.

And that was pretty much how things went for us over the next few years.

As time passed, we got even closer. Older. Feelings that had nothing to do with friendship started to develop. When I was twelve, I started seeing Ramsey in a different light. I finally had to admit to myself that I like-*liked* him, which meant I immediately told him. There were no secrets between us. Not even that I thought he was cute and got jealous as hell when earlier that day he'd chosen to pair up with Tiffany Martin for science lab.

I assumed Ramsey like-*liked* me too when, two seconds after I'd told him how I felt, he'd jumped out of the tree—thankfully without breaking my leg—sat down beside me, and bumped me with his shoulder, stating, "About time. I knew the Tiffany thing would get you."

"She's such a snob."

He threw his arm around my shoulders. "She really is."

Later that weekend, Ramsey asked me to be his girlfriend.

Okay, maybe *asked* was an overstatement. We'd been playing baseball with the guys when a new kid wandered over and laughed that there was a girl on the mound. I'd just gotten my glove off, ready to hurl it at his head, when Ramsey yelled, "Shut the hell up. She's my girlfriend."

He looked at me.

I looked at him.

We both shrugged and then I struck the new kid out—twice.

While our friendship was no secret, our new label set the seventh-grade girls on fire. It didn't change us in the least. He wasn't writing me poems or bringing me flowers or anything. He did, however, still sit with me on the bus every day and pound down my door every Saturday morning after my dad left for work. He and Nora would bring over a box of cereal and I'd provide the milk and bowls. We'd spend the morning watching cartoons, the afternoon exploring the woods, and the nights sneaking around in the shadows, scaring the crap out of each other.

That was who we were. Simple, average, yet utterly extraordinary.

The normal "us" changed all over again a year later.

"Thea, you in there?"

"Go away!" I yelled inside the bathroom.

This was not happening. No way. No how. It was *not* happening.

"Nora told me she thinks you started your period. Good news, you probably won't die from that."

I closed my eyes and leaned on the sink. Jesus Christ, it was really happening.

It had started as a regular old day. Ramsey had shown up early that morning, cussing about his dad's girlfriend getting high and eating all the cereal. He'd stolen some of my Cap'n Crunch, and then while I was getting dressed, he spent the next ten minutes yelling down the hallway about why the cartoon guy on the box had never been promoted. Same old, same old.

Oh, but Mother Nature had other plans for me that day.

RELEASE

We rode our bikes out to the park near the school, where there was a massive pick-up game of dodgeball happening. Not to brag, but also to brag, Ramsey and I made a pretty badass team on the court. We were in the middle of destroying Josh Caskey and Nathan Pollard when the game suddenly came to a screeching halt.

"What the fuck is that on your pants?" Josh yelled, jumping to the side as I hurled a ball at his head.

Positive it had been a ploy to make me drop my guard, I grabbed another ball and chucked it at him. "Shut up, idiot."

No one fired back.

There were chuckles as the herd of teenage boys congregating around us began elbowing each other and pointing at me. The hairs on the back of my neck stood on end as I looked over at Ramsey.

He was frozen. Eyes wide. Mouth hanging open. His face pale and filled with horror as he stared at my shorts.

They were white cotton, by the way.

Clearly, I'd yet to get back in God's good graces.

The laughing got louder, and panic and embarrassment ricocheted inside me, but through it all, Ramsey never moved. That's right. Half of the boys in junior high were laughing at me, and my best friend, my freaking *boyfriend*, said nothing.

I took off at a dead sprint, grabbing my bike on my way past, never slowing as I swung my leg over it and peddled home as fast as two bald tires could carry me.

So, there I was, hiding in my bathroom, knowing I'd just started my period.

Embarrassed that the whole school would know about it on Monday.

Wanting to crawl into a hole and die because Ramsey knew.

Fighting the desire to punch the wall because Ramsey had known and done *nothing* but stare at me.

And feeling more alone than ever because I didn't know what the hell to do about any of it.

My mom would have known though. I still missed her like crazy, but thinking about her didn't eat me away anymore. However, it was times like that when I would have given anything for just one more conversation with her.

"Go away!" I yelled when he knocked at the door again.

"Come on, Sparrow. Open up."

I'd long since given up on fighting the nickname. He didn't use it in public, and truth be told, I liked it a lot when he'd whisper it real sweet when he left each night.

But that was neither here nor there at the moment.

"I think we should break up," I told the bathroom door.

He barked a laugh that infuriated me that much more. "Quit telling jokes and come out of there."

I yanked the door open an inch and pressed my lips to the opening. "I'm not joking. You're the worst boyfriend in history. You just stood there while everyone laughed at me."

His smile fell. "Thea, I…"

"Just go home, Ramsey." I slammed the door again, putting my back to it as I listened to the boards creak under his heavy steps. I waited for the front door to close, but either he'd climbed out the window or hadn't left at all. I was betting on the latter.

"Put these on," he rumbled, suddenly reappearing on the other side of the door.

His voice had gotten deeper recently. It had been preceded by a few months of cracks and squeaks, but I wasn't a jerk who laughed at him when it happened. And you better believe I would have leveled anyone who had.

Ramsey didn't have much need for protection from me though. He'd grown several inches since we started eighth grade and was easily over six feet tall. He didn't participate in any of the organized sports our school offered, but the two of us spent more than enough time outside playing whatever sport was in season with the other kids in the neighborhood to add bulk to his once lanky frame.

I, on the other hand, had grown approximately one inch, still had no boobs, and closely resembled the offspring of a flamingo and a mongoose. Okay, so maybe on top of this ridiculous period business, I was starting to feel slightly insecure about my relationship with Ramsey.

Whatever the case may be, I was still positively fuming as I screamed, "Go home!"

"You know, I didn't take you for a girl who would wear pink hearts on their underwear. They're kinda cute though."

My eyes bulged and I yanked that door open so fast that you would have thought the room caught fire. "What are you doing!"

His eyes twinkled with mischief, but his face was serious. "I got you some shorts and underwear. Change and then come talk to me. Nora will be back soon. I gave her cash to ride her bike to the gas station and buy you some…well, whatever it is that girls need"—he pointed to my shorts but kept his gaze firmly locked with mine—"for that kind of thing."

If I hadn't been so embarrassed that I was contemplating how I was going to convince my father that we needed to move to California, I would have laughed. However, I was that embarrassed and suddenly realizing that the continental United States wouldn't be far enough away for this kind of mortification. So I snatched the clothes from his hand, slammed the door, and turned the shower on.

By the time I got out and retrieved the bag of Nora's gas station shopping spree from the doorknob, I'd cooled off a bit. Just enough for the guilt over how I'd talked to Ramsey earlier to sink in. I still wanted to lock myself in my bedroom and hide from the world, but that wasn't how Ramsey and I worked. We were a team who faced our problems, apparently even the biological kind, together.

"Hey," I whispered when I found him sitting on the couch, staring at the blank screen on the TV.

He immediately stood up and turned to face me. "You okay?"

I'd expected my Ramsey Stewart special grin, but what I got was the same pale-faced boy who had been frozen on the dodgeball court.

I padded over to him, studying him closely. "That depends. Are *you* okay?"

He gave his head a twitch to clear the hair from his eyes. "Yeah. Why?"

"Because you're giving me the 'oh my God, I'm freaking out' puke face. I can't decide if I should take this personally because of what happened or if maybe—" That was all I got out before he reached out with both hands and dragged me into his chest.

Now, it should be noted that Ramsey and I weren't all that affectionate with each other. We high-fived. He sat close when we needed to whisper about someone. And on occasion, he'd hold my hand while we hung out at the tree. But that was as far as things had gone—at least physically. Emotional intimacy was a different story.

His whole body was tight as he held me, our fronts flush top to toe.

"What are you doing?" I mumbled against his chest.

He gathered me even closer until I was unable to move. Not

that I was really trying to get away or anything. We'd shared a few pretty awesome hugs over the years. This one was no exception.

"I'm sorry, Thea. You're right. I shouldn't have just stood there, but I saw all that blood and I freaked out. I thought something was wrong. I know your mom died and thought maybe you had the same thing she did."

I craned my head back to catch his gaze, but he was hunched over with his face buried in my neck. "You thought my mom died from having her period? What the heck? I told you she had cancer, like, a million times."

"I know. I know. But you were bleeding, like a lot. I thought maybe that's how it started and then you were going to die too. I can't lose you. Oh God, Thea. I just can't."

Abandonment. It was Ramsey's biggest fear. He'd never come right out and said it, but even as a kid, I could read between the lines.

When we'd sit in the tree after dark and he couldn't see me, he'd often call out, "You still down there, Sparrow?" He'd ask like I was going to randomly disappear at any minute.

The world could have fallen out of orbit and plunged into a black hole and I still never would have left his side.

Secretly, I loved the way Ramsey needed me. At least someone did. The words had never been uttered between us, but we loved each other. Fierce. Patient. Unconditional. Which was probably why it scared him so much. I understood how he felt because it scared the hell out of me too.

It probably wasn't the healthiest mentality, but the two of us were a pair of wings. One was worthless without the other.

"I sound like an idiot, don't I? Just tell me to shut up."

A blanket of warmth enveloped me as I snuggled deeper into his arms. "You're not an idiot. Don't say that."

"Okay, but you're right. I am the worst boyfriend in history. Tomorrow I'll kick the ass of anyone who laughed at you, I swear."

I giggled. "That's a lot of ass kicking."

His head popped up, and thankfully, the color was starting to return to his face. His eyes flicked between mine as he whispered, "Don't scare me like that again."

"I hear it's a once-a-month thing. But I can promise I'm not going anywhere, okay?"

A chill went down my spine as his gaze dipped to my mouth. "Swear to me."

"I swear. It's me and you forever, Ramsey."

"I swear too."

His voice only became more urgent. "I can't do this without you."

"Do what?"

He lifted one shoulder in a half shrug. "Breathe."

It was one simple word, but it held the weight of a thousand promises. We were two lonely people who relied on each other. We'd never been brainwashed enough to believe that the world wasn't a horrible place. We'd been disenchanted with the beauty of life since the day we'd met. But we had each other. That was the one constant we needed for happiness.

He stared deep into my eyes. Searching. Imploring. Vowing things I'd never be able to understand as a kid. But my sweet Ramsey was silently promising them to me all the same.

And I loved him for it more than an entire dictionary of words could adequately express. The beat of my heart though. That was where the truth was always found. And mine was thundering in my chest under his scrutinizing gaze. As if it had a mind of its own, my tongue snaked out to dampen my lips.

That was all the invitation Ramsey needed. As he held my gaze, his lips came down, oh so gently brushing across mine.

Yes, I was his girlfriend.

Yes, he was a fourteen-year-old boy.

Yes, a lot of the other kids at school were already making out—a few had even graduated to talking about sex.

Was I prepared in any way, shape, or form for Ramsey to kiss me? Nope.

However, one taste of Ramsey Stewart and the tomboy inside me who was kissing her best friend was silenced by the shriek of a teenage girl.

His lips were soft.

His tongue was timid.

And his hands were gentle as they glided up my back.

Compared to the frenzied passion we'd later discover with each other, that kiss was tame.

But with that first kiss, Ramsey sealed our promises. Promises that would change us for the better, for the worse, and for everything in between.

Unfortunately for us, not long after that, the worse became all we knew.

EIGHT

Thea

"OH MY GOD, ARE YOU SERIOUSLY GOING TO BE WEIRD now?"

"I'm not being weird," I lied. I was totally being weird.

"Bullshit," he mumbled under his breath. But Ramsey being Ramsey changed the subject. "So, where are we going on our tenth trip?"

Staring up at the fabric ceiling, I pretended to play it cool. "We might be able to afford to fly by then. Dallas or LA?"

"LA. And I'd rather go to Austin than Dallas. I'll get us both fake IDs and we can hit the bars."

"We'll both be old enough to drink by the time we take our tenth trip."

"Not if I can get a job at the factory when I graduate next year."

He wasn't getting a job at the factory—mainly because I wouldn't let him. We had plans. Big plans that involved us getting the hell out of Clovert and traveling the world. We'd been making a schedule of our trips for the last six months. I had a Ramsey-and-Thea notebook and everything. It contained a budget and a list of things we would need. We'd thought of everything including Nora, who was going to move with us and finish up high school wherever our feet landed. The world was just on the other side of the horizon for us.

So, no, Ramsey was not working at the Clovert meat packing plant. Being that I was naked and all, now was not the time to have that argument with him though.

"Okay, eleventh trip. New York or Seattle?" I asked.

"Paris."

I rolled my gaze his way. "We won't be able to afford Paris yet."

"Nah. But it made you finally look at me." He grinned like the cat who ate the canary.

"Stop smiling," I ordered, dragging the blanket up to cover my body.

"No can do, Sparrow. I'm afraid this thing might be permanent now." He rolled to his stomach, the tips of his fingers grazing my breast as he pulled the blanket down.

"Ramsey!" I slapped his hand away.

"Oh, come on. I was just taking a little peek." He winked and then kissed my bare shoulder. "It's the least you can do after all the filthy things you just did to me."

"So they're filthy now, huh? Guess that means you'll never want to do it again?"

Curling his arm around my waist, he flipped to his back and dragged me on top of him. "Now, I didn't say all that."

It was Ramsey's seventeenth birthday. While finally caving in to the constant desire to tear his clothes off probably wasn't what my father intended when he'd loaned me twenty bucks to buy Ramsey a gift, it was definitely what my guy had wanted. I was one of the lone hold-outs in eleventh grade. I didn't particularly care that stupid Tiffany Martin and Thomas Vaughan had been going at it like animals since sophomore year. Ramsey and

I were on our own schedule. It wasn't a competition or anything. Unlike Tiffany, I actually intended to spend the rest of my life with Ramsey, so there was no rush.

With as much time as we spent together (read: every waking minute and a few times he'd snuck into my room at night and accidentally fallen asleep in my bed), waiting had been hard. A year earlier, he'd saved up enough money to buy a broken-down sedan, which I'm almost positive had a cameo in the Bible.

With wheels came freedom.

And with a back seat came temptation.

I'm not too proud to admit that Ramsey and I did our fair share of "parking." He was a gorgeous almost-man. And I was a reasonably attractive almost-woman. But we never took it past the front seat. He didn't complain, either. If I threw on the brakes, Ramsey was there nodding like a fool and backing away like I'd caught leprosy.

It was time though. I wanted to be with Ramsey in every way I could be, and his birthday seemed perfect. The planning and lies that had gone into that night were astronomical.

First, I'd had to ask the Wynns if *Nora* and I could camp out at the old tree. I wasn't sure if they'd have cared if I had told them it was actually me and *Ramsey*. But I couldn't risk word getting back to my dad. He'd become a tad more attentive since I got boobs. He liked Ramsey and all, but camping together was pushing it. Thankfully, Lacey Wynn had agreed no questions asked.

Next, I'd had to borrow a tent. Josh Caskey was the only kid I knew who had one of his own; thus he wouldn't have to clear it with his parents. Perks of being the mayor's son, I guessed. He'd asked me a million questions about why I needed it. I told him the same story about Nora and me that I'd told the Wynns. After a few perverted questions about whether we'd be sleeping naked, he gave me the tent just in time. I'd been only seconds away from kicking him in the balls.

Lastly, we had our parents. Nora would cover for Ramsey. Not that his dad would care. He was too wrapped up in his new girlfriend. His dad was fat, balding, and broke. Though based on the speed with which he went through women, he clearly had some of his son's charm. Or vice versa, I wasn't sure.

In a spectacular show of how well my dad knew me, he hadn't questioned me when I told him I was staying the night with Tiffany Martin. I'd considered telling him I was staying with Nora, but on the off chance he'd need me for something, two doors down was too close.

Two ham sandwiches, a bag of chips, and a couple cans of Coke later, I was set for the most romantic night of my entire life. Or, more accurately, a night of laughing, bumbling out of clothing, teeth clanking, arguing about why Ramsey had a condom in his wallet, and then finally giving myself to him completely.

Sex was funny like that. It didn't change us or make us closer. That was an impossible feat. But it was special in its own way because we'd done it together.

He was my first boyfriend.

My first kiss.

My first love.

My first everything.

A laugh bubbled in my throat as he kissed up my neck.

"Stop giggling, Thea. You know what that does to me."

Straddling him, I murmured, "I don't know anything."

He lifted his hips, revealing that he was very *ready* again.

I moaned, suddenly feeling ready too. "We don't have another condom."

He growled and threw his head back against the pillow. "See, this is what happens when you get a condom from the gas station vending machine."

Right, so the reason for our argument about why Ramsey had a condom in his wallet was because the condom I'd brought had popped before he'd even gotten it out of the wrapper. I guess you get what you pay for in the Quick Stop men's restroom. Lesson learned.

I slapped his chest. "Hey! I've never done this before. Do you have any idea how many packs of gum I had to buy to get eight quarters for that thing without looking suspicious?"

He smiled, magically producing a chewed-up piece of gum from somewhere under his tongue. "I do appreciate it."

"Were you kissing me with gum in your mouth?"

"Sparrow, I think *every* time I've kissed you I've had gum in my mouth."

I rolled my eyes and shifted to the side to lay beside him, carefully taking the blanket with me.

"Whoa, where ya going?"

"We should probably get dressed. Before things…happen."

"Okay, hold up. First of all, I'm going to need you to stop with that getting dressed crazy talk. Secondly, it will take me all of three minutes to run to my house and grab more condoms."

I narrowed my eyes. "Why the hell do you have more condoms at home?"

"And here we go again."

"Ramsey, I'm serious."

"Oh, I have no doubt that you are. But I already told you that my dad keeps a gigantic box under his bed, and tonight, I'm grateful he does for more reasons than just that he won't be reproducing again."

I curled my lip. "Can we please stop talking about your dad reproducing?"

"Sure thing." He sat up and snagged his shirt and his shorts. "Now you lay there and I'll be right back." His gaze dropped to my exposed breast and his face heated. "I'm bringing the whole damn box."

Pulling the blanket up, I hissed, "You're going to get caught." I swayed my head from side to side. "And possibly get a little brother if you bring the *whole* box."

He tapped the tip of my nose. "Good thinking. I'll leave a few."

Unzipping the door to the tent, he looked at me over his shoulder. If I had known it was the last time I'd ever see seventeen-year-old Ramsey smile, I would have stared longer, engraining every dip and curve into my memory so I would never forget how utterly beautiful and carefree he looked in that moment.

But most of all, I would have begged him to stay.

"Don't move," he ordered as he bent down and scooped up my pile of clothes, taking it with him.

"Ramsey!" I scolded without any way to go after him.

"Three minutes." He laughed before his footsteps disappeared into the night.

Ramsey and I lived unique yet completely common lives.

We'd grown up hard. We'd grown up fast. We'd grown up fearless because we'd already faced some of life's greatest demons when we were only in elementary school. But experiencing that had only lulled us into a false security because we honestly believed that we could handle anything the world threw at us, as long as we were together. And maybe that had been true.

But that night, we weren't together.

Minutes after Ramsey had left, Josh Caskey showed up. I

wasn't concerned. I mean, I was naked and pissed the hell off when he crawled through that doorway. Josh was a prankster and my first mistake was telling him where "Nora and I" were going to be camping in his tent that night.

He was drunk, the smell of alcohol on his breath nearly burning my nostrils. I asked him to leave no fewer than a dozen times before giving up and waiting for Ramsey to get back and handle him. While he slurred random conversation, I stared at my watch, counting the seconds as time ticked on.

It took ten minutes and sixteen seconds for Josh to snatch my blanket.

It took eleven minutes and fifty-five seconds for him to pin me to the ground after I'd punched him.

Twelve minutes and twenty seconds for him to cover my mouth, silencing my screams.

In the end, it took only nineteen minutes and thirty-nine seconds for him to ruin my entire life.

I'd been right. Ramsey had gotten caught trying to snag the condoms, which had resulted in a huge fight with his dad.

It was twenty-two minutes and three seconds before he got back.

Time had never been my friend.

NINE

Ramsey

EVERYTHING HAPPENS FOR A REASON IS THE BIGGEST bullshit adage that has ever been spoken. It's incredible if you think about it though. One tiny change in a sequence of events could alter your entire life.

What if we hadn't rented that house when we moved to Clovert?

What if I'd picked a different tree to hide in the day my mom left?

What if Thea's mom had died an hour later?

What if I hadn't broken her leg?

What if I hadn't failed fifth grade?

What if I hadn't caught Hairy that day in the woods?

What if her dad hadn't sucked?

What if she'd never stopped hating me?

What if she hadn't become my world?

What if...I'd never left her that night?

None of that happened for a *reason*. It was all pure chance. I should have expected it and been ready for life to once again snatch the rug out from under me.

I guess I never expected it to snatch it out from under Thea too.

After a near brawl with my piece-of-shit dad, I finally

got back to our tent in the hayfield. She was on her hands and knees, simultaneously crying and dry-heaving. In all the years I'd known her, I'd never, not once, seen a single tear fall from her seafoam-green eyes.

It was the most ludicrous thought in the entire world given the situation, but for a minute, I panicked that maybe she'd regretted having sex with me. I mean, seriously, how fucking self-centered could a person be?

God, if only I'd been right.

The earthy fragrance of freshly cut grass hung in the air, and the cicadas sang on an otherwise silent night. The blankets were a mess, and wrappers from our food were haphazardly strewn around the small tent. It was the same as it had been when I'd left.

However, when she threw her arms around my neck, violent sobs shaking her shoulders, and stammered out the rusty knives disguised as words detailing what Josh had done to her, nothing was ever the same again.

My mind raced, frantically trying to piece together the who, what, when, and most of all *how* this had happened. My Sparrow—the girl who had held me together more times than I could count—was falling apart in my arms, and I had not one damn clue how to fix it.

Shit like this didn't happen in our small town. Kids got in trouble for smoking weed or bribing one of the homeless guys to buy beer. But assault and rape? From someone we knew?

It didn't take long for the anger to find me. It all became too real when I helped her get dressed. A thunderstorm of razorblades rained from the sky as I took in the red welts and purple bruises covering her body.

A body she'd just given me.

A body I should have been able to protect.

Her tears soaking the shoulder of my shirt burned like acid straight to my soul. Because that's exactly what Thea was.

My soul.

I honestly only remember snapshots in time over the next few hours. How they started and ended were jumbled in a sea of pain, guilt, and helplessness.

I carried her home. We argued that she didn't want to tell her dad because he'd find out what we'd been doing before it happened. And I snapped at her like the dick I so obviously was that she was being ridiculous.

Yeah. I said that. I'd spend the next twelve years regretting it too.

She begged me to stay with her, and despite the adrenaline firing through my nervous system demanding for me to find Josh Caskey as quickly as possible and make him pay for every single one of those tears, I agreed.

I didn't sneak in that night. I walked in the front door with her tucked under my arm and went straight to her room.

She took a shower while I paced a path in the carpet in her bedroom.

I think she spoke to her dad to let him know she was home, but my mind was lost in a toxic storm of failure and revenge.

I told her we should call the cops.

With hollow eyes that shattered a piece of me I would never be able to reclaim, she told me she wasn't ready, and it wouldn't matter anyway. She trembled in my arms as she spoke in broken whispers. Josh was rich. His dad was the mayor. She'd borrowed his tent, told him where she was going, and then had been waiting in it naked.

All of which was my fucking *fault*. She didn't say that part. She didn't have to.

It was around two in the morning when she finally fell asleep in my arms. Her back was to me and I stared at the side of her face, her sparrow-colored hair tickling my nose. I thought about my mother.

She'd never looked back in the six years since she'd left. No phone calls. No Christmas visits. Not even a birthday card dropped in the mail. I tried to forget about her as much as possible. However, as I watched Thea sleeping, I closed my eyes and thought back to when I was a kid.

We'd had woods behind our old house, and when my father was on one of his tangents, she'd take Nora and I out to feed the sparrows. I remembered one particular day when I was eight. It was in the beginning when the abuse first started, or maybe it was only beginning to me because I was finally old enough to see my father for who he truly was.

Regardless, we were hanging out with a bag of bird seed. Of course, the birds were hidden, waiting on us to drop the food and go. But I was pissed, probably more about the fact that my dad had slapped my mom before we left. The birds caught all my wrath that day. I yelled, kicking and screaming like a toddler and not a kid who in less than a year would have to wrestle my father off my mother. Nora cried at my outburst and I told her to shut the hell up. That was when my mom had had enough.

She snatched me up by the back of my shirt, tears streaming down her red cheeks, and got in my face. "The sparrows don't come because you need them, Ramsey. They come because they need *you*."

I'm sure all of this was followed by a quit-yelling-at-your sister lecture and threats that the sparrows would never come if I didn't shut up and be patient. But the only thing I heard in that scolding was that somebody needed me. For an angry kid who felt worthless and out of control, it gave me a purpose.

My mother was my first sparrow. I did everything I could for her until the day she left us.

Nora was next.

And then there was Thea.

Yes, I still believed that *everything happens for a reason* is the biggest bullshit adage that had ever been spoken, but the minute I discovered Thea Hull—with all of her flowing, dark hair and her sad, green eyes—was just as broken as I was, I knew without a shadow of a doubt that someone had sent me another sparrow.

I'd never been more wrong. Thea hadn't shown up at that tree that night because she needed me. She'd appeared because I needed her.

Thea was a fucking eagle—majestic, fierce, and strong.

I was the sparrow.

But that night, Josh Caskey had turned my warrior into a sparrow too. I couldn't let him get away with it. She was never going to tell her dad or call the cops. The spotlight wasn't Thea's place. And if she went to the police, that was exactly what would happen. Gossip would make its way around school, and with Josh's father being such a public figure, the whole town would know before the week was over.

I wanted to respect her decision.

But I couldn't lie there in her bed while she suffered emotionally and physically, knowing what he'd done to her. I couldn't let him get away with it.

Something had to be done.

My sparrow needed me.

And for that reason alone, I kissed her shoulder, crawled out of her bed, and then destroyed us all.

TEN

Thea

Twelve years later...

I STARED AT HIS BACK AS HE GAVE UP SHAKING THE GATE and walked away. Nora chased after him, but he snatched his arm out of her grip.

"You're a coward!" I yelled, crossing my arms over my chest.

"Would you stop?" Nora seethed at me while jumping in front of Ramsey to stop him.

"Why the fuck did you bring her?" he snapped.

"You know why," she replied.

"No. I really fucking don't. She was my *middle school* girlfriend. You got Suzie Jenkins from third grade hiding in the trunk too?"

Yeah. That hurt. But pain was the name of my game where Ramsey was concerned.

I couldn't see her face, but she cocked her head to the side. After all these years, I knew Nora well. I'd bet my bank account that she had her eyebrows pinched and her chocolate-colored eyes narrowed into slits. She was tall. I was five-five and she had me by at least four inches. But there was literally nothing menacing about Nora Stewart. Willowy was the adjective that came to mind. However, don't for a second think her stature made her weak. I'd seen her verbally destroy far bigger men than her brother.

Ramsey probably knew this too, because when she failed to answer him with words, he turned his fury on me. With tight fists and an angry scowl, his gaze hit me like a sledgehammer. I held my ground, twelve years of heartbreak and hatred fueling my courage.

"What is wrong with you asking her to bring you here today?" he snarled. "How many times do I have to scrape you off before you finally get it?"

I locked my greens with his browns. "After everything we've been through? More than *once*, that's for damn sure."

Once.

That was exactly how many times Ramsey had "scraped me off" while he was behind bars.

Once was actually the *only* contact he'd made with me at all.

Six years of promises.

Six years of never leaving each other's sides.

Six years of planning a lifetime together.

Six damn years and he'd written me one letter the entire time he was gone. If I hadn't realized that it was going to be his last, I would have lit the damn thing on fire and mailed him back the ashes.

Move on, he'd written.

Start a new life, he'd urged.

I don't love you anymore, he'd lied.

I'd sobbed the day I got that letter—big, fat, grief-stricken tears. I hadn't believed it any more then than I did now, but each and every word on that page had felt like a stake through the heart. My Ramsey never would have written that. Not to me.

For over a year, I'd traced my fingers over the sloppy

handwriting just to feel him. It was as close as I could get to him after he'd refused to add me to his list of visitors. I'd never been given the opportunity to speak with him in person. I wrote letter after letter. Each one containing a million questions. A million apologies. A million I-love-yous. A million pleas for him to let me come visit.

They all went unanswered.

Once, when I was at the end of my rope, desperate for him to know the truth, I snuck a note inside one of Nora's letters. I still had no idea if he'd read it. Nora was the only connection I had to Ramsey at all, and he hadn't mentioned it to her.

Two years, five months, one week, and six days after Ramsey had gone to prison, I was forced to accept that he was done with me.

However, I had been nowhere near done with him.

I'd told him I'd never leave. *I'd sworn it.* He'd sworn it too. So there was no damn way I was accepting a breakup *letter* a month after he'd been sentenced to sixteen years in prison.

If he didn't love me anymore, fine. I couldn't change that. But if he expected me to truly move on with my life, then he was going to have to tell me to my face. I didn't give a fuck if that was said sixteen minutes or sixteen years later. Until then, I was going to keep my word and be there for him if, and when, he was ready.

With a renewed spirit, I'd tucked his stupid letter under my mattress and set about making a life for myself, because one day, when he got out, that life would extend to Ramsey too. Whether he wanted it to or not.

"You're still holding on to that shit? Jesus, woman, you have issues," he stated matter-of-factly.

I nodded. "Yep. And I can trace every last one of them to

when I was ten years old and this kid jumped out of a tree and broke my leg."

He cocked his head and then cut me to the core as only Ramsey could do. "Funny. I can trace all mine back to that same goddamn day. Considering you were the reason I ended up in this hellhole, you got a lot of fucking balls showing up here today."

"Ramsey!" Nora scolded. "Don't you dare!"

I deserved that though.

The color drained from my face. It was his one valid argument. I'd considered it countless times over the years. I'd spent a lot of nights sitting under our old tree, wondering if he would ever forgive me. God knew I'd never forgive myself.

He'd never cast any blame though. Not in his one letter. Not to Nora. Not until that moment outside the prison when he revealed the only scenario in which I deserved exactly what he'd given me over the years—nothing.

I rocked back a step, the sheer force of my guilt becoming more than I could withstand.

He stared at me with a malevolence that was so unlike the boy I'd once known that it felt like a physical blow. I'd prepared myself for him to be different. Nora had warned me over and over again. There was no way a person could have lived through everything he had and still be the same sweet boy who'd spent the majority of his youth hiding in trees.

It burned like the hottest fire to witness it in person.

It would have been one thing if I'd been there to watch him grow. To see his heart callous over and harden. But I hadn't been there. He wouldn't let me.

"I…" I shook my head as tears welled in my eyes. "I'm sorry… You have to know that I would never hurt you on purpose."

His jaw ticked, but he cut his gaze to the side.

Desperate, I took a step toward him, the tears finally escaping. "Ramsey, please. Can we just talk? Or maybe you just listen. Anything?"

He flinched and then shook his head. "I can't do this. I gotta get out of here."

"Ramsey, please!"

Suddenly, a man in a uniform came strutting out of the building, walking straight to the gate. "Hey!" he yelled. "Everything okay out here?"

Head to toe, Ramsey turned to stone. To a stranger, it would have only been his posture that changed. But I saw it, and being so close, Nora felt it.

A wave of panic crashed into him, momentarily washing away his anger and stealing my breath. His Adam's apple bobbed and then his face fell tragically blank.

The hair on the back of my neck stood on end as Nora and I exchanged knowing glances.

"It's fine," I chirped in my telephone voice, the one I usually reserved for obnoxious clients.

Nora moved first, hooking her arm through Ramsey's. "Yep, all good. We were just leaving."

The officer swung his gaze over the three of us, seemingly convinced when Ramsey started walking with Nora and slowed only to snag his trash bag of belongings off the ground.

I swear I didn't breathe again until Ramsey was in the back seat, his seat belt on, and Nora pulled out onto the main highway.

Well, that's not totally true. As I used the rearview mirror to watch him sitting in the back seat, his elbows on his thighs, his head hanging down, not peering out the window with wonder, reveling in his newfound freedom, a pang of guilt hit me so hard that I wasn't sure I'd ever breathe again.

Suddenly, for the first time in twelve years, eight months, three weeks, four days, thirteen hours, and eighteen minutes, I was terrified that this wasn't a fight I could win.

Twelve years earlier...

"Thea," my dad called, knocking on my bedroom door.

Confused and still half asleep, I mumbled an unintelligible, "Go away."

"Thea, honey, you need to get up. There are some police officers here that want to talk to you."

I sat straight up in bed, my heart lurching into my throat as memories from the night before came crashing down over me. My watch read six forty-five and the sun was barely peeking over the horizon, but Ramsey's side of the bed was blisteringly cold.

"Thea? Did you hear me? You need to come out here and talk."

Oh my God, Ramsey had told them. He'd told them about Josh. I'd begged him not to say anything. He had no right. I wasn't ready to even think about what had happened much less talk to my dad and a bunch of strangers about it.

"Thea? Are you—"

"I'm coming," I croaked. "Give me a second to get dressed."

Bruised and aching from head to toe, I swung my legs over the side of the bed.

What the hell was I supposed to tell them? Maybe I could lie. It'd be Ramsey's word against mine. It's not like he was actually there or anything.

I walked to the full-length mirror in the corner of my room and peeled my pajamas off. My wrists and my arms were black and blue, and so were the inside of my thighs. I had a bite mark on my shoulder and one on my breast. None of which had come from Ramsey. Bile crawled up the back of my throat and I fought the urge to throw up.

Summer still lingered in the Georgia air. I wasn't going to be able to pull off long sleeves and jeans without ringing alarm bells, so I put my pajamas back on and snagged a hoodie from my laundry hamper. As I tugged it over my head, I practiced my lies:

"Nothing happened."

"I don't know what you're talking about."

"I think Ramsey must be confused or something."

My stomach wrenched when my dad knocked again.

With my pulse thundering in my ears, I opened the door and flashed my father the best smile I could muster, which admittedly wasn't much. Things with my dad had gotten better over the years. Or maybe I'd gotten used to the distance between us. He liked to know where I was going and when I was going to be home. Which at least showed he cared. But he rarely asked questions or told me no. Really, it was more like a roommate situation rather than a father-and-daughter relationship.

Concern like I hadn't seen my dad wear since the day my mom was diagnosed with cancer was etched in his face. "Are you okay?"

Damn Ramsey and his big mouth.

"Yeah. I'm fine, why?"

He swept his hand down the hall, where two uniformed officers were standing.

"Miss Hull," the older of the two men greeted. "Sorry to wake you. Can you come have a seat and maybe answer a few questions for us?"

I made my way to our small den, asking, "About what?"

"Ramsey Stewart."

Yep. I was going to kill him.

I settled on the couch, while my dad and the officers stood around me. "What about Ramsey?"

"He told us that he was with you last night. Can you tell us a little about what you two were doing?"

I blinked. What the hell did they want to know what *Ramsey and I* were doing for?

"We…were, uh, we were just hanging out."

"I thought you were with Tiffany?" my dad interjected.

The younger cop lifted his hand to silence him. "What does that mean, *hanging out?*"

Nerves rolled in my stomach, not quite understanding where this was going. If they knew about Josh, why were they asking me about Ramsey? "We have this tree on the Wynns' property that we go to sometimes. We just kinda sit around and talk."

"Drinking?" he asked.

My head snapped back. "No."

"Mr. Stewart do any drugs while he was there?"

My pulse quickened. "No way."

He stared at me for a long second, searching my face. "Okay. Then can you tell me about what time Ramsey left last night?"

Alarm bells started screaming in my head. Something wasn't right. This wasn't about Josh. Or at least not about what he'd done to me.

I crossed my arms over my chest. "I don't know. Can you tell me why you want to know?"

The cops looked at my father and I followed their gaze.

He was pinching the bridge of his nose. "Thea, please just answer the question."

What the hell was going on?

"Not until someone tells me what the hell is going on." Panic bloomed in my chest. "Where's Ramsey? Did something happen?"

And then my dad spoke the words that ended my life as I knew it. "He's in police custody, Thea. Josh Caskey was hit by a car last night. It was Ramsey's car. Josh didn't make it, so please, this is important. You need to tell them everything you know about what happened and where Ramsey was last night, because right now, he's about to be facing some pretty serious charges."

My heart stopped and my lungs felt as though I was breathing poison. I was safely in my den, but I felt the blowback of the entire world as it exploded.

"No," I breathed, shooting to my feet. "That's not possible. Ramsey wouldn't…" Oh my God. After what Josh had done to me, there was no telling what Ramsey would have done. Tears sprang to my eyes as I stood there shaking my head. "You don't understand."

One of the officers stepped forward. "Then make us understand, Thea. We can't help Ramsey if we don't know what happened."

Help him. They were going to help him. I was mortified about what Josh had done to me, but there was literally nothing I wouldn't do for Ramsey. Not even burning at the stake to save him.

But as I frantically yanked off my hoodie and began showing the police my bruises while word-vomiting every disgusting, filthy detail of what Josh had done to me, I had no idea I was tying Ramsey to the stake beside me.

I found out later that Ramsey had told them that it was an accident and that he'd thought he had hit a deer that night. The police had no reason not to believe him.

RELEASE

That is until I had unknowingly handed them the gift of a motive.

It wasn't my fault Ramsey went to prison. He'd made his own choices that night. But it was absolutely my fault that the prosecutor had been able to charge him with first-degree murder. The fact that he'd taken a plea deal, reducing it to voluntary manslaughter and sentencing him to sixteen years in prison, had not eased my conscience.

It clearly hadn't eased his resentment, either.

ELEVEN

Ramsey

"**T**HIS IS BULLSHIT AND YOU KNOW IT," I RUMBLED AT Nora. "I could get in trouble with my PO for having someone else living in the house."

She rolled her eyes. "Relax. I reported her on the parole paperwork."

"Just not to me though, right?"

She shrugged. "Pretty much."

We were sitting in a fancy steakhouse Nora and I had been talking about since the day I got word of my release. It was my big celebration. Nora had insisted on steak and I'd agreed, telling her as long as it didn't come from a can and wasn't served on a plastic tray, I was game.

I was regretting everything about that conversation now though.

I'd just found out that my new home was Thea's home too. Did I get a choice in the matter? Not fucking one. You'd think I'd have been used to that after so long in lockup.

Fucking Thea.

She was the last person in the world I'd wanted to see when I took my first breath of fresh air. She'd changed. Not that I'd assumed she was still sixteen or anything, but on the rare occasions I'd allowed my thoughts to drift to her, I had nothing but my memories and those didn't age.

I couldn't tell if she was taller or not, but she'd filled out into a woman. Boobs, hips, butt. All the things I'd been looking forward to when I got out. But not with her. For fuck's sake, she was wearing a damn dress and heels. That was more than enough to turn my stomach.

When I had seen her climb out of that car, I'd had some sort of visceral reaction. Every pain I'd experienced over the years sliced through me. It was a wonder I'd stayed on my feet.

I'd nearly suffocated in that car on the drive over to the restaurant. And Nora was now telling me I was going to be living under the same roof with Thea too?

Fuck. That.

But that argument could wait until I wasn't on the verge of a panic attack. The restaurant was too busy. Too many people. Too much talking. Too much moving around when we were supposed to be eating at the fucking table.

Only *we* weren't supposed to be doing anything. Everyone was on their own schedule. Coming and going at will rather than on orders.

It was too late for lunch. Too early for dinner.

It was…too much. All of it.

And Thea was there. That was pretty much the definition of *too much* for me. I glanced up to the bathroom she'd disappeared inside only seconds earlier. How was she there? Better yet, *why* was she there?

I was a dick. This was not something new. But even with as much as my vision had flashed red when I saw her standing outside of that prison, I'd had no right to lay into her with the bullshit about her being responsible. I just had no idea what else I could say to her to make her leave me alone. Letters—all the fucking letters over the years. If she would have just moved the hell on the way I'd told her to, we could have saved half a damn rainforest and all of my sanity.

It had been almost thirteen years. She should have been married and two kids deep. Or at the very least living in Paris and traveling across Europe on the weekends. But not Thea. I have no idea why I was surprised. She'd always been stubborn as hell. It didn't help my cause that she and Nora were obviously ganging up on me.

I was free but trapped all over again.

If I could paint a picture of what prison life was like, it would be nothing more than a black canvas with the tiniest speck of white in the center. That speck was the only light I'd had to navigate the darkness. Hell had more flames, but there were a lot of nights I would have rather been burning alive. The loneliness was debilitating, and growing up in prison was paralyzing. As a six-three seventeen-year-old back in Clovert, I had been the big man on campus. In lockup, I was nothing but a child men got their kicks trying to break. My smile was no protection in there. Grinning like an idiot made me a bigger target. That was when I lost it.

Adapt or die, right?

And for the first year, dying was exactly what it was. The person I was had to die in order for me to survive in that place. Yes, I missed Thea. I missed Nora. I missed our tree and having somewhere to escape to when life got rough. I missed stars and the summer breezes. I missed belonging and trusting and loving and being loved. I missed living in a world where it didn't feel like the walls were going to close in at any second.

But obsessing about everything I was missing only made the days harder and the nights longer.

I had to let them go. Longing and hope were useless emotions that hung around my neck like a noose. With every thought, every memory from home, it got tighter until I was only days away from hanging from a bedsheet in the corner of my cell.

Call me a coward.

Call me a quitter.

Call me an asshole.

But you'd be amazed by the things you'd do in order to survive.

Hate was easier. And God knew I'd needed something in my life to be easier.

I tore my attention off the door of the women's restroom. "I'm going to ask my parole officer if he can find me a room to rent for a while."

"Uh…no, you aren't."

"I'm not fucking living with her."

I loved my little sister. She was smart and funny and honestly the only reason I was still alive. But Christ, the woman excelled at bitchery.

"I want to care how you feel right now, Ramsey. I want to sit here and give you everything you could possibly want, but what you *want* is not what you *need*. Living in some trashy glorified cell where you have no idea who is coming or going in the rest of the house is not a safe place for you. You're on parole. Having a place to live is only part of the requirements." She lifted her hand and started counting off using her manicured fingernails. "You also have to maintain employment and avoid criminal activity, drugs, and *alcohol*. Plus, you can't travel within sixty miles from home. One step out of line and you're right back in there to serve out the rest of your sentence. That's three years, Ramsey. *Three*."

I ground my teeth. "I *can't* live with her."

"Can't or won't?"

"Both."

"Fine. You want to bullshit me that you don't love her—"

"It's not bullshit," I rumbled.

"It *is*. But if you want to lie about it, then fine. I'm not going to stop you. But, right now, you need to be surrounded by people who love you. I'm not asking you to put a ring on her finger."

Panic hit my chest. "That's not fucking happening, Nora. Do you understand me? Let go of whatever fairytale bullshit you've made up in your head. She is nothing to me."

"Then you should have no problem living under the same roof as her."

"Nora," I warned.

"She was your best friend once. It's not too late. You could have that back."

"I don't want it back."

"You don't want what back?" Thea asked, suddenly appearing beside me.

Surprise was not a positive emotion in prison.

Rational thinking told me that it was just Thea. Twelve years of experience caused me to shoot to my feet, knocking my chair over behind me.

Thea scrambled back.

Nora shouted my name.

And my heart pounded as my head tried to separate reaction from reality.

It was Thea.

It was Nora.

I was at a restaurant.

I was free.

Only this didn't feel like freedom. There were no bars. There were no guards. There were no cells. But after years and years of conditioning, the prison was inside my mind now.

Nora's voice was careful like she was talking a man off a ledge. "Ramsey, it's okay. Let's sit back down."

Drawing in a deep breath that I hoped like hell didn't sound as shaky as it felt, I bent over and picked up my chair while avoiding Thea's gaze. I didn't know if I'd scared her or if pity was going to show in her eyes. I told myself I didn't care. It was fucking Thea.

But that was exactly the problem.

It was *Thea.*

"Oh look, it's our waitress," Nora announced loud and clear as we all took our seats.

I wasn't too blind to see that it had been spoken as a warning that someone was approaching. I offered her a tight smile in gratitude.

The short, blonde woman who'd delivered a round of waters when we first sat down approached the table wearing a friendly smile. "Are y'all ready to order?"

"Yes," Thea and Nora answered in awkward and unscripted unison.

She pulled out a notebook and a pen and looked to Nora. "Okay, what can I get you?"

"You go first," Nora prompted me. "Get whatever you want."

I swallowed hard as anxiety scorched through my veins. I stared at the menu, seeing words and knowing I was supposed to say something, but I just didn't know what. I was a teenager the last time I'd gotten to pick my own food. I could order snacks at the commissary when I'd had money in my account. This was different. Some things were meals; some things were sides. They even had an entire list of sauces, though I had no fucking idea what the hell those were supposed to go on.

Pressure built in my chest as I scanned the page. "I'll…um… have a steak."

"All right, do you want the filet, the center cut, the rib eye, strip, or porterhouse?"

My mouth dried. "Just a steak."

She half laughed. "Okay, let's try it this way. Are you going to want that *steak* six, eight, twelve, or sixteen ounces?"

I kept staring at the menu like something was going to jump out at me. When, really and truly, I wished she'd shut the hell up and bring me a tray of food. Whatever was on the menu that day. Just bring it out.

"A steak," I repeated roughly when I gave up on trying to figure out how many ounces would fit in the large section of the yellow trays at home—no. Not home. Prison was not home.

"Okay…" she drawled. "How would you like that cooked?"

Oh, for fuck's sake. I banged my fist on the table, which made everyone jump. "I just want a fucking steak. You pick. Whatever you want. Just stop asking me questions."

"Ramsey, relax," Nora whispered, covering my hand with hers.

The touch set me on edge. We hadn't been allowed to touch or hold hands. Not even at visitation. A hug when she arrived and a hug when she left. That was all we had been permitted.

I snatched my hand away. "Stop touching me. Everybody, just fucking *stop*." I put my elbows on the table and dropped my head into my hands.

Yeah, this was definitely too much.

"Okay," Thea mumbled. "He'll have a twelve-ounce rib eye, medium-rare, house salad with ranch, and a loaded baked—"

She was doing me a favor. Clearly, I was overwhelmed and about thirty seconds from losing my shit, and Thea had come to my rescue. But I didn't want *Thea* to rescue me from anything. I didn't want her to be there at all.

RELEASE

My head snapped up. "Don't fucking order for me."

She jerked to the side as if she were trying to dodge my words. When she opened her mouth to speak, I knew with an absolute certainty it was going to be an apology. I could see it in those damn green eyes that had haunted me for too many years. I wasn't going to be able to handle another apology from her. The first one had been bad enough. I'd have rather served the last three years than experience that again.

Pushing off the table, I stood up. "I gotta get out of here."

"Ramsey, wait," Nora called, but there was no stopping me.

I was done.

And as sad as it might have been, part of me actually longed to go back to that cell. It was a horrible and soul-sucking place, but I knew how to navigate life on the inside.

Freedom was foreign territory.

TWELVE

Thea

THERE WERE FEW TIMES IN MY LIFE THAT I'D BEEN MORE devastated than when I was watching Ramsey unravel while attempting the simple task of ordering lunch. I shouldn't have stepped in and tried to help. I was already crossing a scorching desert barefoot when it came to him, but I couldn't just sit there while he'd been floundering.

After he'd stormed out, Nora followed him, while I apologized to the waitress and handed her a twenty-dollar bill for her time. I couldn't convince myself to go after him. Not with my emotions on the verge of overflowing. So I stood at the restaurant door, watching through the glass as Nora opened her car and Ramsey slid into the back seat. She didn't climb into the driver's seat though. Instead, she got her phone out of her bag, casually leaned against the hood, and gave Ramsey a few moments of solitude.

My heart broke all over again.

Nora was handling this so much better than I was. I could barely breathe. My emotional grid was all over the place—hate, love, regret, pain, happiness. I'd been waiting for that day for so long. Dreaming about it, really. And while I'd managed to keep my expectations low, I'd *hoped* for a lot.

I'd hoped seeing me would make him remember that we were made for each other.

I'd hoped being out of that hell would make him smile again.

I'd hoped he could finally start his life the way it was supposed to be.

Yes. I loved Ramsey. I would always love Ramsey. But if that life didn't include me, I could be content until the end of my days as long as he was *happy*. That's all I'd ever wanted for him.

Though, on what should have been the best day of his life, he was crumbling in the back seat of a car, his head leaned back on the headrest, his absent stare aimed at the roof.

When Nora saw me standing at the door, she curled two fingers for me to come out. I ran a hand over the top of my hair to smooth it down. It wasn't messy. I'd brushed it a dozen times while I'd been hiding in the bathroom, willing my heart to slow after nothing more than sitting next to him at a table. It was something so common that I hadn't realized how much I'd missed it.

But I had.

Oh God, how I'd missed it.

He was pissed off and overwhelmed, but I'd missed feeling him next to me.

A thick blanket of unease shrouded the car on our way home. Nora put on the radio and she and Ramsey made small talk about how shitty music was these days. I offered no opinion. He was more comfortable that way—when he could forget I was there.

We lived almost two hours away from the prison, so I had plenty of time to think on that drive. Everything I'd ever wanted was riding in that car with me, but the emptiness within me was more prominent than ever.

What if that was my natural state of being now? What if this was my life, sitting in the front seat while the man I'd been in love with since I was old enough to understand the concept sat behind me completely out of my reach?

By the time we pulled into our driveway, I was in full-on Debbie Dooms Day mode.

He hated me.

He resented me.

My Ramsey was gone forever.

Insert a million other the-sky-is-falling references here.

"Nice place," he mumbled to Nora when she opened the front door.

I trailed behind, not wanting to get too close, all the while wishing I could.

"I know. I picked it out." She smiled. "Though Thea paid for it. So I guess she gets some of the credit."

His back stiffened at the mention of my name, but he made no comment.

Nora hung her keys on the hook beside the door and set her purse on the table. Drawing in a deep breath, she walked into our den and swung her arms out to her sides. "Welcome home, big brother."

An unlikely smile crept up my face as I imagined seeing our house for the first time through his eyes. Photos from throughout the years, including several of Ramsey, hung in a massive collage above our tan microfiber sectional. With white distressed end tables and a rustic wood coffee table, thrift store chic was our style of choice. It also happened to be our style of necessity. Penny by penny, I'd saved up the money for a hefty down payment on that three-bedroom, eighteen-hundred-square-foot ranch home. Nora had pitched in and gotten a credit card at a furniture store so we could buy couches. After a solid hour of begging us not to go, my dad told me we could take the bedroom furniture and then offered to rent the U-Haul for us.

He'd disappeared to his room for the rest of the night after that. I'd felt horrible leaving him all alone like that, but if Nora and I wanted a life, we needed to get out of Clovert. It was impossible to heal in the place that had broken you. The new house was only twenty minutes away and we both still commuted back for work, but having our own little safe haven did wonders for our emotional wellbeing.

I was proud of that house. Proud of us for what we'd made of our lives. And now I was proud to give a little piece of it to Ramsey too.

My voice shook as I chanced asking, "You...um...want to see your room?"

He didn't answer, but when Nora started walking toward the hall, he followed without argument.

"You're gonna love it," she said as she opened the last door on the right. "Thea's decoratively challenged, so I picked out everything."

She walked in first, and it took several beats before Ramsey entered the bedroom. I silently lamented the fact that I was behind them and unable to see his reaction. We'd spent almost every day for the last week getting that room ready.

A midnight-blue comforter covered the king-size platform bed. Pillows—at least eight of them—were stacked at the top, waiting for someone to dive into the middle. There was a faux mahogany dresser on the opposite wall and two cherry nightstands on either side of the bed. Nothing matched. We'd changed the knobs to make it look like that was the purpose. We—well, Nora—had gone for minimalistic with the rest with hopes that Ramsey would want to put his own touches on his new space. But there was one single framed photo of the three of us that hung on the wall. The picture was my contribution to his room.

On and off, depending on what stage of grief I was experiencing at the time, that picture had hung in my room for over twelve years. In it, Nora and I were laughing. I have no memory of what was so funny, but Ramsey was in the middle of us, his shaggy, brown hair hanging over his forehead, his eyes bright, and his smile so wide that it almost looked photoshopped.

That was how I'd chosen to remember him—happy and carefree.

And now I hoped it would help him remember too.

"Is this the master?" he asked, roaming around the room, before dumping his garbage bag of belongings in the corner.

"Yep," Nora answered. "We drew straws to see who was going to be forced to share the hall bathroom with you, but Thea forgot to cut a short one, so we both won." She walked over and flipped on the light to the adjoining bathroom. "So now you get your own."

That wasn't exactly how it had happened. After he'd spent so much of his life in a six-by-eight cell, giving Ramsey the master was the obvious choice. Nora and I hadn't even discussed it before calling my dad to help us lug all my crap across the hall. My bed wouldn't fit in the small room we'd been using as a home office, so I left the king for Ramsey and downgraded to a double.

"You shouldn't have done that," he rumbled. "I'm not gonna be here long anyway."

Surprise—and okay, fine, panic—hit me like a ton of bricks. "What? Where are you going?"

Nora shook her head and rolled her eyes. "Nowhere. He's not going anywhere."

"We'll see about that," he muttered, running his hand over the top of the bed, pressing into the soft pillowtop.

I pointedly flared my eyes at Nora in question, but she waved me off.

"We bought you some welcome home presents." She opened the drawer on his end table and pulled out a new silver iPhone. "You know my number, but I programmed Thea's into the contacts in case I'm not around and you need something. Your phone number is on the Post-it note in the box. Memorize it and give it to your parole officer tomorrow, okay?"

He flipped the phone in his hand. "You gonna teach me how to use this thing first?"

"Yep. You'll be ignoring me to check your Instagram in no time." She reached back into the drawer and retrieved my gift, which suddenly seemed paltry compared to hers. When I'd been shopping though, I'd been damn near giddy picking them out for him. "This one's from Thea."

As if it were an involuntary reaction, his eyes flicked to me for the first time since the restaurant.

One glance and my whole body came alive. It only lasted a heartbeat, but the hum in my veins remained long after he'd looked away.

It only hurt a little when he tried to hand it back to Nora.

She dodged the bag. "Open it, silly."

With a ticking jaw, he glared at her for a long second, but in true Nora fashion, she stared back at him, smiling like she'd escaped from a 1950's mental institution.

Nerves fluttered in my stomach as he stabbed his hand inside the bag.

And then he froze.

And then I froze.

And then I wished like hell I'd never given it to him at all.

He pulled out a pack of red-and-green gum. Watermelon. The wrapper was different now, but it had been his favorite when we were younger. And, most recently, it had been what he tasted like in my mind each and every time I touched myself. His words from all those years earlier flittered through my brain.

"Sparrow, I think every time I've kissed you I've had gum in my mouth."

His dark gaze came back to mine, and this time, it lingered. Tangible, as though it were the tip of a finger, his gaze swept from my mouth to my breasts before taking the slow path back to my eyes.

My breath hitched and a chill traveled down my spine even as I feared I might burst into flames.

Gum had been the likely choice when it came to picking out a present for him. Ramsey had never gone anywhere without at least one pack in his pocket. It was as much a part of him as the way he'd walked in the grass so I could have the sidewalk or the way he'd inhaled as if he could consume me each time he'd kissed me. I'd flown into a fit of hysteria the day Nora had told me he wasn't allowed to have gum in prison, and that was after he'd already "scraped me off."

A pack of gum could have been an innocent gesture from an old friend.

However, as my lungs burned while he plundered my emotions with nothing more than a stormy stare, we both knew there was nothing innocent about it.

He had been chewing gum the first time he kissed a path over my breasts.

The first time he timidly inched his fingers into my panties.

And the first time he made love to me under the stars before time stopped.

Oh, yes. I had fond, fond memories of Ramsey and his gum.

Which was probably why it felt like a slap to the face when he turned and dropped the entire bag in the trash can beside the bed.

"Jesus Christ," Nora mumbled.

The remnants of my pride told me to run as far as I could and never look back.

But it was my heart covered in ugly scars and lesions that kept my feet rooted and my gaze locked on his. Rejection burned thick in my throat, but I refused to give him that victory.

"You're welcome," I snapped.

An arrogant smile that had never suited someone less curled his lips. "I don't remember saying thank you."

I slanted my head and ignored the festering desire to cry. "There seems to be a lot you don't remember, Ramsey. Starting with how to be a decent human being. But don't worry. We'll get you there. And yes. I mean *we*. As in me and you. Because unlike you, when I make someone a promise, I actually keep it."

And with that, I walked out of his room, straight to the hall bathroom, and proceeded to throw up the contents of my empty stomach. And for the way it felt, it contained a fair amount of my empty soul too.

THIRTEEN

Thea

RAMSEY NEVER CAME OUT OF HIS ROOM AGAIN THAT night.

I cooked steaks. Nora carried one to his room. He invited her in. They had dinner together. And I stood in the hall, listening to the magic that was their laughter, while tears of longing dripped off my smile.

Their voices had become muted, but his light was still on when I went to bed. I'd been so excited for his release that I hadn't been sleeping well for over a week, but my good pal Anxiety was hell-bent on making sure we didn't break the streak.

The numbers on the clock read one thirty-six when I heard my bedroom door crack open. My heart lurched with fantasies that he'd come to talk to me. Or *not* talk to me. I didn't care which as long he was there to wrap me in his strong arms and erase twelve years of hell.

It was Nora who pulled back the covers and climbed into bed beside me.

"How ya holding up?" she whispered.

"Well, the good news is I'm officially dehydrated from crying. Any more and I think I'll wake up a raisin." A lump caught in my throat. "The bad news is I'm *definitely* going to wake up as a raisin."

"Hey," she cooed. "Stop. You knew this was going to be hard."

"I know. I know. It's just… Why is *everything* so fucking hard? When are we going to catch a break? When is *he* going to catch a break?"

"He's fine, Thea."

"I get it. He doesn't love me. But why does he have to be so angry? He has to know that I've spent the last decade blaming myself for telling the cops about Josh."

She rested her palm on the side of my neck, her long, thin fingers curling around as she gave me a gentle shake. "He doesn't blame you. You didn't do anything wrong. He was pissed off that you were there today and looking for a way to lash out. We had a long talk tonight and I made sure he knew exactly how messed up it was for him to bring that shit up."

"But he didn't say he didn't mean it, did he?"

"He doesn't say much of anything anymore. He listens a lot though and observes everything. But you know who's more observant?" She released my neck and used one finger to tap me on the nose like I was one of the kids in her class. "Me. And I'm telling you right now, the same thing I have told you for oh… twelve years, eight months, three weeks, four days, and however the hell many hours we're up to at this point: My brother loves you, Thea. Ramsey is stupid. Ramsey is an idiot. Ramsey is emotionally stunted. But Ramsey fucking *loves* you."

She'd said it so many times over the years that I'd started to believe it. There were mounds of evidence to say otherwise, but each time Nora hugged me and whispered those words to me, it gave me the strength to make it through another day.

It had been lonely growing up without him. I'd watched as people we'd gone to school with grew up, posted stupid shit about their relationships on social media, got engaged, got married, had babies. A few had already added a divorce and marriage number two to their relationship résumé.

Meanwhile, I was twenty-eight and had never been on another date since our night in the tent on his seventeenth birthday. Forget about a relationship or even a one-night stand. I was in the never-ending holding pattern of hating Ramsey for what he'd done to us while simultaneously waiting for him to come home.

He was in the bedroom across the hall and I was still waiting.

"There's nothing there when I look in his eyes, Nora. I used to be able to tell. I don't feel anything when he looks at me now."

"He's overwhelmed. Just give him some time."

The room was dark, lit only by the moon and dim rays from a streetlight. My vision swam as I stared at Nora's silhouette. "How much time do I need to give him before I accept that it's really over? Twenty years? Thirty? My entire life? Because you know I'll do it. If there is one single sliver of hope that I'll finally get him back, I will wait for that man." When my voice cracked, she slid her arm under my head and wrapped me in a hug.

"Ohhh-kay, let's slow down. It's been, like, twelve hours, Anxiety Angie. Nobody is asking you to wait the rest of your life. Let's start with like…two weeks. Tops. Ten bucks says I'm falling asleep with earplugs in by the end of the month."

"It's not even about the physical stuff. I just want my best friend back."

"Hey." She feigned injury. "I'm your best friend now. He can have all the other gross stuff like seeing you naked and watching all those cheesy Christmas movies you try to force on me every year." She hooked her arm through mine before rolling to her back. "I read a study recently about reintegration and it said there are two common reactions when it comes to reacclimating into society. Some men go full steam ahead, making up for lost time and filling their days with missed experiences. That was what I thought was going to happen with Ramsey. For weeks, he's been planning the things he wanted to do as soon as he got out. Apparently, he's not that type though. At least not yet. We just need to be patient with him."

"What's the other type?"

She sighed. "The ones who can't leave prison life behind. Nothing feels familiar anymore, not even the most mundane chores. I read a story about a guy who got out after twenty years. His first day home, he sat on the couch for over two hours watching the TV Guide channel because he had no idea he could change it."

"Jesus," I breathed.

"Ramsey's relearning how to live. He did it twelve years ago when he went in. He'll do it again, and this time, he has us to help him."

My eyes stung, and my throat got thick. "I'm pretty sure he doesn't want my help."

"Probably not, but you have to remember where you two started. How many times have you told me that you hated him when you first met? You were depressed and miserable, and Ramsey stormed into your life with nothing but a smile and the finesse of a tornado. Now it's your turn. It was a good start putting him in his place tonight. But you gotta stop all the woe-is-me wallowing. Not when you've already come this far. You're the strongest woman I know, Thea. It's time for you to do what you do best."

"What's that?"

"You need to beat the absolute shit out of him with kindness and love, the same way you did with me."

I laughed. "For the record, you were right. I shouldn't have gone today."

"Now, that I'll agree with. But here we are, and this is our new normal. We have to accept that whatever happens, good, bad, or ugly is part of the process. Every step, no matter how heart-breaking or difficult, brings us closer to truly getting him back. We're all fighting the same fight here." She gave my arm a pointed squeeze. "And trust me. He's fighting *hard*. That's nothing to be sad about. That's fucking beautiful."

If Nora was right—and, God, I was praying Nora was right—I had to be patient for a little longer.

If he was fighting, then I was fighting too.

"You're right," I whispered.

"I know. And you can name your first born after me as a show of gratitude."

I smiled, and it wasn't even fake. "You're that confident this is going to work out, huh?"

Her face warmed and her lips tipped up into a breathtaking smile that was an exact replica of her brother's. "Yeah. I am. I accepted a long time ago that something good had to come from all this. I still don't know what it is exactly, but knowing that something is yet to come, it fuels me to keep searching. Maybe it's in him. Maybe it's in you. Maybe it's in all of us. But whatever it is, we'll find it. We just gotta keep looking."

Right then, I had a strong suspicion that the universe giving me Nora Stewart was hands down the best thing that was ever going to come from this tragedy.

Twelve years earlier…

As crazy as it sounded, I wasn't sure how I felt about Ramsey killing Josh.

A part of me didn't believe that he was capable of something like that.

A part of me was devastated that he loved me so much that he'd killed a man over me.

A part of me felt relieved that Josh couldn't hurt me again.

And then, in some sick and twisted place hidden deep in my soul, a part of me was mad that Ramsey was the one who had gotten to do it.

For a few days after Ramsey had been arrested, I prayed so hard for a miracle that I invented new religions. I begged anyone who would listen at the police station to let me see him, but they wouldn't budge. Surprisingly, it was my dad who jumped into action, calling around, trying and failing at every turn to find out what was going on. No one was talking—at least not about anything other than gossip.

I wasn't eating or sleeping, and time passed at a staggering crawl.

The sun rose.

The sun set.

And he never came home.

Hollow.

I was so damn hollow.

It took just over ten days for the prosecution to offer Ramsey a plea bargain. The news hit our small town like a wildfire. Those who had known Josh were screaming for the death penalty. I was a minor, so my identity had not been revealed in the public court documents, but it wasn't hard to figure out who Ramsey had been defending that night.

Josh was well-liked. His dad was the mayor, and his mom was the president of the prestigious *Ladies of Clovert*. In the eyes of our town, there was no way he could have done what I'd claimed.

A rape kit at the hospital the morning I had thrown Ramsey under the proverbial bus said otherwise though. It was the only reason the prosecution agreed to a deal so quickly.

Unfortunately, the court of public opinion found me guilty of fabricating the entire story. Rumors began circling back on themselves, forming a vicious cycle of exaggeration and straight-up lies. Some people thought I was covering for Ramsey. Some thought I was in on it too. Whatever the case was, the Hulls and the Stewarts became the town's most hated families.

Our house was egged three times. Fireworks were shot through the front windows twice. And, once, the Stewarts' lawn was set on fire.

The cops did nothing.

Coincidentally, that was the same thing Ramsey's dad did after Ramsey had been arrested. He spoke to the police when questioned, and during a TV interview with the local news, he told them all about his son's "violent side" at home. After that, he went back to sitting on his ass and being a worthless waste of oxygen. Nora stayed locked in her room, and I was too lost in my own grief to entertain the idea of helping another person through the darkness.

I was dealing with a lot those first few weeks. I couldn't differentiate between the emotional torture of what Josh had done to me and the devastation of having lost Ramsey. The pain was unbearable.

A lot of it stemmed from guilt.

What if I'd fought harder against Josh?

What if I hadn't told Ramsey what he'd done to me?

What if we'd reported it to the police as soon as it had happened?

In every scenario, there was a "what if" in which I was to blame.

The story the police decided on was that Ramsey had flown into a blinding rage when he'd found out what Josh had done to me. I'd already caused enough damage to his case, so I didn't bother to tell them that he'd taken his shoes off and lain in bed with me for well over an hour while I cried in his arms. Ramsey wasn't violent, but they painted the picture of a monster.

As I forced my legs to carry me into the courtroom the day he was to be formally sentenced, I decided that if he was a monster, then I was a monster too. I still loved him with my whole heart and my entire being.

The stares I got that day with my father standing tall at my side made me want to peel out of my skin. I had no idea that was the last time I was going to see him for over twelve years. In my mind, the fact that he was going to prison changed nothing.

There'd be phone calls, visits, and a future where we could pick right back up where we'd left off. We were still a team. When he looked at me over his shoulder just before he was escorted out of the courtroom and mouthed, "I love you," I naively believed we were on the same page. He was gone before I had the chance to reply to him that day. He knew though.

Our love wasn't defined by time or circumstance. Or, at least, that was the romantic musing of a sixteen-year-old girl who had no concept of how much a person changed in the sixteen years he'd been sentenced to.

Just like the day my mother died, the clock started. But instead of counting to how many minutes he'd been gone, I was officially counting down.

My father drove me home and it was the strangest feeling. Mainly because, for the first time since we'd lost my mom, it wasn't strange at all. We had a newfound respect for each other. We'd both loved and lost. And now we were both going to survive. Simple as that.

When we pulled into our driveway, the sound of Nora screaming could be heard up and down the street. Without the first thought or concern, I took off at a dead sprint.

Ramsey had told me a lot of stories about their dad. He was an abusive drunk who hated his children for no other reason than they reminded him of their mother. The bastard hadn't even gone to his own son's sentencing.

Nora was fourteen and a freshman in high school. She didn't need a babysitter anymore. But there was no fucking way I was abandoning her with that asshole now that Ramsey was gone.

"Thea!" my dad yelled after me. "Stay out of it."

I couldn't stay out of it. Nora and Ramsey were my family. I didn't slow as my ballet flats pounded against the grass through the neighbor's yard to their house.

"You didn't even try to help him!" Nora screamed.

I slung the door open without knocking and then my blood caught fire as I watched him charge Nora, pinning her to the wall with a hand around her throat. Streams of crimson dripped from her lip, and her eye was already starting to swell shut.

"Get your fucking hands off her!" I yelled, giving him a hard shove that did nothing to move him.

"You fucking whore!" her dad roared, releasing Nora and turning his anger on me.

Pain exploded inside me as I T-boned my back on the open door in my frenzied attempt to stay out of his reach.

His vile breath ghosted across my skin as he leaned in close. "You ever put your hands on me again and I will slit your throat. Do you understand me?"

And then he was gone. He went stumbling back, falling flat on his ass and cracking his head on the coffee table.

My father stepped in front of me, fury rolling off him in waves.

"You son of a bitch," Mr. Stewart said, touching his temple to check for blood. There was plenty of it.

My dad didn't say anything for a long second, but he reached back and took my hand, giving me a reassuring squeeze. I moved in close to his back, feeling his chest rising and falling with labored breaths.

Joe Hull wasn't a fighter. He was a quiet man who owned a barbershop. But that day, he was my hero. And it had nothing to do with him physically stepping between me and Ramsey's father.

"Nora," he rumbled. "Get your things. You're moving in with us."

"What?" she croaked.

"Now, Nora," my dad ordered. "Thea, go help her. Throw the stuff out the window and we'll get it from the side of the house after we get her cleaned up."

I slapped a hand over my mouth and peered around him to look at Nora. The relief in that young girl's shoulders as she started to cry would stay with me for the rest of my life.

She didn't have much, so it only took us about ten minutes to pitch it all out of her bedroom window. I was tempted to crawl out after it so we didn't have to walk back through the house and see Mr. Stewart again. But my dad was still in there, and there was no way I was leaving without him.

I have no idea what they were discussing as we entered the den. Nora's dad was still sitting on the floor, but he was holding a towel to the back of his head and my dad was squatting in front of him, whispering inaudibly. They weren't brawling, so I took it as a positive sign.

I curled Nora into my side, and together, we hurried to the front door. We'd almost made it out the door when Mr. Stewart called out. "Have a nice life. God knows, you ruined mine."

She choked on a sob, and then we left her father's house for the very last time.

One week later, Nora's dad moved in the middle of the night. He'd left Ramsey's room untouched, so we were able to sneak over and gather most of his belongings before the landlord cleaned it out.

The very next day, my father produced signed and notarized papers granting him temporary guardianship of Nora. We all knew it was permanent though.

And the day after that, my father added Nora to his health insurance and our new family of three started therapy.

FOURTEEN

Ramsey

UNDER THE CRISP WHITE LIGHTING OF MY NEW BATHROOM, I leaned toward the mirror and inspected my face. Jesus. When had I gotten so damn old?

Yes, there were mirrors in prison. They were small rectangles of metallic painted plastic bolted to the wall. They would have been more useful as funhouse mirrors rather than anything else.

Drawing my eyebrows together before popping them up, I watched thin lines dance across my forehead. Had those always been there? Making a mental note to look at Nora's forehead later, I ran a hand over the top of my hair, smoothing down the styling cream. I needed a trim. I should have asked Jared before I left, but I'd been too damn busy working my way through the line of guys I'd promised to cut one last time before I flew the coop. It was the downfall of being one of only two guys in the cell block allowed to work in the barbershop.

The day I'd been handed a pair of clippers almost eight years earlier, I'd thought it was Karma's way of sliding my naked ass down a rusty razor blade straight into a sea of salt. The last thing I needed was a fucking reminder of Thea, much less to follow in her father's footsteps with a set of scissors. I'd hated the man for the way he'd abandoned Thea after her mom died, but when I'd found out he took Nora in, I'd felt nothing but gratitude.

I learned to love cutting hair. The job kept my mind occupied and my hands busy. I made friends with almost everyone who sat in my chair, including a few of the guards who would come in for a cleanup when they didn't have time to go after their shift.

Working in the shop wasn't exactly manual labor, but it was far from a cushy job like pushing the book cart or mail delivery. We had at least four lice breakouts while I was there. People were supposed to go to Medical for that shit, but those lazy fuckers just turned them around and sent them to me. I pretended like it pissed me off, but I didn't mind. I got extra hours in the shop when there was lice. I'd work my ass off shaving everyone's head and then spend even more time teaching them how to pick the nits off each other with a comb. By the time I'd get back to my bunk, I'd lie down and pass the hell out.

There was no staring up at the ceiling. No tossing and turning on the mat masquerading as a mattress. No counting down the days until Nora came for a visit. Nothing but thoughtless sleep while time melted off my sentence.

That was the main goal. Stay busy, try not to think, and sleep as much as allowed. Time passed faster that way.

Shower. Eat. Cut hair. Work out. Eat. Read. Sleep.

And that had been it. That had been my entire life since I was seventeen years old, minus a few months while I was working to complete my GED.

Now that I was free, I was standing in a bathroom, staring at myself in the mirror because I was so fucking bored and I had not one goddamn idea what to do.

I'd woken up before the sun.

I took a shower, not realizing until halfway through that I didn't need to wear my shower shoes. I shaved with an actual razor that didn't leave a red burn on my neck. I brushed my teeth with a toothbrush that hadn't been snapped in half for fear someone would use the handle end to make a weapon. I walked around the room naked for a solid ten minutes, just to remember what it was like not to be surrounded by a roomful of other naked dudes. This led to some other naked activities when I remembered I wasn't surrounded by a roomful of other naked dudes. This led to another shower, and when I got out, I sat on the bed and rubbed my toes in the carpet for twenty minutes.

After that, there was still no sign of life outside of my room. I knew this because, like a completely well-adjusted person, I put my ear to the door and didn't hear any movement on the other side. I was too scared I'd run into Thea if I went out to check.

It was funny. I'd spent almost half my life surrounded by the biggest, baddest criminals the state of Georgia had been able to capture. Yet, I was terrified of a five-foot-five woman who for some asinine reason was still in love with me.

I couldn't be around her. Not if I wanted to keep my head straight and my eye on the prize. I had three years before I got off parole. I needed to get a job, tuck away some cash, and, the second I was allowed to leave Georgia, get the fuck out of there. Maybe, if I was lucky, I'd be able to convince Nora to come with me. We didn't have to go far. We could stay in the south if she wanted. South Carolina, North Carolina, Alabama, Tennessee— there were schools everywhere. She wouldn't have trouble finding a job. The hardest part would be convincing her to leave Thea.

However, maybe if she did, Thea would finally move on with her damn life and stop obsessing about me.

I'd known they lived together for a while. I didn't want anything to do with Thea while I was locked up, but I was happy as hell Nora had someone to lean on. I had been under the impression that Nora had gotten her own place when she found out about my release. I had been under that impression because Nora had straight-up *told me* she was getting her own place after I'd declared there was no fucking way I was living with Thea.

Now, I was hiding in my room, waiting for Nora to wake up, open my door, and escort me to breakfast like a fucking bodyguard so I could avoid confrontation.

Next up in my efforts to kill time was a workout. Sit ups, push-ups, planks, running in place. This was when I realized Nora hadn't bought me any deodorant.

Another shower.

Another naked lap around the bedroom, and this time, I managed to keep my hands off my cock.

Finally, I got dressed. This required me to pick through a bunch of preppy shit Nora had bought for me to find tattered jeans and a fitted green tee that clung to my chest like a damn glove. In my closet, I found a belt and a pair of distressed brown lace-up boots that maybe could have doubled as combat boots if the war was taking place on a runway. But what the hell did I know about style? I'd been wearing orange or puke beige for almost half my life.

When I was done with all of that and there was still no sign of Nora, I sat on the edge of the bed and decided to give the phone thing a try. I wasn't totally out of the technology loop. We had computers at the library and we were allowed to use them if we earned the privileges. But they might as well have been dinosaurs compared to the phone she'd bought me. I couldn't even get it to read my face with the fancy secret laser thing. I gave up trying pretty quickly.

So there I was, bored out of my fucking mind, starving, and poking at my newfound wrinkles in the bathroom mirror, when I heard a knock at my door.

"Ramsey?"

I froze, my eyes locked on the mirror, panic staring back at me.

Thea.

Jesus. I needed to find somewhere else to live.

Leaning out of the bathroom, I stared at the door. If I was super quiet, maybe she'd think I was still asleep and go the hell away.

When I didn't reply, she knocked again. Her voice was timid and sweet, not at all like the fearless girl I'd grown up with. I fucking hated it.

"Ramsey? You hungry? I'm making breakfast? I was wondering if you wanted something?" Everything from my name to the fact that she was making breakfast was a question, as if maybe she was asking permission to cook in her own damn house.

My stomach was currently feasting on my backbone. Still, I said nothing.

She sighed. "Okay. Well, if you change your—" There were several seconds of silence.

I quirked my eyebrow at the door, trying to figure out why she'd abruptly stopped talking, and then cursed my inability to develop x-ray vision.

I held my breath, hoping to hear her footsteps as she walked away.

No. Such. Fucking. Luck.

The door swung open and she came walking inside with her hands stacked over her eyes. "Look, I know you're awake. I heard you running earlier. I also heard you take at least three showers. Sorry, but the house isn't that big. Neither is the hot water heater. Are you at least dressed so I can open my eyes?"

Brave. Unapologetic. And completely oblivious to boundaries. Now *that* was the Thea I knew.

"Get out," I barked.

"Dressed? Not dressed? Help me out here?"

"Get. Out."

She kept her eyes closed. "You gotta eat, Ramsey. You can't stay locked up in this room forever."

I wanted to tell her to get the hell out again. Honestly, it was on the tip of my tongue. But it never made it past my lips because my traitorous eyes stole a head-to-toe of her lithe body. She was barefoot, wearing jeans—tight ones that tapered at her ankle. They looked like mine in the sense that they had a rip in the knee. They didn't look like mine in the sense that they hugged the curve of her hips and more than likely her ass too. A pink tank top stretched across her chest, and I swear on my life, fuck x-ray vision because I could see the pebble of her nipples beneath the fabric.

It wasn't a ridiculous dress.

It wasn't stupid fucking heels.

She wasn't wearing a face full of clown makeup.

She was just Thea.

The nostalgia pumped through my veins like acid even as my cock stirred. Fuck, I should have jerked off again in the shower.

"I'm dressed," I bit out, desperate for her to put her damn hands down and maybe use them to cover her tits instead.

Her long, brown lashes fluttered as she opened her eyes. Those fucking eyes had once owned me. As a huge smile lit her face, I felt the claim all over again.

"Oh, look, you chose one of the outfits I picked out for you."

Of course I had. Of fucking course. As soon as I got her out of my room, I was going to take the outfit off and light it on fire.

I ground my teeth. "Where's Nora?"

"She had an emergency at work and had to go in about an hour ago. I'm supposed to take you to meet your parole officer and then take you shopping to get whatever you need that we might have forgotten." She smiled. Well, she smiled wider. She had already been fucking smiling to begin with.

"What the hell kind of a work emergency can a first-grade teacher have?"

She shrugged. "Ran out of glue? Dripped the blue paint in the white? Substitute used permanent markers on the dry erase board?" She shrugged again. "Take your pick."

"Or maybe she was trying to force me to spend time with you when she knew good and damn well I can't miss this meeting with my PO, so I'll have no choice but to let you drive me there."

She blinked all innocent and sweet. "Or that."

"Right," I muttered, gripping the back of my neck and wishing I could snap it to put myself out of this misery once and for all. "What are you playing at here, Thea? You think if we spend the day together, I'm going to suddenly realize I can't live without you and drop to a knee and propose?"

I waited for her to cower. Maybe burst into tears like she had outside the prison. She'd come at me with some shit after I'd thrown the gum in the trash, but it had been for show. She wasn't the only one who could eavesdrop. I'd heard her puking in the bathroom not two minutes later.

This time, she didn't even flinch. "God, I hope not. I haven't had a manicure in ages."

I glared at her.

She pushed up onto her toes and glared right back. A burst of laughter escaped as she dropped to her heels. "You need to relax. I'm not trying to marry you, Ramsey. You're a felon without a job. Even I have higher standards than that."

Yeah. It stung, but at least she recognized the truth.

She strolled past me into the room, and fuck my life, I was right about the way those jeans hugged her ass.

"What are you doing?" I rumbled.

She pointed to the picture of us hanging on the wall. "I'm surprised you left it up."

I'd wanted to rip that damn thing down as soon as I'd seen it. Serious as a heart attack, Nora had threatened to tell my parole officer she found a bag of weed in my stuff if I took it down. I didn't believe she'd send me back to prison, but Nora could be crazy as shit sometimes, so I'd opted to hang a T-shirt over it while I slept instead.

"Do you remember when this was taken?" Thea asked.

Last week of tenth grade. After Nora's middle school graduation. We had gone out to grab burgers. Nora ditched us halfway through dinner to hang out with some of her friends, so we went home early. I snuck in Thea's window. We made out for over an hour and then I finger-fucked her until she came on my hand. I left with blue balls and a shit-eating grin.

"Nope."

"It was after Nora's middle school graduation. You didn't ask me to go that night. You didn't have to. I went because the three of us were a family. We did everything together and that wasn't because you were in love with me. Long before there was love, there was friendship, Ramsey. We relied on each other. Trusted each other. Cared about each other in ways that had nothing to do with holding hands or kissing." She sucked in a shaky breath that felt like sandpaper to my soul. "I don't care if you don't want to be with me, Ramsey. I'm pissed as hell that you cut me out of your life the way you did. I'm angry that you would do that to me at a time when I was dealing with a lot of shit. You *killed* a kid because he hurt me. But what you did, the way you did it, it hurt worse than anything Josh ever did to me."

Bile clawed up the back of my throat. She was wrong. So fucking wrong. I'd given her a gift. One she couldn't understand because she was so damn stubborn she refused to accept it.

I bit the inside of my cheek and distracted myself with the metallic taste of blood. "I don't love you, and I never did. I was a teenage boy trying to get in your pants. There wasn't much I wouldn't say."

"You fucking liar," she hissed.

"I'm sorry if that hurts you. But you weren't the only one with a lot of shit going on in your life. I'd just stared down the possibility of the death penalty before being sentenced to sixteen *years* in prison. Do you have any concept of how fucking scary that is? 'Cause it's terrifying." I stabbed a finger in her direction, praying she couldn't see it tremble.

She needed to understand. I *had* to make her understand. Even if it meant breaking her again in the process. It was better that way.

My voice rose with every sentence. "I wasn't cruel when I wrote you that letter. I didn't tell you I hated you. I didn't tell you to fuck off. I let you go. That's it. But you wouldn't fucking stop. All the letters and trying to get Nora involved. That's what made me hate you. So if you want to sit here and have a bitchfest about what happened to us, maybe go look in the mirror. Your high school boyfriend broke up with you, and you've spent the last twelve years being pissed about it." I threw my hands out to the sides. "Get over it, Thea. There are real-world problems happening right now and this is not one of them."

I waited for the fallout. The screaming. The fighting. The insults. A sinkhole to swallow me. *Anything.*

She just...stood there. Arms limp at her sides. Disappointment sparkling in her eyes. Lips pursed so tight, as if they were furious and still begging to be kissed.

And I just...stood there, withering into nothingness and silently imploring her to believe me.

It was all a lie. Every single word. There had never been a point in my life that I hadn't been in love with Thea Hull. It was exactly why I let her go.

And because Karma was hell-bent on destroying me, Thea knew it too.

"Where's the gum?"

"What?"

She pointed to the trash can. "Where's the gum I gave you last night?"

Chewed up and flushed down the toilet, every goddamn piece. "I don't fucking know. Maybe Nora took the trash out."

A slow, victorious smile crept across her plump lips. "Insult me. Lie to me. Try to paint me as a crazy woman. I don't give a shit how you have to spin this in your head to make yourself feel better." She prowled toward me like a lion hunting its prey. Stopping only inches away, she craned her head back and peered up at me. "You don't have to love me, Ramsey. But just so you know, I do love you. I always have and I always will. But right now, I really just want my best friend back." She tapped my pec. "He's in there. I know he is. And you are seriously underestimating me if you think your petty lies are going to stop me."

My throat closed and a tidal wave of heat roared through me as she trailed her finger down my chest, stopping above the button on my jeans.

"We'll worry about the rest later." She walked to the door, calling out over her shoulder, "So…breakfast?"

Yeah, I'd been right to be scared of running into Thea in the hall. Less than twenty-four hours after release and I was out of the frying pan and into the fire.

Eight years earlier…

"Hey, you," I whispered, wrapping Nora in my arms.

She buried her face in my chest, a sob shaking her shoulders.

My stomach knotted as my mind raced, frantically trying to figure out what the hell had her so upset. She'd cried a lot the first two years. Pretty much every time I saw her, she spent the entire visit in tears. I smiled and reassured her that I was fine. She never believed me, which only proved she was as smart as I thought she was. At year three, she only cried when she hugged me. And as of six months ago, we'd made it through almost all the bi-monthly visits without tears.

So when she promptly burst into tears as she walked through the door, I knew something was seriously wrong.

And it was the worst kind of wrong, because I could feel it in my soul that it had something to do with Thea.

It had been ten weeks since she'd mailed me a letter. I didn't read them. I wouldn't allow myself that kind of reprieve. My life was already hard enough without being reminded of what I was missing—*who* I was missing. But it had been radio silence recently.

Nora loved to torture me with all things Thea. We didn't go a single visitation without her filling my ears with some kind of bullshit, which I pretended to ignore while staring at the table and drinking in every syllable about my Sparrow.

Not anymore though. Nora hadn't brought her up in the last two months. It was crazy. She lived with the Hulls, so how was it possible that she never had anything to say about Thea?

She had to have been dating someone and Nora didn't want to tell me. I would have been happy for Thea. God knew it had taken long enough for her to finally give up on me. Fuck, why did it feel like I'd been filleted open to think she'd given up on me?

It was what I'd wanted.

It was what I'd told her to do.

It was the inevitable.

But what if something else had happened?

"What's going on?" I whispered into the top of her hair.

"That's enough, lover boy. Break it up," the guard overseeing visitation droned from his perch in the corner.

I gritted my teeth. "She's my sister."

He cocked his head to the side with a challenge. "I don't care if she's Mother Teresa. I said break it up."

A low growl rumbled in my chest. I wanted to punch that motherfucker in his throat, but it only would have bought me more time. I had no interest in spending even one second longer than I had to in that hellhole. I minded my Ps and Qs. Kept my head down. And avoided trouble like I was Keanu Reeves in the Matrix.

But this guy—this *asshole*—had it coming. It would have given me great pleasure to turn his ass in for the amount of contraband he smuggled in. Everything from heroine to women's dirty panties, this fucker had it. But being a good person in lockup was a lot like being a bad one on the outside. And I did not have the time or desire to watch my back for getting the unit's main supplier canned.

I glared at him as I continued to hold Nora. Toeing the line did not mean being a pushover. My sister was sobbing. It wasn't going to hurt anyone for me to have an extra ten damn seconds to console her.

"Stewart!" he barked, rising to his feet.

It took everything I had to let my arms fall away from her.

Nora sniffled as she backed up. "It's okay. Don't get in trouble. I'm fine."

We settled across from each other at a small table while the other inmates scattered across the open room with their loved ones.

"What's going on? Why are you so upset?" I asked.

"I just really missed you." She started to reach across the table to take my hand, stopping when she remembered touching wasn't allowed.

"Is everything okay at home?"

"Yeah. It's good."

I searched her face for clues. She'd been fine two days ago when we'd talked on the phone. "You seen your therapist recently?"

She laughed and swept the tears from under her eyes. "Every two weeks, alternating schedule from the days I come here."

She traveled two hours every other Saturday, and it was rare for her to miss a visit. Thea or Joe had been driving her before she got her license. I refused to think about Thea being that close. Nora liked to rub it in though.

Yet two months and not one fucking peep about the woman who haunted my dreams and lived in my fantasies. I couldn't ask. She'd read into it. Tell Thea. Then she would read into it too. I couldn't give her that kind of hope. Not when I needed her to forget.

"Nora, come on. You're killing me here. What's going on? Why are you crying?"

She stretched her long legs out under the table, leaving the toe of her shoe resting against mine. "Did I tell you Joe started dating Misty Martin?"

Not who I wanted to hear about, but shocking all the same. "Tiffany Martin's mom?"

"Yep."

"Like what kind of dating?"

She shrugged. "I don't know. I guess the kind you do a million years after your wife dies and you finally decide to get back in the game."

That was my chance. An opening. I could ask a subtle question about Thea that I could disguise as a question about Joe dating. Something along the lines of *Has Tiffany clawed Thea's eyes out over it yet?* I could add a laugh to make it sound like a joke. But it would force her into telling me how Thea was feeling about her dad dating and hopefully segue into every fucking detail about Thea over the last two months.

Battery acid pooled in my stomach when a thought struck me. Tiffany had an older brother. Kyle Martin was a cocky jock a few years older than we were. He had gone off to college before I'd been arrested. He would have been home by now though. My stomach rolled. Maybe that was how Joe had met Misty. Thea and Kyle were getting hot and heavy. Time to introduce the parents. Boom! Built-in double dates for life.

"Why do you look like you're about to puke?"

She'd been hanging out with Thea too much. She even sounded like her now. It was a kick in the balls almost as much as it was a gift.

"What? I don't."

"Is everything okay with you? Anyone giving you any trouble since they transferred Paulson? You need more money in your commissary account?"

Now, that felt like a kick in the balls sans the gift. I hated that she had to take care of me. And more than that, I hated that there had been money deposited in my commissary account before Joe had allowed her to get a job. Which meant it had been either Joe or Thea buying me snacks and deodorant. Everything had tasted bitter in those years.

"No, I'm fine. I've got plenty. I want to know what the hell is going on with you."

"I already told you I just miss you."

"Right. Which means you've already lied to me once since you've been here. Don't make it twice."

She cut her gaze over my shoulder. "Ramsey..."

"Spill it."

She put her foot on top of mine and pressed down. It was the visitation equivalent of a reassuring squeeze. "Last week was the four-year anniversary of Josh's...ya know."

My stomach sank, and I didn't give one fuck what the guards had to say about it. I reached across the table and caught her hand.

"Nora, he was a shit human being. I don't feel bad about what happened."

"I don't either," she whispered. "Though I kinda wish he was the one behind bars and not you."

"Stewart!" the guard shouted. "I'm not going to tell you again. I catch you touching again and visitation's over."

I silently fumed while Nora yanked her hand away and kept talking.

"Anyway. They did a whole special for him on the local news. His parents were on there, crying and holding on to each other. His dumbass brother, Jonathan, gave his part in his police uniform. He held up a picture of them as kids and did some seriously bad acting as he reminisced about what a great guy Josh was. It was all I could do not to break the TV."

I closed my eyes and pinched the bridge of my nose. "Jesus. What the hell is wrong with that town? That piece of shit doesn't deserve to be remembered."

"Oh, he definitely deserves to be remembered. Just not like that."

I scrubbed my sweaty palms over my thighs. Shit. I bet Thea was a mess, having watched that douchebag's family completely ignore what he'd done to her. Parading it around on TV, forcing it down her throat, and pouring salt in her wounds. I couldn't imagine how she lived with—

My heart stopped as yet another thought dawned on me.

What if she wasn't living with it anymore? What if she hadn't been able to handle it? What if that's why she stopped writing me letters? What if she'd gotten so dark and the fucking Caskeys had come out of the woodwork and pushed her over the edge? What if that was what Nora's tears were about?

What if…

What if…

What if…

What if Thea was gone?

I shot to my feet, and the words were out of my mouth before my brain had the chance to filter them. "Is Thea okay?"

Nora's eyes grew wide and her mouth fell open.

"Sit down, Stewart. Last warning."

Bile blazed a trail up the back of my throat. Slowly sinking to the chair, I begged, "Whatever it is, just tell me. She hasn't been writing me and you haven't been talking about her."

She closed her mouth and didn't say a word.

My pulse skyrocketed as my fears assaulted me. "Please. Nora, I'm dying here. Tell me she's okay."

A slow Cheshire cat grin stretched across her face as she whispered, "I knew it. I freaking knew it."

The smile helped, but it was a lot like throwing a bucket of water on a forest fire. I needed the words. I needed proof. Fuck, I needed Thea.

Her smile fell and she leaned across the table. "Tell me you love her. Tell me you are a *dumbass* who still loves her. Tell me she's your person and I'll tell you what Thea has been up to."

She wasn't *my* anything anymore. But I loved her. Every minute of every day, even when I didn't want to.

Emotions four years in the making flooded my eyes. I refused their escape and shook my head. I couldn't say it. I'd been through hell trying to forget her. I couldn't close my eyes without seeing her. She was never smiling or laughing the way she had done almost every day during the six years she had been mine. When I closed my eyes, all I saw was Thea crying—broken and shattered. I needed it to stop. I needed her to be able to smile again. It was ripping my heart from my fucking chest to stay away from her, but I wanted her to be able to truly live again.

"Tell me you love her," Nora demanded.

I sucked my lips in, trapping them between my teeth. I couldn't tell her that. I didn't want it to be true.

A tear teetered at the corner of my eye and I scrubbed my hands over my face before it had the chance to fall. No one needed to see that kind of weakness from me. Not Nora. Not the guards. Not the other inmates no doubt gawking from across the room. I was twenty-one years old; collapsing into a puddle of tears wasn't an option anymore.

"Good enough, Ramsey. Good enough." Her smile returned. "Thea's fine. She just got home from Australia."

My head snapped back, and I coughed to clear the emotion from my throat. "Australia? Really?"

"Yep. She's been touring the great Outback for the last few months. She got home middle of last week. She asked me not to tell you. I know you guys made plans to travel the world and stuff. She didn't want to rub it in."

I nodded, relief coating the inside of my chest. She was better than okay. She was traveling. Exploring the world. Moving on with her life without me. Yeah, it fucking hurt. But it also reaffirmed that I'd done the right thing by setting my Sparrow free.

"Thanks," I mumbled.

Nora shot me a wink. "Any time. All you have to do is ask."

I wouldn't. Not ever again. But after that day, Nora went out of her way to make sure I got a Thea update with every visit.

"So, now that we're on the topic of Thea, I guess I can tell you the other thing she asked me not to mention."

I looked at the table, not sure I wanted to hear but also hanging on her every word.

"After the Caskeys' interview, she bought a billboard in downtown Clovert. Two days later, pictures of her bruises and bite marks from that night along with a few magnified lines from her medical records were plastered fourteen feet high, forty-eight feet wide for the whole town to see. She put this big black stripe across the top that said *Remembering the real Josh Caskey.*"

My mouth gaped. I didn't want to remember the way she'd

looked that night. But knowing that Thea was a badass who wasn't hiding anymore made an unlikely laugh bubble from my throat. God, I was proud of that girl.

Nora laughed too. "It was hands down the most amazing thing I've ever seen. His old man got it removed the next morning, but it was incredible while it lasted."

I bet it was incredible. It made sense. Thea was incredible.

Nora and I chitchatted about everything and nothing for the next hour. A sense of peace washed over me as I watched her walk out that day.

I'd done the right thing. I could feel it coursing through me, icing the lava in my veins.

Everyone was finally moving on with their lives.

Nora was doing well. She still cried sometimes, but it was progress. She was going to college to become a teacher and had her whole life ahead of her.

Thea was traveling. If it wasn't already douchcanoe Kyle Martin, she'd eventually start dating someone else. And that was a good thing.

I was dying a little more each day.

But *they* were okay.

FIFTEEN

Thea

Me: He chewed the gum! I repeat he chewed the gum.

Nora: Duh. It was gum and it was Ramsey. He probably still has a piece hidden in his mouth. Tell him to open up so you can check…with your tongue.

Me: I'm thinking we are still a long way from tongue cavity searches. He basically told me that he never loved me, that he was only a teenager trying to get laid, and I needed to get the hell over it because I was insane to still be pining over my high school boyfriend.

Nora: Oh. My. God. He did not say that to you.

Me: Oh, he absolutely did. That was the abridged version though. The full version had a lot more F-bombs.

Nora: Please tell me you didn't fall apart.

Me: Nope. I took your advice, told him that I still loved him and there was nothing I wouldn't do to get my best friend back, and then I made him a rasher of bacon, a plate of maple sausage, and a southwest omlette. Oh, while I'm thinking about it, there is a rasher of bacon, a plate of maple sausage, and a southwest omlette in the fridge if you're hungry later.

Nora: Jeez, he's a stubborn one.

Me: He snuck a piece of bacon when he thought I wasn't looking, so I'll chalk it up to a victory.

Nora: Did you get him to his parole officer on time?

Me: Yep. I'm chilling in the car, checking some last-minute flight prices, and waiting for him to finish up.

Nora: Flights for you or for a client?

Me: Client. You know I've got three years before I'm flying anywhere again.

Nora: I know. Just making sure that hasn't changed in the last twenty-four hours.

Me: It didn't change for twelve years, it's sure as hell not going to change in twenty-four hours.

Nora: That's my girl. Give him hell, wildcat.

Me: Lol. So what are you really doing today?

Nora: Sitting in Starbucks, in the middle of the day, doing not a damn thing while my kids are probably running around the classroom like a bunch of wild banshees and bringing a substitute teacher to her knees. It's glorious. Truly glorious.

Me: You love those wild banshees though. Even the snotty nose one who always wipes it on your pants. Ten bucks says you've actually been sitting there stressing about them instead of enjoying your day off.

Nora: Witchcraft! Get out of my head and go babysit my brother.

I laughed and clicked back to the flights. I was in a much better place mentally and emotionally after my late-night chat with Nora.

I'd come into this expecting a war, yet at the first sign of trouble, I'd been ready to lie down and die. Ramsey wasn't the only one who was overwhelmed. I'd had high—and yes, slightly delusional—hopes about finally being able to press play on my life again. But just because Ramsey wasn't behind bars didn't mean I had him back.

We'd get there though. Losing him again wasn't an option.

Nora had been right. I had been a miserable drip once and Ramsey had won me over. I could do the same. I hadn't yet perfected the smile the way he had when we were kids. Though after seeing the way Ramsey's muscles had strained against the confines of that plain cotton tee that morning, I wasn't having a lot of childlike feelings toward him at all.

God, he had grown into a gorgeous man. I'd seen pictures of him that Nora had snapped during holiday visits at the prison, but seeing him in person was an entirely different experience. From his shoulders all the way down to his hips, his body was formed of sharp angles and contoured planes that a camera couldn't possibly do justice. He'd always been taller than me, but he was bigger now, rugged and purely masculine. When we were younger, Ramsey didn't have much. Jeans, T-shirts, and boots were his high school uniform. But the way he filled them out now, using them to enhance his body rather than simply covering his nakedness… God, it was sexy.

If I hadn't been two seconds from bursting into flames when I'd seen him standing in that bedroom, I would have laughed at how neat and meticulously styled his hair had been. It was a far cry from the shaggy mop he'd worn when we were younger.

It looked good on him. All of it.

Then again, it was Ramsey. He could have been wearing the prison scrubs—as Nora called them—and I wouldn't have cared.

The door to his parole officer's building swung open, drawing my attention from my phone. Ramsey came jogging down the steps, a folder in his hand and his eyes aimed at the ground.

Butterflies swarmed in my stomach, and it didn't matter one bit that he hadn't looked at me or spoken to me again since our argument in the bedroom. He was there. That was all I needed.

"Hey, how'd it go?" I asked when he opened the door on the new black Toyota 4Runner.

The SUV had been a recent splurge, one I didn't need considering my old Camry was sitting in the garage. I'd paid cash for it a few weeks earlier and it drove like a freaking dream. I didn't plan to be driving it long though. As soon as Ramsey was allowed to get his driver's license, it would be his. Nora had rolled her eyes when I'd asked her to drop me off at the dealership. I was usually the more frugal of the two of us, choosing to squirrel away money in investment accounts rather than spending them on frivolous purchases. But Ramsey coming home was exactly what I'd been saving for.

I worked my ass off as a travel agent. I'd started when I was eighteen. It had been slow at first. Planning vacations for the people of Clovert usually consisted of a two-night stay at the closest budget hotel that had an indoor pool so the grandkids could swim in January. I had my eyes on bigger adventures though. Things like seeing the giant tortoises in the Galapagos Islands, driving classic cars in Havana, and getting lost inside Istanbul's Grand Bazaar. They were extravagant vacations I hadn't been sure I would ever be able to afford, but I planned them all anyway.

It wasn't until I started a website called Travel For Me that things really took off. It wasn't the normal travel agent gig where people would come to me and I'd put a vacation together around their specifications. No, these were trips I'd made around my specifications, and people would come and purchase them like a floor plan on a home. There were different packages and price ranges. Add-on or bonus itineraries. But for the most part, I was selling my dreams to strangers, all the while banking the money so I could one day share that dream with Ramsey.

When I'd first started the website, I'd set a countdown for sixteen years in the top right-hand corner. Not a single one of my thousands of customers knew what it meant. A ton had asked. I lied to some. Played dumb with others. But I'd never told anyone the truth. Anyone who truly knew me assumed it was a countdown to when Ramsey was scheduled for release. An homage of sorts. It was more than that though. So much more.

That countdown was a reminder of how long I had to save every single penny I would need for both of us to retire and travel the world the way we'd discussed so many times growing up. I lived on around ten percent of what I actually made each month. Taxes and insurance took a solid forty percent of the rest. But that remaining fifty percent that I deposited into an investment account each month was how I fell asleep with a smile every night. Pinching pennies and living cheap was a small price to pay for that kind of security.

Ramsey slid into the black leather passenger seat. "I need to find a job."

"Nora told you I was going to add you to my payroll, right? Did they give you the paperwork? I can fill it out now if you want and you can run it back in there. Get it ticked off your to-do list."

His gaze never flickered my way as he buckled his seat belt. "A *real* job."

"Uh, it is a real job. I have boxes you can move. Filing that needs to be done. I'm not sure you have the cheerful demeanor needed to deal with my good customers yet, but I have a few assholes I'd really enjoy listening to you cuss out."

He opened his folder, took out a piece of paper, and passed it my way. He gave no explanation as he stared out the windshield.

"What's this?"

He. Said. Nothing.

Ohhh-kay. It appeared as though I was on my own to figure out what the hell he wanted.

The top of the paper read *Potential Employment Opportunities*. It was a short list that contained a random smattering of everything from restaurants to scrapyards.

I turned in my seat and looked at the side of his face. "Blink once if you want me to drive you to all these places so you can apply for a job even though I said I'd give you one. Blink twice if you're a robot from the future sent back in time to save our world."

His lips thinned and I leaned toward him, making a show of watching his eyes.

I jumped back when his head suddenly turned my way.

"I don't want to fucking be here with you," he growled. "But thanks to you and Nora and your stupid games, I don't exactly have a choice in the matter. I don't want to work for you, Thea. I don't want to live in the same house with you. I don't want to fucking *talk* to you. So quit with the goddamn jokes and just drive. The sooner I can find a job, the sooner this nightmare can be over."

Hurt swirled in my stomach, but I didn't let it show. "See, now I'm not sure what to do. You blinked three times."

153

He stared at me, angry and unimpressed. But while he was doing it…he blinked.

"Oh, okay. There we go. One blink." I straightened in my seat and got busy putting my seat belt on. "You had me worried there for a second. Though I'm kind of disappointed. I've never chauffeured a robot before."

Before we pulled out of the parking lot in order to start the impossible felon job hunt, I sent one last text to Nora.

Me: Plan worked perfectly. He told me to take my job and shove it. Initiating Part B of Gainful Employment.

We drove around for hours. Most places didn't even give Ramsey the chance to mention the part about being a felon before the door was slammed in his face. Clovert was a small town. Someone had to die, retire, or move for there to be a job opening. Not to mention that people remembered when Josh had been killed. And they definitely hadn't forgotten that it was Ramsey who had done it.

I drove him out to a few of the places that were closer to our house in Thomaston, hoping he could gain some anonymity, but the dejected look on his face each time he walked back to the SUV told me it wasn't helping.

We went to a drive-thru for lunch. I feared it was going to go as well as it had at the restaurant the day before, but Ramsey had no problem leaning over me to order.

"Two number fours with a Coke and a large chocolate shake."

We sat in the car and ate.

He didn't talk.

I did.

He didn't reply.

I pretended not to notice.

I smiled a lot that afternoon.

He scowled pretty much the entire time.

It was still the best day I'd had in over twelve years.

Deflated and exhausted, Ramsey gave up the job search around five o'clock. He signaled this to me with a grunted, "I'm done."

I was sure he was expecting me to drive him home so he could lock himself in the bedroom with Nora again. Instead, I took him to meet his new boss.

Yep. I'd been well aware that he was never going to take that job from me. Not in a million years. Probably not even if it meant breaking his parole and going back. But there was no way he was going to be able to turn down Joe Hull.

"What the fuck," he breathed as we pulled into a parking spot in front of my dad's barbershop.

My dad loved Ramsey. Yes, he wished that that night hadn't ended with a dead body, but he wasn't all that heartbroken that it had been Josh Caskey after hearing what he'd done to me. Seriously, sometimes I thought my dad loved Ramsey more than he loved me. Okay, not totally true. But it felt like that when I was in the middle of a fit of rage, huffing and puffing about how Ramsey had abandoned me, and my dad would jump in and defend him. His favorite line was, "I'm sure he has his reasons." It was like my dad wasn't on my side at all.

Ramsey had written my dad two letters from prison—yep. *Two.* For accounting clarification, that would be one more than he'd sent to me. I'd snuck into my dad's room to read the first one.

It was filled with profuse gratitude, thanking my dad for taking Nora in. He'd hidden the second one from me though. I assumed it contained the same message since it had been received shortly after Nora had graduated college.

Ramsey "hated" me. Yes. Those are air quotes. But he *respected* my father. He owed him a debt of gratitude, and I was banking on the fact that even though he was a cranky prick, Ramsey wouldn't be able to withstand one of Joe's good ol' guilt trips.

"Why are we here?" Ramsey growled.

I grinned at him, but it was my turn to play the silent game.

My dad came walking out of the double glass doors before I had cut the engine.

Pressed slacks. Tailored button-down with his sleeves rolled up to his elbows. Thinning, gray hair combed to the side. It was just the way Misty liked him.

I was thrilled when they'd gotten married. Dad had needed someone to take care of him. In a strange way, that had been the hardest part after he'd lost my mom. His heart was shattered, but she had always been the one to pick up the pieces. It took a lot of years and a lot of therapy for me to truly forgive him for the way he'd checked out after she'd died. But much like Ramsey, I'd never be able to thank him enough for the way he'd stepped up for all of us when our lives suddenly exploded.

And I loved him that much more as he rounded the hood of our SUV with a warm smile aimed directly at the man in my passenger seat.

When Ramsey looked at me, I was prepared for more of his anger, but his face paled and his gaze was pleading.

It almost made me feel bad for springing this on him.

Almost. But not really.

"Ramsey Stewart," my dad greeted as he snatched the car door open. "I was wondering when my girls were going to bring you around to see me. How ya been, son?"

Ramsey blinked rapidly. "Um…Hi, Mr. Hull. I'm uh…good."

I bit my bottom lip to stifle a laugh. Big, tough Ramsey had cussed me seven ways from Sunday, but he turned into a bumbling kid when it came to my dad.

"Come on in. We've got a lot of catching up to do."

He followed my father's direction so quickly that he forgot to unbuckle his seat belt and it yanked him back when he tried to get out.

I couldn't hide my laughter that time.

With jerky movements, Ramsey managed to escape the merciless belt of confinement and climb out of the car. My dad shook his hand and pulled him in for a back pat.

Contentment washed over me the likes of which I hadn't felt in years. I liked seeing them together. My two guys embraced in a hug.

I tucked my phone and my keys into the back pocket of my jeans and then met them at the front door to the shop.

"How's it going, buttercup?" my dad asked while pulling me in for a side hug.

I sucked in a deep breath. "Well, it turns out Ramsey never loved me. He was just trying to get laid in high school."

Ramsey's mouth fell open, the most incredulous shock contorting his handsome face.

My only response was a shrug.

"Hmm," my dad hummed. "That true, Ramsey?"

"Well, I… That—That's not what I meant, sir."

"What did you mean, then?" I asked, innocently batting my eyelashes at him.

Oh, yes. This was going to be fun.

Ramsey bulged his eyes at me. "All I was saying was that we were kids when we dated. Things are different now. We've both changed a lot."

"So, you did love me then?"

His jaw ticked as he shot lasers my way. "We were kids."

"Right. I got that. I'm just trying to establish if you loved me or not. Were you lying then or are you lying now?"

My dad's head bounced between us like he was watching a ping-pong match. Nora and I were not exactly known for being "well-behaved women." My father encouraged us to step out and be heard, even when the entire town was against us. Besides, he was no delicate daisy, either. He'd heard far worse than this from us over the years. He was used to it.

Ramsey, however, was not.

He clenched his teeth so hard that I feared he was going to need a dentist when we left. "I think we can have this conversation later."

"Okay, but to be clear, since I was so tragically bad at reading the situation last time. After we have this talk, are you hoping to get laid again? Or was that just a high school thing?"

My dad coughed and became enthralled with his shoes, and my Ramsey, my sweet Ramsey… His face turned bright red as he stared at me in absolute awe—and not the good kind.

But deep in my heart of hearts, it was the *best* kind because that was an emotion I recognized from him. Giving each other shit had been a way of life before he'd gone to prison. We loved each other fiercely, but we also loved to torment each other as if we didn't.

I was actually quite proud of myself. His face had shifted through the full spectrum of colors in the three minutes since we'd arrived. That was no easy feat with a man like him.

He stared at me.

I stared back.

My dad probably prayed to disappear before finally saying, "How about you don't answer that right now, son. Knowing you're trying to get my daughter between the sheets is going to make working together pretty damn awkward." And with that, he opened the door and went inside.

"*What the fuck?*" Ramsey mouthed at me as he caught the door with a hand at the top.

I had no idea what part he was pissed off about: the fact that I was talking about sex and his stupid lies in front of my dad or the fact that he'd insinuated they would be working together.

It was funny either way.

The bells on the door jingled, announcing our entry, and Misty rose from her permeant seat at the check-in desk. "Thea," she cooed, walking around the wooden counter, her short blonde bob brushing her round jawline. "Come give me some love."

There was no arguing with Misty when it came to her "love." My dad wasn't particularly affectionate, but that man's smile could light up a solar eclipse when his woman wrapped his baby in a momma-bear hug.

She pulled me in for a tight embrace, whispering, "How ya doing with all this?"

"Pretty okay actually."

When she was done with me, she turned her attention on Ramsey. "Mister, I've heard a lot about you." She gave him exactly zero warning before her arms were around his middle and her cheek was pressed against his chest.

Ramsey's body went solid, and his face flashed yet another shade of discomfort.

I laughed. Again.

He scowled at me. Again.

"All right, babe. Let the boy go. I need to show him his new station."

Ramsey once again looked at me. The emotion of the minute was accusation. "My station?"

Dad walked down the long aisle with four chairs and mirrors on each side. The shop was empty, which was strange for that time of day—something he'd no doubt planned with Nora. He stopped at the last chair on the left. "I lost a man to Gentleman Clips a few weeks ago. I've been trying to replace him, but the combination of talent and a good work ethic is harder to find than Atlantis." He patted the back of the chair in a silent order for Ramsey to sit down.

He obeyed, and my dad wrapped him in a cape.

With a set of clippers buzzing in his hand, he asked, "My girls tell me part of your parole means getting a job."

"Yeah. I got a few leads today."

Using his free hand, Dad nudged the back of Ramsey's head until his chin hit his chest. The buzzing returned as he went to work shaping up Ramsey's hair on the back of his neck.

It was something so simple. He'd probably had hundreds of haircuts since he'd been gone. But seeing my father take care of Ramsey with a gentle touch and a skilled hand made my heart swell.

He kept the clippers to his neck, rendering Ramsey immobile as he said, "Well, this isn't a lead. You start tomorrow."

"No offense, Mr. Hull, but I'd rather—"

"How's Nora doing? She good? Happy? Healthy? Safe?"

And there it was. The guilt trip.

I smiled, crossing my arms over my chest, preparing for the show.

"She's great," Ramsey answered, his eyes finding mine in the mirror. "We were both really lucky she had you and Thea while I was gone."

My exhale became painfully lodged in my throat as I held his gaze. Holy shit, had he actually said something positive about me? It hadn't been grumbled or rumbled, either. No cussing or seething. My vision swam, hope spiraling in my chest that this was some kind of magical turning point for us. And even if it wasn't, it was a start.

I lost his eyes when my dad guided his head to the side to trim around his ear.

"We were lucky to have *her*. And I'm going to be lucky to have you here as well. I need someone I can trust, Ramsey."

"I'm a convicted felon, Mr. Hull. That guy isn't me."

The buzzing sound suddenly stopped. "That's not what I heard during our visit a few years back."

I was relatively sure there hadn't been an invasion and there were no bullets falling from the sky, but each one of his words pierced through me all the same.

"What?" I gasped. "You visited him?" I looked at Ramsey. "You let him visit you?"

Why did that hurt? After all this time, why did that feel like a knife of betrayal landing in my back, knowing that my own father had been allowed to visit him while I'd been emotionally and physically locked out of his life?

My dad ignored me, kicking back on the clippers and leaning Ramsey's head to the opposite side. "I mean, I remember a lot of that conversation. Maybe I should refresh your memory in case you forgot about it."

Ramsey's gaze bounced to mine in the mirror, and like an oasis in the desert, apology was etched across his face. Just as quickly as it had appeared, it vanished, but Ramsey's eyes never left mine. There was a weight to his stare that hadn't been there before. Something hidden beneath the surface that I couldn't quite read, but I desperately wanted to. If for no other reason than maybe it would help me understand this new version of my Ramsey.

The buzzing stopped again and the room fell painfully silent. My dad walked to his station to grab a comb and spray bottle, but Ramsey was out of that chair like it had been struck by lightning.

He ripped off the cape and tossed it in the seat. "I don't have a license. I can't work here."

"You got your hours though. All you need to do is take the exam. Sit back down and let me take a little off your top."

"Nah, I'm good," Ramsey said. "Thanks for the cleanup, but we have to go now." He marched toward the door, slowing to grab my arm and drag me after him.

Electricity licked at my skin as his finger bit into me—not rough, definitely not gentle.

"Eight a.m. tomorrow, your tail better be in my shop. You got it?" my dad called after us. "That's not a request, son."

Ramsey's jaw turned to granite as he stopped at the door, his fingers still wrapped around my forearm. He stared at his reflection in the glass, his chest heaving and the thick cords of muscles at the base of his neck straining against his shirt. I didn't have to know Ramsey the man to recognize that he was about to explode.

"Hey," I whispered. Turning toward him, I rested my hand on his stomach. "Relax. You don't have to take the job. We'll figure something else out."

His lids fell shut, and his brows drew together painfully. That day wasn't supposed to end like that. I'd assumed he was going to be mad that Nora and I had set him up. But this was something else altogether. He was hurting. I didn't know why or what was going on in his head, but it slashed through me.

"Ramsey," I breathed, shifting into him until my front was flush with his side. He probably hated the contact, but it was all I had to offer. "It's okay. Just breathe. It's not a big deal."

His eyes popped open, a feral emotion blazing within. Releasing my arm, he shoved the door open and walked out, saying, "I'll be here at eight."

It was a warm Georgia afternoon, but the chill his sudden departure left behind was arctic.

Confused, I looked at my dad and then to Misty and then back to Ramsey as he climbed into our 4Runner.

"What the hell just happened?" I asked everyone and no one.

My dad walked over and threw his arm around my shoulder. "Just be patient, baby. It's going to be okay now."

It didn't feel like it was going to be okay. It didn't feel like anything was ever going to be okay again. It felt a lot like the man I was in love with was shattered beyond repair.

And once again, it felt like it was my fault.

Fighting back tears, I nodded and walked to the car.

Our drive home was silent.

So were the next seven days.

SIXTEEN

Ramsey

HER BROWN HAIR SCORCHED A PATH DOWN MY FEVERED skin as it brushed my abs.

"Wait," I breathed, not yet ready for it to be over.

Her small hands pumped my cock, twisting and gliding in a relentless rhythm.

"Wait, wait, wait, please," I begged, fisting the blanket.

Her large breasts swayed with the movement of her hands, the tips of her peaked nipples teasing my thigh as she continued to work me hard and fast.

The coil in my stomach tightened and my breathing shuddered. Fuck, I was close. Just a little more. Fuck me, just a little more.

Her rhythm faltered as I arched into her grip. My hips rolling to match her speed.

"Stay with me, Sparrow. Stay with me, baby, please."

My lungs burned as I held my breath, the pain drawing me closer to the edge. I wasn't ready. Not to lose her.

"No, no, no, no," I chanted as my cock swelled.

It was too late. My mouth fell open, and my head slammed back into the pillow as I erupted, crumbling in the wake. A guttural moan escaped, agony and ecstasy mingling into one emotion as I emptied on my stomach.

I could keep my eyes shut, pretending she was still there as I continued to stroke my cock to ride out the waves of my release.

It was always so damn hollow after I got off. She'd be gone, and I'd be left alone, holding my deflating cock and feeling like a part of me had been carved out all over again. I hated the aftermath that followed so much that it was rare that I let myself think of her. But it had been a week since I'd gotten out and I was buckling under the pressure of having her close again.

She drove me to work each morning, usually wearing a fucking skirt so unlike her that I couldn't decide if I wanted to bunch it at her hips as I spread her legs wide or rip it off and burn it.

Her office was next door, so she came over periodically to check in and talk to her dad. She was always smiling and laughing. It was fucking torture because I became Pavlov's dog, my mouth watering each time the bell on the door would ring.

Nora had started back at work, so Thea drove me home too. She'd talk and tell me about her day, groaning as she vented about her crazy clients and giggling as she made jokes about her clients who weren't crazy enough.

Each night, she'd settle into her corner on the couch, wearing one of her many pairs of baggy pajama pants. Most of them had a ridiculous pattern like dueling bacon and eggs or Bill Murray's face. It pissed me off how much they made me want to laugh. Worst of all though, she paired the damn things with a tank top that hugged her breasts and left me holding my cock every time I got a minute alone.

It was hell. Absolute hell. My PO had a lead on a room for rent in a privately-run halfway house of sorts. But not living with Thea only solved a few of my problems. I was still working for Joe. He'd blackmailed me into taking the job, so I assumed that leverage extended to me *keeping* the job as well. My sister was still living with her, which meant she'd still be a part of the equation no matter where I rested my head at night.

And there was Thea. Stubborn, determined, and hell-bent Thea.

Cutting her out of my life hadn't dissuaded her. Neither had being a dick. It seemed prison walls were the only thing that could keep her away.

I needed to step it up a notch. Though I had no fucking clue what that entailed.

Opting out of another shower when I remembered the way she'd looked on her knees in my fantasies the night before, I used a washcloth to clean up, and then I got dressed.

When I opened my bedroom door, I was hit with the sound of Thea's laughter ringing down the hallway. Like an emotional masochist, I froze, hidden out of sight, and allowed myself a second to absorb it.

"She called it pot roast." Thea laughed. "But it tasted like that mystery meat they used to serve in the school cafeteria."

"Oh, come on now. It wasn't that bad," Nora replied.

"Yes. It was. I haven't had to hide food in my napkin since I was six."

"She caught you, didn't she? Oh, God, please tell me she caught you."

"Would it be my life if she hadn't?"

Together they burst into a fit of laughter that washed over me like a cool summer breeze. That made it worth it. All twelve years and listening to them make jokes and tell stories, breathing free and easy, made it absolutely worth it.

I was still grinning when a woman appeared at the mouth of the hall.

"Shit!" she yelled when she saw me. She clutched her pearls and blew out a ragged breath. "Jesus, you scared me."

She was familiar, but my brain couldn't pinpoint who she was or why she was standing in our house at seven thirty in the morning.

Pink, glossy lips.

Long, blonde hair.

A flowy dress and towering high heels.

It clicked. Tiffany Martin. Thea's once archnemesis-turned-stepsister.

It was odd, running into people from my past. A few of our old classmates had been into the shop. Jeremy Dantis had greeted me with a handshake. Mike Shriver had turned around and walked right back out, slamming the door to his car before peeling out of the parking lot.

I waited to see which type Tiffany was.

A row of white teeth nearly blinded me as she smiled. "I brought some donuts. You want one?"

I wedged a hand inside my front pocket. "I'm good."

"He won't eat if I'm here," Thea called out. "Sometimes I sit at the kitchen table and read just so he has to go hungry."

Tiffany's smile grew. "You're like that deer repellent my mom sprays in the garden to keep the does off her tomatoes."

"Pretty much." Thea laughed. "Come on, Ramsey. I'm going to be late if we don't leave soon."

Like my own personal superhero, Nora rounded the corner to save me, holding a chocolate donut no less. "Here. I saved you the custard-filled one."

"Thanks," I mumbled, taking the donut. My stomach rejoiced that it wouldn't have to settle for a banana for the seventh morning in a row.

"I packed you a lunch for today too. Misty called and ratted you out about not eating the takeout Thea brought over yesterday."

"See? Deer repellent," Thea said from the kitchen.

Tiffany cocked her head to the side. "You know, 'snitches get stitches' is not a concept my mother has ever embraced."

"Apparently neither is pot roast." Nora gave my arm a tug. "Come on. Thea's been waiting on you. She has a call at eight fifteen and she needs to be at the office to take it."

"I'll be in the car!" Thea called out. "See ya, Tiff."

Tiffany's silver bracelets jingled as she lifted her hand and waved. "Bye, sweetie. Have a better day."

Better day? Had yesterday been bad? She sure as shit hadn't acted like it as she'd followed me around while I swept the shop, updating me on every single asshole we'd ever so much as crossed paths with.

I followed Nora out of the hall, passing Tiffany without speaking to her again. I pretended that wasn't because of six years of Thea training me not to.

Demolishing my first donut in over a decade, I watched Nora swirl around the kitchen. She wrapped up another donut and poured coffee into a travel mug. Then she handed them to me along with a brown paper sack.

"There ya go, buddy. All set for the day."

I grinned while still chewing. "Thanks, Mom."

She rolled her eyes and gave me a shove. "Go. And be nice to Thea. She's been up since three."

My eyebrows jumped up my forehead. "Why?"

She curled her lip. "What do you mean why? Because you're a dick. Why else?"

"What did I do?"

She gave me another shove toward the door. "Nothing."

Juggling my coffee and my donut as I walked, I looked at her over my shoulder. "So why am I a dick?"

"Nothing doesn't mean you didn't do anything wrong. It means you did *nothing*."

"I have no idea what that means."

She swooped in front of me and opened the front door. "It means you're a dick."

I stared at her for a long beat. "Women are freaking crazy."

Shooting me a bored glare, she retorted, "Says the man who will starve to death before eating anything Thea touches."

As usual, my glare was better than hers.

"All I'm asking is that you be nice. You don't have to reveal your undying love—" She shoved her hand in my face when I opened my mouth to object. "Shut it, Ramsey. This bullshit silent treatment you're giving her is really starting to piss me off. You have a roof over your head because of her. A bed to sleep in. Clothes in your drawer. A job. A ride to your job. A ride home from your job. Everything."

"I didn't ask her for any of that."

She poked my chest. "I know. Which is exactly why she does it. She feels guilty. If you want to get rid of her so bad, stop acting like an injured puppy she can't catch. She's never going to let go if she thinks there's a possibility you might need her again. Show her you're okay. Be nice. It won't kill you."

I wasn't sure I agreed with her about that last part.

Thea was not a woman who was going to accept casual conversation. If I so much as cracked open the door to more, she was going to barge right through, dropping me to my knees. And once she was in, I was terrified I wouldn't have the willpower to make her leave again.

Mainly because I didn't want to leave.

I wanted to go to our tree, back before Josh Caskey had ruined it. I wanted to sit in the branches and listen to my Sparrow

169

talk about anything and everything that happened to pass through her mind. I wanted to climb down and pull her into my arms. I wanted to kiss her so I could finally breathe again. I wanted to get to know the woman she had become and I wanted to give her the life we'd planned and then take selfishly that for myself.

But that's exactly what following through on my desires would have been.

Completely. Totally. Utterly *selfish*.

"Please. For me?" Nora begged.

I let out a loud groan. "I'll try. No promises."

She squeaked, jumping on her toes and clapping her hands. "Start with something simple. Like, like… Oh, tell her she looks nice today."

"No."

"Okay, what about complimenting her perfume? She has to smell better than sweaty guys in prison."

She did. She smelled like flowers dipped in honey. And every time I walked past her, I held my breath because of it.

"Not doing that either."

Crossing her arms over her chest, she narrowed her eyes. "Fine. Then tell her she has nice boobs. God knows you stare at those enough."

"And we're done here." I started to turn away, but she caught my arm.

"Okay. Okay. Just make conversation. Things like *good morning* and *thanks for the ride* go a long way when you've been up with nightmares since three."

My shoulders got tight. "What kind of nightmares?"

"The kind where you go back to prison and you're a *dick* who cuts her out again."

"Jesus," I cussed under my breath.

"She doesn't deserve this. You know that."

I leaned in close and lowered my voice. "This is *exactly* what she deserves. And you know *that*."

She pressed her lips together and stole the donut from my hand, but she had no argument. I'd spoken the truth.

"I'll see you tonight." And with that, I was gone, walking to Thea's car, giving myself a motivational speech with every step.

I could do this. It was going to fucking gut me, but that was nothing new. I could be nice, set her mind at ease, and maybe just maybe she'd let go of the past in order to find her future. But one way or another, it had to end.

When I climbed into her SUV, she was surfing through channels on the radio, passing the various morning shows in the hunt for music. The constant skipping grated on my nerves, but it was part of her morning ritual, and if I was being honest, it was pretty fucking cute, so I let her have it. At the first stop sign, she'd run a frustrated hand through her hair, flipping it to one side only to flip it right back. At the second stop sign, she'd huff and stab at the buttons harder, sometimes changing fingers if she was really annoyed. At the exit of the neighborhood, she'd mumble a curse, plug in her phone, and put on the same damn playlist she listened to every freaking day, like clockwork.

Sipping on my coffee, I waited until we were on the highway before asking, "So you and Tiffany are friends now, huh?"

Her head swung my way so fast that it was a wonder it didn't fly off her neck. "Did you just speak to me?"

I shrugged. "Nora said I'm an injured puppy that you can't catch."

"Ah, well, that explains nothing."

My lips twitched. "Pretty much."

There was a long pause, neither of us knowing what the hell to say. Who knew being nice would be so damn hard?

"She was on the yearbook staff our junior year," Thea blurted.

"Who?"

"Tiffany. She always had a camera around her neck. You probably don't remember because you weren't giving her the evil eye twenty-four-seven the way I was."

"Ha! The evil eye? I wasn't even allowed to look at her without getting in trouble. I almost broke into a cold sweat when I saw her today."

Her face softened, and her perfect crescent lips curled into a smile. "She wanted my man. I wasn't about to sit back and let that happen."

Something inside me stirred at the memory of when I was hers. When I belonged. When I wasn't fighting the way I felt for her every single minute of every single day. When I could touch her any time I wanted and hold her when she needed me. I missed the days when she was my Sparrow.

When I didn't reply, she kept her eyes on the road and continued talking. "A few weeks after you were sentenced, she came over to my house with a shoebox of pictures. It was everything she could find of us. Sometimes we were tiny and in the background. Other times, you were all blurry. There were a couple decent ones of us laughing at lunch together."

Surprise wasn't a strong enough word. "Why would she do that? Tiffany wasn't known to be…well, not a bitch."

Thea's gaze flicked between me and the road. "You really didn't read any of my letters, did you?"

Shit. "Thea…I—"

"It's okay. The letters were more for me anyway. It was

172

therapeutic. I got to write down how much I loved you…or hated you…or missed you…or wanted to punch you." She flashed me another smile. "I could have saved a lot of money on stamps though."

"Sorry," I muttered.

"Anyway, back to Tiffany. I wasn't the only one Josh hurt. I know of at least three others."

My back shot straight, and bile clawed up the back of my throat. "No fucking way. Tiffany?"

She swayed her head from side to side. "And Jessica Lathem. And Ashley Rowlan. There's one more, but she hasn't said anything publicly, so I don't feel it's my place to out her. Her family is friends with the Caskeys. It would be a whole big thing if she came out with the truth."

My voice echoed off the windows as I boomed, "Thea, he was raping girls. It *needs* to be a whole big fucking thing!"

"I agree," she said, calm as a cucumber. Like that kid hadn't ruined her entire freaking life. "But how she deals with what he did is her choice. He's gone. He can't hurt anybody else."

"The Caskeys can though. Did you know his brother, Jonathan, wrote a letter to the parole board, trying to block me from getting out? I heard they didn't give it to me at the eight-year mark because his dad called in some fucking favors. He was a serial rapist, and yet somehow I'm the criminal."

Her hands tightened on the steering wheel. "I know, Ramsey. I promise you I understand your frustration better than anyone else."

Blood thundered in my ears, and guilt took up root in my stomach. Me flipping my shit probably wasn't what Nora had had in mind when she'd told me to be nice. Neither was snapping at Thea over something as painful as memories of Josh Caskey. Christ, she was right. I was a dick.

173

"I'm sorry," I told the window.

"You don't have to apologize to me. It's okay to be mad. I was pissed at the world for a really long time too." She flashed me a weak grin. "See, this is why you should have written me some letters."

I smiled. God, she was a good woman. She did not deserve the life I had given her. Even, and especially, the one when I was trying not to give her anything at all.

I sucked in a deep breath and willed my heart to slow. "So, if I'm an injured puppy that you can't catch, what the hell has Nora been saying to you about me?"

"What makes you think we talk about you when you aren't around?"

"Because it is physically impossible for Nora to keep her nose out of our relationsh—" I bit the inside of my cheek. Fucking. Fuck. Fuck. Fuck. I was horrible at this shit. "I didn't mean that we have…a *relationship* or anything."

Thea let out a laugh. "Relax, Ramsey. I've come to terms with a lot of things over the last week. That being one of them."

I ignored the way my stomach rolled. "Good. That's good."

"You know it doesn't have to be all or nothing though. We were friends before love entered the picture."

I swallowed hard, the distance between us suddenly measuring in oceans rather than inches. "You think that could actually happen?"

She slowed to a stop at a red light and turned to face me, beautiful destruction breaking in her eyes. "I would give up over twelve years of my life for the opportunity to try."

"Thea," I breathed when all other words failed me.

"We've established I love you. I can't and won't take that back. But if that ship has sailed, then we need to find a new ship. I'm not giving up on you, Ramsey. I don't care if you want me to. I don't care if it means you ice me out for all of eternity. I don't even care that you've already quit on me. I once promised that it was you and me forever. Do you remember that? You made me swear it."

Oh, I remembered it. It was why I'd let her go as quickly as I had. It was going to take time to convince Thea to give up on me, and that clock was still ticking.

I sighed. "I was a scared kid who needed reassurance."

"I was too." Her hand suddenly came down on my wrist, her fingerprints branding me from the outside to match the marks she'd already left on my heart. "I *am* too. Tell me why you hate me. Give me a reason for why you cut me out of your life. Give me anything so maybe I can finally understand. Is it because of what I told the cops about Josh—"

"No," I said firmly. "It was never that. I swear to you none of this is your fault. And I've never, not for a single day, thought it was."

"That's not what you said when—"

Unable to take the sizzling at my wrist any longer, I moved my arm out of her reach and rested my hand on the back of her seat, bringing us closer without actually touching her. "It was bullshit. That day outside the prison, I said a lot of shit that I didn't mean because I was pissed that you were there. You should have been married or dating or raising kids. Maybe off on one of your adventures to Australia or Fiji or China, not standing outside of a fucking prison."

She laughed soft and entirely sad. "A husband and kids? Jesus, Ramsey, Joe didn't have that kind of therapy money."

I rolled my eyes, but she kept going.

"Besides, I ran out of countries to visit when I was twenty-five."

"What?"

The light turned green and she slowly eased on the accelerator. "Places to visit. I ran out. I spent two weeks in Japan on my twenty-fifth birthday and then hung up my passport."

"You've traveled to every country?"

"No. I've traveled to every country that doesn't allow a felon to get a visa. I saved all the others for us."

My heart stopped, and a brick of emotion lodged in my throat. Fuck, why did that feel good? I didn't want that. I'd never wanted her waiting for me for anything. Thea had found the one loophole.

She'd done well for herself. She had a business and a website, and while I hated the idea of her planning trips for people instead of taking them herself, I was proud that she'd found something she loved and made a career out of it. She had a nice car. She owned a house. She was currently taking care of my broke ass. She could have floated through life, bouncing from one plane to the next, but she was waiting for *me*. And I couldn't even be mad about it because before she'd done it, she'd lived the life I wanted for her. Not with a new man who could actually offer her something, but she was only twenty-eight. She had time.

I moved my arm to my lap and righted myself in my seat. A myriad of conflicting emotions swirled inside me.

"Ramsey," she breathed.

I had no words. It was already happening. One conversation and the carefully crafted walls I'd painstakingly built brick by fucking brick were starting to shake. It was what I'd feared would happen if I let her in even an inch.

"Please don't shut down on me again." She covered my hand with hers. "Come back. Please."

I couldn't go back. I'd ruined her life once. I'd never forgive myself if I did it again.

Nora was right. Thea was never going to stop until I was happy. After the hell I'd put her through, I had no idea why she cared at all anymore. Misplaced guilt or a sense of responsibility, I couldn't be sure. But whatever the reason, it had to end.

I'd fooled her when we were kids. Wearing my smile as a mask when in reality my world had been crumbling around me. It had been a long time since that smile had been a part of my arsenal.

It was time to bring it back.

Giving her hand a squeeze that was as much of a goodbye as it was a hello, I split my lips into a smile so painful that it felt as though it had been created with the blade of a knife. "Let's try the friends thing."

Her head swung my way and her whole face lit like the New York City power grid. "Really?"

"Sure. Why not? It can't hurt, right?"

It was a lie. It was going to fucking slay me.

But there wasn't much I wouldn't do to set my Sparrow free.

SEVENTEEN

Thea

"THEA?" RAMSEY CALLED AS HE PADDED BAREFOOT down the hall.

The grin I'd been wearing all day stretched across my face. "In the kitchen."

It was well past seven, and Nora was out having drinks with a few of her fellow teachers. She didn't go out often, and it was awful convenient that the day I'd texted her the good news about Ramsey and me giving the friends thing a shot, she'd suddenly had plans and wouldn't be home until "late." She'd followed it up with a GIF of Daisy Duck covering Donald's face with lipstick kisses, so I thought her hopes for my first evening alone with Ramsey were slightly more aspiring than mine.

Ramsey and I had been busy at work that day, so our paths had only crossed a few times since our conversation that morning and our interactions had been limited. My dad and Misty had eaten with us when I'd walked over to have lunch, and when Ramsey had popped over to return a package that had been mistakenly delivered to the barbershop, I'd been on the phone with a client. That afternoon, he'd spent the ride home on the phone with his parole officer discussing the paperwork he needed from the prison so he could schedule the exam for his barber's license. He had years more than the fifteen hundred hours of experience required, but until the prison signed off on his hours worked and he passed the exam, he was stuck cleaning and observing at my dad's shop.

As per usual, when we'd gotten home, Ramsey had gone straight to his room, shut the door, and turned on the shower. I swear he was the cleanest man I had ever met. My water bill was going to be a bazillion dollars, but I couldn't bring myself to care.

"Question," he said, settling on one of the barstools that overlooked our kitchen.

I nervously toyed with the tie on my *Yeti for Bed* pajama pants before turning to face him. "Answer."

He ran his finger down the yellow page of the open book and asked, "What do you know about Peach Ink?"

My chin jerked to the side. "What is that?"

"It's a tattoo shop."

"No, I mean, what is that you're looking at?"

"A phone book?" He frowned adorably—and a lot hot too. *Dammit! Just friends, Thea. Just. Friends.*

"Right," I said. "But where did you find it? I didn't know they made those anymore. You do know you can look up all that stuff on your phone, right?"

"Yeah, I'm not using that thing again. It's possessed by that deaf Siri woman." He looked back down at the phone book, shaking his head and mimicking, "I'm sorry, Ram-zay, I didn't catch that."

I barked a laugh. "You can turn her off, ya know?"

"I don't even know how I turned her on. You think I can figure out how to turn her off?"

I walked around the bar, my hand outstretched. "Here, give it to me. I'll show you."

He pulled his phone out of his back pocket and slapped it

in my hand. "So anyway, Peach Ink. What do you know about it? Are they any good? From one to ten, what are the chances I'll catch hepatitis?"

I handed the phone back to him. "You gotta open it first." Biting my bottom lip to stifle a laugh, I watched as he moved his head from side to side, trying to get the facial recognition to read the different angles of his face.

"Dammit," he muttered, starting the process over.

"Oh my God. You and this phone." I laughed, taking it again. "Sit still. You don't have to move it around. Just look at it and it will open." I held it up in front of his face, and not a second later, the sounds of a woman moaning and skin slapping filled the room.

Ramsey's face contorted with horror and he jumped off the stool, yelling, "Siri off! Siri off!" He plucked it from my hands and frantically pressed the buttons on the side, cussing when the moans grew louder. "Goddamn it, Siri. Turn it off!"

The room suddenly fell silent, followed by, "I'm sorry, Ramzay. I didn't catch that."

We stood there staring at each other, my surprise meeting his mortification.

And then it happened. Twelve years, nine months, five days, nineteen hours, and four minutes after I'd lost him, Ramsey came home. A full-blown Ramsey Stewart special split his face.

"Well, that wasn't awkward at all."

A loud laugh bubbled from my throat and I leaned against the bar to keep from falling over. "So let me get this straight. You can't work Siri and you're using a phone book to look up a number, but you were able to find porn?"

"Shut up." He laughed, deep and throaty. It was the Ramsey Stewart masterpiece to match the Ramsey Stewart special and it made my knees weak.

"That does explain all the showers."

"Sweet Jesus, we're really going to talk about this, aren't we?"

"I'm just happy Nora got you the waterproof model."

His laughter abruptly stopped. "Wait, it's waterproof?"

That was when I lost it. I collapsed onto the floor, holding my stomach, and laughing my ass off.

Ramsey was right behind me, groaning, "Shoot me!"

We laughed. And we laughed. God, did we laugh.

I started crying at one point.

Ramsey laughed harder.

He hit his leg on the barstool as he rolled over.

I laughed even harder.

"Siri off!" I mocked.

He was laughing so hard that he started coughing.

When he crawled over to me on his elbows and covered my mouth with his hand to make me stop talking, I continued to shout around his fingers.

It was stupid, but it felt like some of the pieces of me I'd lost over the years were finally clicking back into place. I had no idea how long it was in actual minutes, but it felt like twelve years' worth of humor was trying to escape. By the time we sobered, we were both flat on our backs, not touching, but close enough that we could have.

I'd have given anything to inch over, rest my head on his shoulder, and curl into his side. He would have kissed me on the top of my head, and I would have tilted my head back and smiled up at him. He would have dipped low, telling me I was crazy before planting a toe-curling kiss on my lips. We'd have made out like we were high schoolers again, and then he would have picked me up and carried me to bed, where he'd have made love to me hard and fast like the adults we'd become.

But that wasn't this version of Thea and Ramsey. They were just friends.

It would however be Ramsey and someone else one day.

As I lay there, staring at the side of his smiling face, love warmed my chest. I'd missed him so damn much. I didn't need it to be physical with us. If keeping him as a part of my life meant not being the center of his, I could do that. Having him back was enough.

He'd been home just over a week, and as crazy as it was, I'd never thought about Ramsey watching porn or getting himself off. But now, it seemed so obvious. After all, I'd gone through my fair share of batteries over the years. He was a gorgeous twenty-nine-year-old man who had been arrested the same night he'd lost his virginity. Even if he was content with being alone for the time being, he wouldn't be forever. A time would come when he would want to find a woman, if not for a long-term relationship then at least for a few hot and heavy nights.

He'd made it clear that woman wasn't going to be me. I'd even come to terms with it—kind of. Deep down, I hoped that, when that day came, he didn't feel like he had to lie to me about it or sneak around behind my back. It would break me to know he was out with another woman, but I'd already put myself back together once. I could do it again.

If he was happy, I would find a way to accept it.

"We…are never…speaking of this again," Ramsey panted.

"I did…not agree to that."

"I think Siri's out to get me."

"She's probably jealous of all your porn ladies."

"Nah. She's a know-it-all. She's not my type."

I rolled to the side to face him and propped myself up on an elbow. "What is your type, Ramsey?"

Staring up at the ceiling, he laughed again. "A tree is my type at this point."

I swallowed hard. "You know, if you ever wanted to go out and meet someone, you could tell me, right?"

His smile fell as he looked over at me. "Don't do this. We're finally having a good night. Don't do this."

"Don't do what? We're friends. We can talk about this stuff. Come on. Be real. The showers aren't going to cut it forever."

He shook his head and fluidly climbed to his feet. "I'm not talking about this."

My chest literally ached, but I did my best to cover as I stood too. "Ramsey, it's okay."

"Drop it," he demanded.

I rested my hand on his forearm. "I know it will happen eventually. It's natural for you to want someone. I'm actually impressed you've waited this long. I'm sure it's been tough over the years."

He looked at my hand and then back up again, his dark eyes straddling the line between fury and fire. "Who said I've waited?"

Well, hello there, gaping hole in my chest. So nice to see you again.

My breath lodged in my throat as I mentally told myself it was okay. Wasn't that the message I'd been trying to give him? That he was allowed to have someone else? And he hadn't lied to me about it, which was also what I'd thought I'd wanted. Only now it stung.

I had no idea when he could have met someone. He was always with me or Nora. But the when and the how didn't matter. He was officially moving on.

I quickly turned away, knowing that no matter how much

I wanted to, I wouldn't be able to smile through that kind of pain. Jesus, it had been twelve years. Why couldn't I just let him go?

Oh, right. Because I still loved him as if it had been coded into my DNA.

"That's good. Great. I'm happy for you," I whispered, ready to bolt to my room but without an excuse to make my escape.

I heard his feet shuffle across the carpet just seconds before his suffocating proximity stole the oxygen from my lungs. He wasn't touching me, but he loomed so close that his body heat licked at my back.

"What about you, Thea? There had to have been a lot of cold nights since you were sixteen?"

My breathing shuddered as I stared at the way our shadows erotically melded into one. "There were."

"I know you were mad at me for a lot of years. You find someone to warm you up while I was gone?"

I gasped when his hands landed on my hips, his fingers sneaking under the hem of my tank top and brushing the sensitive flesh above my waistband.

"No," I replied, chancing a step backward to bring his front flush against me.

He was hard. And not the ripples of his abs or the curves of his defined pecs. His cock was long and thick, straining against the denim of his jeans where they met my ass.

He hissed at the contact, and every nerve ending from my nipples to my clit, all the ones that had long since been dormant, came to life like wildfire.

His head dipped and his hot breath fluttered across my skin as he asked, "No one?"

Fiery butterflies hummed in my stomach as I boldly turned

my head toward him. His nose swept my cheek. "You smell like watermelon."

His fingers spasmed and he pulled me deeper into his curve. "Answer me."

I didn't want to answer him. Jealousy was the only thing keeping him in that moment.

Well, jealousy and need.

I lifted my arm, terrified of breaking whatever spell had been cast over him but unable to stop myself, and wrapped my hand around the back of his neck, drawing him closer. "I have hands too. I even know how to look up porn. Though I didn't need it most nights."

His chest rose and fell against my back, my heart working at a similar marathon pace.

I probably should have cared that he'd been with someone that week. I was a woman who knew my worth. And I deserved far more than being someone's sloppy seconds.

But I just couldn't bring myself to care.

It had been too long. And it was Ramsey; he could use me all he wanted.

I'd use him too.

We could be two broken people numbing our pain with sex and orgasms.

Distracting each other.

Giving to each other.

Taking from each other.

It was such subtle movement that I don't think he was conscious of the way his hips rocked against my ass. Stroking and teasing.

"You think about me?" he rumbled, but it was laced with thick insecurity.

I nuzzled my cheek against his nose again and raked my fingernails across the back of his neck. "I don't know. You think about me?"

My lungs seized as his hand glided up my stomach, his thumb stopping so close to the bottom of my breast that it caused an ache between my legs.

He licked his lips. "When I'm in the shower, you're fucking beautiful on your knees, Thea."

I moaned, arching my back to add more pressure against his hard-on, and smiled. "Good, because when I'm in my bed at night, you're fucking beautiful between my thighs, Ramsey."

A deep groan vibrated against my back. "Dammit, this can't happen."

"We're two consenting adults. It can definitely happen." I covered his hand and guided it to my breast.

His entire body stiffened at the contact, but his hand kneaded like it'd found its way home. "Fuck," he groaned, plucking at my nipple through the fabric of my thin bra.

Throwing my head back to rest on his shoulder, I sagged against him.

His arm hooked around my hips, holding me up as he continued his delicious assault on my breast.

"I don't want you," he snarled, but his teeth nipped at my neck.

I thrust a hand between us and gave his hard length a pointed rub. "You're a liar."

His hand left my breast and traced up my throat, squeezing my jaw as his thumb dipped inside my mouth. "We're not fucking doing this."

"Ramsey, please."

"No," he growled before biting me again, harder this time, sending sparks to my clit.

One touch and I would unravel.

I tugged at his wrist, desperate to shift his frenzied attention into my panties, and I thought I was successful until he roughly shoved his hand into the front of my shirt.

Palm to breast. Skin to skin. Reckless and wild.

It was fucking magical.

My lids fell shut, and his mouth opened and I could taste the watermelon on his breath as he hovered out of my reach. "Kiss me."

The rocking of his hips intensified. "No."

"Then let me touch you." I twisted in his arms, going for the button of his jeans, but I never made it.

In less than a second, he had me off my feet and I hit the floor hard. I was face down and his hand beside my head was the only thing to soften the blow. He came down on top of me, his heavy weight pinning me to the carpet.

"I can't do this with you," he choked out, emotion overflowing in his voice. It was such a stark dichotomy to the relentless rhythm of his hips as he ground into me. "You're going to kill me. I can't handle this, Thea. I can't do it. I can't."

I reached back, trying to hold him.

He pinned my hands out to my sides. "I'm not strong enough for this."

"Ramsey, stop," I urged, turning my head, trying to get a read on his face. The only progress I made was carpet burn on the tip of my chin.

He suddenly stopped moving over me, but his heavy weight slumped on top of me, head to foot, making it difficult to breathe.

"Stop," I coughed.

As if he'd been propelled by a greater force, he flew off me all at once.

That day had been one of the biggest roller coasters of my life.

It'd started with nightmares.

Then elation after our conversation on the way to work.

Giddiness as I'd waited for that friendship to start.

Heartbreak when I'd realized he was already moving on.

Red-hot desire as his hands had traveled over my body.

But as I sat up, finding him on his knees across the room, I'd never seen such soul-crushing devastation in my entire life.

"Ramsey," I whispered.

His chest heaved, and his wild eyes scanned my face before landing on my neck. I hadn't looked in the mirror, but I was positive there was a bite mark. I could all but see the reflection of it in the agony twisting his face.

"No," I breathed, slapping a hand over the side of my neck. "I'm okay. I promise."

I knew what he was thinking. Who he was comparing himself to. It wasn't true, but there would be no convincing Ramsey of that.

"I didn't tell you to stop because you were hurting me. You aren't like him."

It sounded like the words traveled over broken glass before escaping his throat. "Oh, God, Sparrow. I'm so sorry."

Sparrow.

Sparrow.

Sparrow.

The dimensions folded in on themselves, like thin sheets of paper forming one whole. In that moment, it hadn't been twelve years. It hadn't even been twelve minutes.

In that moment, he was hiding in the branches of our tree and I was sitting at the base, waiting for him to finally find me.

The ground shook and the few remaining shards of my heart began rattling.

He was in there. I was his Sparrow, and my Ramsey was in there.

My chin quivered, and tears sprang to my eyes. "You came back," I choked out, scrambling to my feet. I raced toward him, not thinking or considering, just needing to be in his arms. Distance had separated us; time had divided us. But we were a team. There was nothing we couldn't face as long as we were together.

He was gone before I got anywhere close.

"Ramsey," I called after him as he swirled like a tornado bumping into the walls, heading straight for his bedroom. "Wait for me."

He didn't.

He slammed his bedroom door, clicked the lock, and then killed the light.

It was my house. My home. My safe haven from the cruel outside world. Yet I'd never wanted to be somewhere less. He was only one door away, but that door might as well have been an entire universe.

With open hands, I pounded on the door. "Let me in. Take me with you."

I tested the door handle, knowing it was locked. Shaking it hard, I tried to break it off the damn hinges. Sobs racked my chest as I gave up and slid to the carpet with my back against the wall.

I cried myself to sleep in that hallway. Broken, shattered, and more lost than ever before.

Twelve hours, fifty-eight minutes, and thirteen seconds.

That was how long Ramsey and I had lasted as friends.

EIGHTEEN

Ramsey

LIKE A COWARD, I HID IN THE BATHROOM.

Bedroom door locked.

Bathroom door too.

I couldn't listen to her beg or plead for a second longer. If I didn't get the fuck out of there, I was going to peel out of my own skin. I didn't have my phone, so I couldn't call Nora. I'd contemplated climbing out the window and making a break for it. Not that I had anywhere I could go.

But truth be told, I couldn't leave her.

I'd never be able to forget the marks on her neck and the tears in my Sparrow's eyes.

"Stop, Ramsey."

I'd heard her the first time. It just hadn't felt real. To have her again. To touch her. The heat of her sweet body pressed to mine as she begged me to kiss her. I could have had her. A few flimsy layers of my denim and her cotton had been the only things dividing us.

I wanted her hard and fast.

I wanted her naked and crying my name.

I wanted to plunder her mouth and worship her body.

But I didn't want any of that *for her*.

One touch—that was all it had taken for her to drive a fucking bulldozer through my resolve. Those damn brick walls I'd spent

190

over a decade building might as well have been made out of tissue boxes when she'd told me there had never been anyone else.

I was so overcome with the feral need to reclaim her that I'd forgotten the unspoken truth.

There *had* been someone after me.

And it hadn't been her choice.

What I'd done to her, throwing her down and dry-humping her like a rabid animal, was the lowest of lows. She'd already lived through hell; she didn't need my emotional breakdown adding to it.

She didn't deserve that.

She didn't deserve a man like me.

I was breaking, emotionally and physically. I couldn't keep my hands off her, but I couldn't keep her, either. It was wrong on so many levels. I didn't even know where to start with the self-loathing.

No, wait. Yes I did.

I'd made her cry.

Again.

When the tears had fallen from her eyes, it had felt like the tip of a knife dragging across my skin. I loved Thea. I'd spent almost half of my life in prison for killing the asshole who had dared to touch her.

But maybe I wasn't any better. Maybe I was the animal who belonged in a cage.

I buried my head in my hands and leaned back against the bathroom door, the winds of guilt and regret storming inside me like a hurricane.

Why the fuck was this happening? I'd done everything I could for her. I'd heard the saying, *If you love someone, set them free. If they come back, it was meant to be.* But Thea had never actually gone anywhere. Nora had never mentioned her dating anyone, but I'd figured the physical stuff had happened at least once. A drunken night. A one-night stand. A friend with benefits. *Something.* But no. Thea was still mine. And it fucking broke me, because God, did I want that.

"*Kiss me, Ramsey.*"

An icy chill rolled down my spine. Soft as a feather. Hard as a sledgehammer. She'd been so close. Her every breath as it had floated through her parted lips taunted me. One taste and I would have snapped. Planting myself between her legs. Putting a ring on her finger. Making babies. Ruining her fucking life all over again.

That's not how you treat a person who saved you. I flat-out refused to repay her for the happiest six years of my entire existence by tying a boulder around her ankle and shoving her into the ocean.

And that's what I was for her. A boulder, guaranteed to sink, regardless of how hard she tried to keep me afloat.

I was almost thirty years old.

A felon.

A murderer.

Homeless.

Employed out of pity.

For fuck's sake, she'd had to buy the clothes on my back for me. And it wasn't going to change. Sure, in three years, I would be done with parole, but the stigma of my crimes would follow me for the rest of my life.

And after seeing what I'd done to her like a dog on the floor of her living room, the way I'd touched her and the bruises I'd left on her silky-smooth skin, in a sick way I thought maybe it was for the best.

Maybe she would finally fucking give up on me once and for all.

NINETEEN

Thea

I PURRED, UNFURLING FROM A BALL LIKE A KITTEN AS fingers sifted through the top of my hair.

"Ramsey," I breathed, forcing my lazy eyes open.

"Sorry, babe. It's just me," Nora said, squatting in front of me.

Blinking, I waited for my eyes to adjust to the bright lights of the hallway before sitting up. I winced when the devastating weight of last night's events crashed over me.

Nora's gaze searched my face, and she reached out with a single finger to touch my neck. "Knowing you were alone with Ramsey all night, I want to say this looks really fucking good on you. But since you're sleeping in the hall outside his door at three a.m., I'll save the party banners for later. You want to talk about it?"

I swallowed hard. "I don't know what there is to say. I was so close tonight. Ramsey was here. Like really and truly here. First, we were laughing. Then he got pissed. Then he couldn't keep his hands off me. It was as if all the stages of our relationship had been wrapped up into one conversation." I rubbed the side of my neck where his mouth had once been. "He thinks he hurt me."

Offering me a weak smile, she tapped a finger over my heart. "Good, because he has hurt you."

"Not like that." I closed my eyes, my body coming back to life as the memories rained down. "He was jealous. He wanted to know if I'd been with anyone else."

"Please tell me you told him you had a line of guys circling the block and not that you turned into a crazy cat lady minus the cats."

I shook my head. "I told him the truth. And then he had some sort of meltdown and things got rough." I sighed and let my hand fall away from his teeth marks on my neck. "I was ready for it though. Every single bit. And when I told him to stop, it was because I thought I was hurting *him*. Not the other way around." I bit my bottom lip, tears welling in my eyes again. "He called me Sparrow."

She grinned. "Well, duh. That's your name, silly."

"It used to be. But he won't let me in. He wants me. He made that clear. He just won't open the damn door. I could fix him. I could fix us."

Her face got soft as she put her palm to the door and gave it a shove. "His door's open now."

My back shot straight. "Did he open that? Is he awake?"

"Nah, I used a bobby pin to unlock it so I could check on him. He's racked out. A marching band could come through the house right now and he wouldn't wake up."

My shoulders sagged. "He doesn't want me in there."

"See, that's where you're wrong. *He* doesn't want to be in there." She cut her gaze over my shoulder. "Ramsey never wanted to let you go, but he couldn't stand the idea of you stuck in a different kind of prison for sixteen years, either. I'll be honest with you. Twelve years ago, I hated it and it broke my heart to watch you mourn his loss, but I kind of understood where he was coming from. Now though? He's lonely. You're lonely.

He won't let you in. You won't let go. Everyone is so damn miserable."

She rose to her full height and then backed toward her bedroom door, her brown gaze locked with mine as she went. "You told me once a long time ago that you would switch places with him if you could. But that still would have left the two of you in separate prisons, when all you really need to be happy is to be together. What if maybe all you have to do is join him? It's not like your side of the bars is any better than his at this point." She jerked her chin toward his door and then offered me another weak smile. "I love you, Thea. And there's not a day that goes by where I don't wish I could magically fix all of this. Unfortunately, my only super power is a bobby pin. Don't let it go to waste." And with that, she walked into her room and shut the door.

I sat in the dim hallway for several minutes. Rational thought told me to get up, shut his door, and go to bed. I wasn't going to accomplish anything that night. Even if I woke him up, he wasn't going to miraculously drag me into his arms and kiss me breathless. It had been a long day. If he'd found rest, I didn't want to disturb that.

However, there was a part of me that ached to see contentment on his handsome face, even if it was only in slumber. I could sneak in, steal a moment of comfort, and then sneak out without him ever being the wiser.

It was selfish and wrong and a clear invasion of his privacy, but as I stood up and gave his door a silent push, I was desperate enough not to care.

The darkness stole my vision, but I knew that room like the back of my hand. The carpet crushed under my feet, the synthetic fibers sounding like tin cans in the otherwise silent room.

As I approached the side of his bed, my heart pounded

against my rib cage, partially from the fear of getting caught and partially because that was the way my body reacted when Ramsey was near. Only as my eyes adjusted to the darkness, I found he wasn't near at all.

His midnight-blue comforter was smooth across the plush mattress, and the pillows appeared untouched. His room was always neat and tidy. Each time I'd passed his doorway that week, his bed had been made. Just not when he was supposed to be in it.

Maybe he'd heard Nora and me talking in the hall and woken up. Curiously, I looked to the bathroom, but the door was open and the light was off.

What the hell?

I turned in a circle, scanning the room, wondering if he'd snuck out before I could sneak in. I'd made it almost a full three hundred and sixty degrees around when I suddenly stilled, my attention honing in on the small walk-in closet in the corner.

Oh, God.

My breath caught, and my stomach churned.

No way he was in there.

I'd made sure he had the biggest room in the house, a massive king-sized bed, and enough pillows to sleep an army. After sleeping in a crappy bed, locked in a cell for so long, he should have been relishing in the comfort.

So there was no fucking way he was in that closet.

I didn't breathe as I tiptoed over and quietly twisted the handle. I put my eye to the door, peering in as though catching a glimpse would soften the blow. He never stirred as I opened the door, but I had to slap a hand over my mouth to keep the sob from escaping.

My sweet Ramsey was sleeping soundly on the floor, his bare chest rising and falling with even breaths. He was on his side, a pillow under his head, one of the decorative throws from the couch in the den draped over his strong body. The blanket wasn't long enough, so his bare feet hung out of the bottom.

It was sad, heartbreakingly so. But because it was Ramsey, it was also beautiful. I couldn't make out much, but his lips were parted and his shadowy silhouette appeared strong and rugged, like a warrior resting from battle.

There was a small space in front of him—a place that had once belonged to me.

In what seemed like a different life, we'd spent a lot of rainy days alternating between napping and making out, curled together on the couch while my dad had been at work. If I'd gotten up to use the bathroom or get something to eat, Ramsey would welcome me back with a sleepy mumble and a half smile. He'd jostle me until he had me in the perfect position, snug in the curve of his front, and when he'd finally sag behind me, he'd let out a content hum. It had always felt like two broken pieces clicking into place.

Now, we were all but strangers and he was sleeping *alone* in a closet.

I wanted to cry and rage at the world. It wasn't right. It wasn't fair. It wasn't the way it was supposed to be. But despite years of trying, I couldn't change any of that. Right then, the only thing I could control was the fact that he was alone.

I'd fought like hell, but he'd locked me out of his original prison. And dammit, I wouldn't let him do it again.

I didn't care if Ramsey was sleeping in hell; if he was struggling, so was I.

And who knew, maybe having a battle we could fight together would free us both.

It wasn't like it could make it any worse.

TWENTY

Ramsey

THE BRIGHT LIGHTS OF THE MORNING SUN ROUSED ME TO consciousness. I stretched my arms over my head, cringing when my back let out a loud crack. That was going to hurt later, but luckily, I didn't have to work. It was Saturday and Joe had given me the day off. If only my internal clock had gotten the memo.

Pulling the blanket up and flipping to my back, I kept my eyes closed and hoped like hell I could convince my brain to drift back to sleep.

All at once, I bolted upright.

It should have been pitch black in the closet. It was easier to pretend that way. It was a delicate balance between the past and the present. The carpet reminded me I wasn't back in prison, but like a newborn in a crib, I used the confining walls to lull me into a sense of security. I'd tried that cushy bed, but it felt like it was going to swallow me whole, and as much as I liked the idea, I wasn't going to be able to sleep through it.

Short of the light that peeked in under the crack of the door, there should have been no sun in that closet with me. When I sat up and saw the woman wrapped in a comforter and sleeping just outside the threshold, the door being open was the least of my worries.

Thea.

Memories from the night before hit me like an avalanche.

Her sexy mouth whispering my name.

Her full breast filling my hand.

Her ass circling against my cock.

And then...

Her pleas for me to stop.

The bite marks on her neck.

The tears rolling down her cheeks.

Fuck.

My stomach soured and I sat up, scrubbing a hand over my eyes, hoping she'd disappear.

What the hell was she doing? My teeth marks still marred her neck, yet she'd broken into my room and slept at my feet? God, if that wasn't bad enough, she was sleeping on the floor of my fucking makeshift prison.

She wasn't supposed to be there. And not because of the bullshit lies I'd told her about not loving her, but because I'd spent half of my life fighting myself—the biggest demon of all— to make sure she never had to be.

Without a second thought, I rose to my feet and scooped her off the floor in one fluid movement.

She woke up with a squeak, hooking her arms around my neck. Her voice contained the proper amount of fear as she asked, "What are you doing?"

"You don't belong there," I replied, marching to my bedroom door. "You don't sleep on the floor, Thea. *I* sleep on the floor. You sleep in a fucking bed. Got it?"

She shook her head. "You don't belong there either. But I wanted to be with you."

Cradling her in front of me, I bumped her legs on the jamb

as I leaned in close to twist the knob. I used my foot to kick the door open. "What the fuck for? You need a matching bruise for the other side of your neck?"

"You didn't hurt me. That's not why I told you to stop. I wanted to see your face. That was all."

The vise in my chest eased a fraction. "It doesn't matter."

"Bullshit. *We* matter, Ramsey."

Right then, the only thing that mattered was getting her out of my arms. My damn peripheral vision was giving me a show down the gaping front of that flimsy tank top I swear she only wore to torture me. Gritting my teeth, I stomped from my room, turning sideways to clear the doorframe as I walked across the hall into hers. I'd never been in her room and I sure as shit wasn't taking the time to look around while I was in nothing but a pair of boxer briefs, nature's lie detector tenting the front.

Get in. Get out. Take a cold shower. And then consider narcing on someone from the inside so I could secure a spot in the witness protection program. *STAT.*

Bending at the hip, I deposited her on the yellow-and-green floral bedspread that I hated almost as much as those damn skirts she insisted on wearing to work.

That should have been the end of it.

But this was Thea and the shitshow was just getting started.

"You have to talk to me at some point," she yelled, scrambling off the bed after me.

"No, I really don't." Long, heavy strides carried me to my room, but she was hot on my heels, so I didn't have time to lock her out.

Goal number two was to beeline to the bathroom.

Oh, but fucking Thea, she charged around me, ducking under my arm and stopping me dead in my tracks.

"Move," I rumbled.

She rested a hand on my chest and I swear it singed my skin. "Look at me, please."

Nope. Not fucking happening. She was still wearing that tank top and I did not have the strength to see her nipples—or look her in the eye without kissing her fucking face off.

"Get out of here. I need to take a shower."

I realized my mistake the minute I'd said it and it was only one of many for the morning. I'd told Thea how beautiful she'd looked on her knees when I was in the shower. It was not a lie. She was a mythical beast I couldn't tame or bring to fruition.

"I could take a shower with you?" she suggested, stepping in so close it was suffocating.

I jumped away before my cock had the chance to sprout arms and claw its way from my boxers. "Jesus Christ, woman. You are so fucking stubborn. There have to be at least five hundred men out there willing to…" I shook my head, unable to finish the thought.

That was mistake number two.

"Willing to what, Ramsey?" She pushed up onto her toes. "Fuck me? Date me? Marry me? What?"

I bit the inside of my cheek, swearing I would give her no reaction. But every single word out of her mouth was a lash from a whip. "Yes."

"But not you though, right? You want nothing to do with me."

"Why the fuck are you so desperate?"

She sank back to her heels, the mere inches giving me infinite space. "Well, that's an easy question. I'm glad you asked." She trailed a finger down my chest and my cock jumped as though it were the flute of a snake charmer. "Because when I was ten years old, I met a boy. I hated him. But I needed him like my veins needed blood. He broke my leg. He broke my patience. And eventually he broke my heart. But there hasn't been a minute that's passed that I haven't loved him with every single broken shard."

My throat closed and I staggered back from the impact of her words. She followed me forward, allowing me no reprieve. Thea. Fucking, fucking Thea. She peeled her tank top over her head. I silently gave thanks to the god of bras, regardless of how see-through the damn thing might have been.

Sexy and wild, her long hair, which I ached to wrap around my fist, splayed across her shoulders. She took another step toward me. "We promised we'd be there for each other. We swore to it. But I was the only one who kept that deal. You, on the other hand, have lied to me with your every breath. You inked words onto paper that you weren't brave enough to say to my face. You blamed me for things that I had no power to change. You robbed me of twelve years of my goddamn life. And at some point this week, you were with another woman while I lay alone in my room, my fingers in my panties with your lips sucking my clit on the backs of my eyelids."

Oh.

My.

Fucking.

God.

My mouth fell open as all the oxygen was sucked from the state of Georgia.

She canted her head, and her eyes sparkled with defiance. "And guess what? I still fucking love you. So yeah. Maybe I am desperate." Her hands suddenly snaked around behind her. I tried not to look. I deserved a fucking medal of honor for that effort. But when her bra fell to the floor, there wasn't enough guilt or hate in the world to keep my gaze from dropping with it. "But I can live with that, because there will never be anyone other than you. I was ten when I fell in love with you. Nothing you say right now is going to change that."

There was so much I should have said to her.

I love you too.

I've always loved you.

I've been rotting away from the inside out for years knowing someone was going to take you from me.

You're my Sparrow, and that will never change.

My brain had it on lockdown though, because that shit was never coming out. However, mistake number three was opening my goddamn mouth.

"I wasn't with anyone else. I've never been with anyone else. I've never even wanted to be."

What. The. Fuck!

She blinked at me for several beats. And then, slowly and triumphantly, her lips curled into a blinding white smile.

Oh, yes. I. Was. *Fucked.* I prayed like hell that I'd survive, all the while preparing myself not to.

Running her thumbs beneath the waistband of her pajama pants, she never tore her gaze from mine. "Tell me to stop, Ramsey. Tell me I'm making you uncomfortable. Tell me you don't want to make me come. I'll walk out of this room and give you your space. One hundred percent, your call."

My mouth watered as her breasts swayed with her hips as she inched her pants down one side at a time.

I clenched my jaw and fisted my hands at my sides. It was my final stand. Completely and utterly worthless too. It was a seriously lackluster effort.

Her eyes filled with heat as her thumbs hooked with the little pink strings on her panties, dragging them down with her pants. "All you have to do is say no."

Mistake number four also came from opening my mouth. *A-fucking-gain.*

My voice shook and my chest heaved. "I'm not sure I can be gentle, Thea."

She stopped the descent of her pants and stared at me with trust sparkling in her eyes. "I'm not scared of you."

Based on nothing more than my brutal need to bury myself inside her slick heat, I thought she should have been terrified. I licked my lips, guilt slashing me as I glanced at her neck. "I won't bite you again though. I promise."

"Okay," she whispered, shimmying her pants down another inch.

Blood thundered in my ears as she came perilously close to revealing herself completely.

"Last chance," she murmured.

She could have stood there, holding my gaze, until we both wasted away into the Earth and I never would have said the word *stop*.

Her smile grew, and then brazen and beautiful as only Thea could be, she dropped her pants to the floor.

Oh, fuck me. Her pussy was bare. Oh, fucking fuck me.

A growl rumbled in my chest.

Do not be rough.

Do not be rough.

Do not be…

I charged forward, our bodies colliding only a split second before our mouths. Her hands went straight into the back of my hair while our tongues tangled in a fiery reunion.

She moaned down my throat when I palmed her round ass.

And then she climbed my body, linking her legs around my hips, pinning my straining erection between us.

"Thea," I groaned, using her ass to slide her up and down my length. Fuck, why was I still wearing boxers? I set her on the edge of the bed, planting my hands on either side of her head when I followed her down, frantic to keep our mouths fused.

Our teeth clanked, sweet pain pinching at my bottom lip when it became trapped between them. With a frenzied slant, she took the kiss deeper, sealing her mouth under mine, air and breathing becoming an afterthought.

Her tongue swirled and she rolled her hips in the same rhythm. Each time she found friction against my hard length, her whimpers crashed into my groans, creating an erotic symphony of lust and longing.

"Off," she ordered, sitting up and tugging at my boxers, all the while shifting her focus to my neck.

My head fell back and I panted up at the ceiling as she licked and teased her way up to my ear.

"You're mine, Ramsey. You can try to fight me. You can hate me. You can lie to yourself for the rest of your life." She raked her fingernails down my abs before diving into the front of my boxers and wrapping her palm around my shaft. "But wherever you are, however long you are there, you are always *mine*." She punctuated it with a hard pull that weakened my knees.

This. Fucking. Woman.

It had been eighteen years since I first saw her at the base of that tree.

And she was right. She had owned me every day since. Maybe that was why I'd never been able to convince her to leave. She wasn't my Sparrow to free.

I was hers.

Feelings far more dense than sexual desire splintered inside me, making my hands rougher than I intended as I pushed her flat on her back.

She cried out as I hunched over her and sucked at her nipple while I shoved my boxers down.

I wanted to do a dozen things to that woman. Lick and explore her every curve. Taste her. Kiss her. Memorize her. But that could wait.

Lifting one of her legs over my shoulder, I spread her wide. My stomach tightened as I stared down at her fucking glistening and ready. I trailed my finger up her opening, spreading her wet over her clit.

She threw her head back. "Oh, God, Ramsey."

I repeated the process. "If I've always been yours, Thea. What does that make you?"

"Yours."

My cock twitched in jealousy as I dipped my finger inside her tight heat. "Say it again."

"I'm yours. I've always been yours. Even when you didn't want me to be."

My eyes jumped to hers and something deep inside me stirred. It was the truth, the dark and dirty truth I'd been wearing like a straitjacket for my soul. "There was never a day when I didn't want you to be mine, Sparrow. I just loved you enough to hope you wouldn't have to be."

The color drained from her face, but I was done talking.

With devastating control, I entered her slow and steady. A growl ripped from my throat and her mouth formed the most incredible O as I disappeared inside her.

"Fuck, baby," I rasped, raking my teeth over her calf when I bottomed out.

I told myself I was giving her a second to adjust, but that breather was as much for me as it was for her. I'd only been inside her once, and while I'd tried to cling to those memories each time I wrapped my hand around my shaft, it was only similar in the sense that my cock was involved.

She was so damn perfect—tight and hot.

But most of all, she was perfect because she was Thea.

Finally.

I forced myself to start short and shallow. But each time she moaned my name, the urge to claim her grew.

I wanted to hear those two syllables tumble from her lips as she came.

I wanted to empty inside her.

I wanted to spend the rest of that day fucking her over and over again until I physically couldn't get hard again.

And then, when my body gave out on me, I wanted to taste her. Lick her and suck her, feeling her pulse against my mouth.

I wanted to shower with her.

I wanted to fuck her again.

But really, I just wanted to keep her.

Before I knew it, I was riding her hard, driving into her with a desperation I couldn't quell.

"Thea?" I rasped through labored breaths.

"Don't stop," she begged, "I'm okay. Don't stop, baby. I'm close."

An aching tension built, and I closed my eyes to delay my inevitable release. It didn't work; the sight of her breasts bobbing with my every thrust was burned into my retinas. I bit the inside of my cheek and licked my thumb before dropping it to her clit. "Come on, Sparrow. Give it to me."

"Oh, God," she cried.

My rhythm never slowed and my release all but shredded my skin as it fought to find a way out. But there was no fucking chance that, the first time I had her in over twelve fucking years, I wasn't getting her off.

Clenching my teeth, my thrusts got harder, faster, more frantic. Leaning forward with her leg still draped over my shoulder, I practically folded her in half, but she made no complaints as I drove in deeper.

"Oh, God, Ramsey." Like a rubber band, my Sparrow finally snapped. Bucking beneath me, she pulsed around me while her nails scored my back.

And as I followed her over the edge, time finally stopped. There was no distance or years spent apart. We weren't broken or beaten down by life. I wasn't a murderer. She wasn't a victim. No. In that bed, naked and drenched in sweat, we were just two halves of one whole, the way it was always supposed to be.

I'd be damned if I didn't want to wage war with the entire fucking world—including myself—in order to hold on to that.

TWENTY-ONE

Thea

MY HEART HAMMERED IN MY CHEST AS I STARED UP AT the ceiling. After Ramsey had moved my leg off his shoulder, he'd promptly collapsed on top of me, burying his face in the curve of my neck while he caught his breath.

I should have been smiling. I'd just had incredible sex with an incredible man, that resulted in an incredible orgasm.

Yet I was only seconds away from a full-blown panic attack.

What the hell happened now? Would he stay? Would he leave? Would he go back to hating me? Could I handle it if he did?

No. The answer was a resounding, blinking neon sign of No.

I was going to crash and burn in that bed if and when he lifted his head and he wasn't my Ramsey again.

I could barely breathe under his heavy weight, but I made no effort to move out from under him. I wasn't ready yet. I wasn't sure I'd ever be ready.

His hips made slow circles as he began to soften inside me. Another minute and I'd lose him completely.

More panic.

What if that was all I got?

What if I'd seduced him into sex, tempting him with my body in a way a man could never refuse?

He'd called me Sparrow. He'd told me he'd always wanted me. He'd kissed me like he'd never let go.

But what if nothing had changed?

My breathing shuddered and he immediately shifted to my side. The loss was staggering, the reality unbearable.

His heart pounded in time with mine, and I wished like hell I'd been wearing my watch so I would have known how long I'd had him. It would have given me something to obsess about later when I was alone in my bed.

"What are you thinking?" he rumbled into my neck. "You're so tense it's freaking me out."

Shocker. Ramsey could still read my body language.

"Nothing," I choked out.

He gave me a squeeze. "Don't lie. Whatever you're thinking, just say it. I can handle it."

I swallowed hard and then cleared my throat. "I guess I'm wondering if this is the part where you kick me out of your bed?"

His head popped up and his thick brows pinched together. "Not unless you want to fuck me on the floor."

It was a joke—a funny one at that. But I burst into tears.

"Hey," he breathed, rolling to his back and taking me over with him so my head was on his chest. "Easy now. There's no crying allowed while I'm naked."

I half laughed, half sobbed. "I don't know what's going to happen now, and I'm so damn scared you're going to go back to pushing me away."

"Would it work?"

My head snapped back as I peered up at him. "What?"

He tucked a stray hair behind my ear and trailed the tips of his fingers down my jaw. "Would it work? If I got up right now and told you to take a hike, would you actually do it?"

I didn't have to think before answering. "No."

The side of his mouth hitched. "Then what's the point?"

My chin quivered. "I can't answer that. I've never known the point in any of this."

He let out a loud sigh and wrapped me in both of his strong arms. "I know, Sparrow. I know."

"I don't think you do." I tried to sit up, but he held me tight.

"We'll talk, okay? I don't know what's going to happen to us. It's been almost thirteen years. You haven't moved on. I can't keep my hands off you and my heart is sick and fucking tired of trying. We have a lot of things to talk about, some of which are going to be an absolute dumpster fire. But I don't know how to stop loving you, Thea. I've tried. And tried. But here we are. Fucked up and in love."

My lip quivered. "Fucked up and in love. That's the sweetest thing anyone has ever said to me."

He grasped my chin between his thumb and forefinger, tilting my head back and pressing a lingering kiss to my lips. "That's sad. And only serves as further proof to how fucked up we truly are."

We.

There was a *we* again.

One word. Two small letters. And the debilitating weight of losing my soulmate ebbed from my system.

Gripping the back of his neck, I kissed him, deep and long. I kissed him like we were kids again and a world of suffering didn't exist between us. Our mouths moved with a practiced ease, but our tongues danced and explored like we were strangers.

And in this life, I supposed we were.

My heart beat for him.

My lungs filled for him.

My veins bled for him.

But this was new and different. And, God, did I need it to be different.

"Shit," he whispered against my mouth. "We probably should have used a condom."

"It's okay. I'm on birth control, and unless I'm mistaken, I don't think you can give yourself an STD."

He chuckled. "Birth control, huh?"

"I started it when I found out you were coming home."

Turning into me, he slid a hand to my ass and dragged me flush with his front. He was hard again, long and thick. The tears were still wet on my face, but sparks ignited between my legs. "You were that sure we were going to end up here?"

I half shrugged. "I'm persistent."

"That you are." Rumbling with approval, he kneaded my ass and rocked me against his length. "You are also fucking sexy as hell."

I smiled and nuzzled his nose. "I'm the only woman you've seen in over a decade. I'll wait a few months before applying for supermodel status."

"That's not true. Tiffany was here the other day."

My mouth fell open, and I gave him a hard shove. "What the hell, Ramsey?"

A loud laugh sprang from his chest as he flipped me to my back. My legs immediately fell open, welcoming him home.

He put his feet to the floor and hooked my thighs to drag me to the edge, his smoldering gaze aimed between my legs. "It's good to see that jealous streak of yours is still alive and well."

I watched with rapt attention as he slid his hand up and down his shaft. "She's practically my sister, and you're about to—" I let out a hiss, pressing my head into the bed as he filled me, slow and torturous.

"I'm about to do what, Sparrow?"

"This," I panted.

He planted himself to the hilt, stretching and filling. "And what's that? What am I doing to you?"

"Ramsey," I breathed.

"That's not an answer." He reached out and caught my hand, bringing it to his mouth, where he swirled his tongue over two of my fingers. Fire blazed a trail straight to my nipples when he guided my wet fingers to my clit. "Show me what you did when you thought about me between your thighs." He withdrew ever so slowly and then drove back in hard and fast.

"Oh, God!" I cried out.

A sudden knock at the door had us both freezing. "Um, Ramsey?" Nora called. "I am really, really, *really* sorry to interrupt you guys, but um… Your parole officer is here." She paused and then nervously finished. "With the cops."

All the color drained from his face, and in the very next heartbeat, my Ramsey was gone.

Suffocating panic filled the room as he snatched his boxer briefs off the floor. Every muscle in his body strained as he tugged them on. "Get under the covers."

I pointed to the floor. "My clothes are just—"

"Covers," he barked, pausing with his hand on the doorknob.

The comforter was still on the floor from when I'd slept with it, so I scrambled under the sheet, my anxiety skyrocketing.

The minute I was fully covered, he yanked the door open. A short, gray-haired man in khaki slacks and a polo shirt was standing next to Nora.

"Hey, Lee. What's going on?" Ramsey greeted, his voice light and almost chipper.

The man leaned around him, sweeping his gaze through the room. "I'm going to need you to step out front with me."

Ramsey nodded. "Okay. No prob. My girl's naked though. Can she have a minute to get dressed?"

Lee, who I assumed was his parole officer, pursed his lips. "One minute. You can get dressed too. Stay out of the bathroom though. Don't let me hear that toilet flush."

What. The. Hell?

Lee disappeared down the hall, and Nora bulged her eyes at her brother before following after him.

Keeping the sheet pulled to my chest, I rose to my knees and whispered, "What's going on?"

Ramsey shut the door and spun on a toe. "I have no fucking clue." He snagged my clothes off the floor and threw them at me.

"Are you in trouble?"

He yanked his top drawer open. "I don't know."

Bile crawled up the back of my throat. "Have you done anything wrong?"

He stepped into a pair of gray sweats and then tugged on a white fitted T-shirt. "I don't fucking know! Just get dressed." He threw a black hoodie my way and then marched to the door. "Put that on. You can see your tits through that goddamn tank top."

Wow. Okay, then. I was too nervous to argue or bitch at him for being crass.

He waited until I was fully dressed and standing next to him before we exited the room.

My apprehension climbed as we walked down the short hallway together. Desperate for reassurance, as much as I wanted to offer him the same, I reached for his hand. He pulled it away.

"Stewart," Lee called, motioning us over.

My heart stopped as I took in the cops removing the couch

cushions and using flashlights to search the cracks. Nora was standing in the kitchen, watching a female officer go through the cabinets. The second our eyes met, she hurried over.

"It's okay. Just relax," she soothed, tugging me in for a side hug. She gave Ramsey an arm squeeze. "You're going to be fine. This isn't a big deal."

My back shot straight when he looked at her and smiled. "I know."

He knew? He was smiling and he *knew*? Funny because, in the bedroom, he was on the verge of jumping out the window and didn't know a damn thing. Though I really liked the idea that things were going to be fine. And he "knew" it, so I let it slide.

"What's going on?" Ramsey rumbled when we made it to the front door.

Lee planted a hand on his hip. "I need all of you to step out front with me for a few minutes. Clovert PD got an anonymous tip that you were selling coke out of the back of Joe Hull's barbershop. They called me. I had to drag my ass out of bed on a Saturday morning, so I'm sure you can imagine how happy this made me."

"What?" I gasped.

And then, as if I weren't already shocked enough, Ramsey barked a loud laugh, nearly causing me to have a heart attack. "You gotta be shitting me? I wasn't even in on a drug charge."

I peered up at him in wonder.

What the hell was happening? I mean, seriously. What. Was. Happening?

Ramsey *knew*. He was *smiling*. And now he was freaking *laughing*?

I was about to lose my mind or possibly dry-heave—I hadn't quite decided which—and he was laughing?

Lee walked out front, calling over his shoulder, "Well aware, Stewart. But you've been out less than two weeks. We gotta follow up on this. Quick search. We'll be gone in an hour. Though I am going to need you to hit my office before end of day and piss in a cup."

"Jesus Christ," he muttered, but he did it pressing his lips into the top of my hair and then guiding me out the door with his hand on the small of my back, so I decided to postpone my freak-out for a few minutes longer.

Unfortunately, I only got a few *seconds*.

And that was because none other than Clovert's finest, Officer Jonathan *Caskey*, was standing in my driveway, leaning against his police cruiser.

Suddenly, everything and nothing at all made sense.

Nora and I had moved the twenty minutes from Clovert to Thomaston for a reason. And while it wasn't completely because Josh's older brother was a decorated officer in the Clovert Police Department, that had made our decision easier. I had no reason to hate Jonathan. He hadn't raped me. He'd never even spoken to me. But his flat-out refusal to see his brother for the deviant he truly was made my skin crawl.

Each year on the anniversary of Josh's death, Jonathan would host a stupid fundraiser for victims of bullying. *Bullying!* Like Josh hadn't terrorized multiple innocent women. For a week, the whole town would wear green—a nod to Josh's St. Patrick's Day birthday—and the local newspaper would write a completely biased, utterly trash article about the Caskeys' devastating loss.

It was a miracle I hadn't needed to be institutionalized during that week every year. Nothing lit me on fire like delusional people who were only delusional because they refused to open their eyes. And Jonathan Caskey was the king of all delusional kings.

And there he was, in my driveway, wearing a smug grin and an impenetrable shield in the shape of a badge on his chest, while officers flipped my house searching for nonexistent drugs for no other reason than he had the power to make it happen.

"Get off my property," I seethed, my body vibrating with an overdose of adrenaline.

He cocked his head to the side and shoved off his car. "You have a problem, Miss Hull?"

I lunged forward, screaming, "Get off my fucking property!"

Ramsey hooked me around the waist, dragging me against his chest while rumbling in my ear, "Thea, stop. You're gonna make it worse."

I couldn't stop though. We'd been through enough without the Caskeys meddling in our newfound happiness.

He'd been home for a little over a week, but I'd only had Ramsey back for a matter of minutes.

We were fucked up and in love.

We were a *we* again.

For God's sake, he'd been making love to me when the cops had shown up.

This asshole did not get to ruin that.

"You are not Thomaston PD." I looked at Ramsey's parole officer and repeated, "He is *not* Thomaston PD. He has no right to be here." My hands shook as I tried to peel out of Ramsey's hold on me. "Do you know his brother raped me?" I looked back at Jonathan, my stomach rolling as I stared into his blue eyes, which matched his brother's. "Your brother was a piece of shit who bit me and hit me and then pinned me down and forced himself on me like I was nothing. He deserved everything he got."

"Thea. *Stop!*" Ramsey boomed.

Jonathan's eyes narrowed. "You sure it was Josh who did all that to you? Judging by that bruise on your neck, it could have easily been your loverboy there."

My body jolted like I'd been shot, and Ramsey turned to stone.

However, it was Nora who exploded first.

"You son of a bitch!" she roared, charging forward.

Ramsey let me go and dove after her, catching her arm before she got her hands on Caskey—an act that would have no doubt landed her behind bars.

Like a hellcat, she kicked and fought against her brother, cussing and screaming incoherently. As pissed off and angry as I was, it was so painful to watch her melt down that it momentarily quelled the storm brewing within me.

Nora was nothing if not loyal.

Ramsey put a hand over her mouth and dragged her away, pleading, "Lee, come on. You know this is fucked up. He shouldn't be here. I'm cooperating. We're all fucking cooperating. But this is harassment."

I glanced around, finding several of the Thomaston cops decorating my front porch. At least three of them had their hands resting on their guns. Their eyes were locked on my entire life as he dragged my best friend away from the brother of the dead boy who had wrecked us all.

How was this my life?

"Officer Caskey," Lee started. "I thought I told you we'd handle this."

Jonathan smirked, never tearing his eyes off of Ramsey. "You did. I just happened to be in the neighborhood. Figured I'd swing by in case you needed an extra hand."

Lee tucked his clipboard under his arm and shot him an un-impressed glare. "I think we got it covered."

"You sure about that?"

Lee's lips thinned as he looked at Ramsey. He was juggling Nora into a hug with her feet dangling off the ground. He didn't appear completely convinced, but he still answered, "Yeah. All good."

Jonathan sucked his teeth and backed toward his cruiser. "You find anything, I want to be the first to know, yeah?"

"No," Lee bit back. "But if you don't get out of here and forget this address, your captain will be." He arched a furry, gray eyebrow and mocked. "*Yeah?*"

My shoulders fell, thankful beyond all reason that the Caskeys didn't own everyone in our area.

Jonathan chuffed, and I held my breath as he folded into his car. His arrogance never wavered as he backed out of my drive-way. The bastard had the balls to wink at me before he finally drove away.

"I'm sorry about that, Miss Hull," Lee said with genuine regret.

"Thank you," I mumbled, adrenaline-fueled tears burning the backs of my lids.

He scratched the back of his head. "He knows better than to show up like that. I'll have a word with his captain. It won't happen again."

Like a moth to a flame, my eyes found Ramsey's only a few feet away. Nora had relaxed in his arms, but a hurricane raged in his gaze as he stared at me.

"That would be much appreciated, Lee," I said absently.

Walking to the door, he jerked his chin at Ramsey. "Let me hurry these guys along. It's too early for this shit."

Ramsey, with Nora in tow, was at my side immediately. "You okay?"

"I think so. Neither of you two are in cuffs. I'll chalk it up as a win." I tried to joke, but my voice cracked, revealing my true emotion.

He caught me at the back of my neck and pulled me face-first into his chest while Nora occupied his other side.

We didn't say anything for a long time. I listened to Ramsey's heart and Nora's sniffles while we waited for the cops to finish up and allow us back inside. Ramsey's hand never stopped soothing up and down my back, and as messed up as everything was, it felt like I finally belonged somewhere again.

Going toe-to-toe with Jonathan Caskey wasn't how any of us had wanted to start our day, but for the first time in what felt like forever, the three of us were a family. Ramsey wasn't angry. Nora wasn't the middleman. I wasn't the elephant in the room.

We were all emotionally drained and fighting our demons, but we were a family nonetheless.

———

"Thanks for dealing with that." Ramsey smiled and shook Lee's hand.

"No problem. Thanks for not having any drugs. That is a mountain of paperwork I did not feel like filling out."

"You sure I can't get you some coffee for the road?" I asked from the kitchen while I put away the stacks of dishes.

Our house was a wreck. Everything from my bedroom to the garage had been flipped on end. If we were lucky, we could get the place put back together before the end of the weekend. When the police had finished, Nora had gone straight to her room, muttering something about going back to bed. She'd been up late—as we all had—so I couldn't blame her. I also didn't try to stop her in hopes of buying myself some time before she launched her what's-going-on-with-you-and-my-brother inquisition.

Ramsey walked Lee to the door. "Do I need any kind of paperwork for the drug test today?"

"Nah. I called it in. Bring your ID and they'll have everything else you need when you get there. Don't bullshit me. Is that thing going to bounce back hot?"

Ramsey's grin stretched and he rubbed his stomach. "I've never touched a drug in my life. As long as you aren't testing for cheeseburgers, I'm pretty sure I'm clean."

"Good to know. Eat a vegetable, Stewart."

Ramsey laughed and opened the door. "Will do." Then he stood at the door, smiling with his hands shoved inside the pockets of his sweats.

I had to give it to him. For a man who had looked like he was on the verge of imploding when the cops had shown up, he was dealing with everything a hell of a lot better than I was.

Or so I thought.

No sooner than he shut the front door, Ramsey's entire handsome face turned green. He bent over and then all at once collapsed to his knees.

"Ramsey," I called, dropping a stack of plates on the counter and rushing toward him.

He lifted a hand to stop me and put his chin to his shoulder, his chest rising and falling at a marathon pace.

I threw on the brakes and allowed him the space, despite my hands aching to comfort him the way I'd been denied for too many years. "It's over, honey. Everything's fine now."

With his hands on the carpet, his muscular back rounded with a gag. "It's not," he choked. "I'm always just one misstep from getting sent back."

The broken shards of my heart clattered at my feet. "You're not going back."

"You don't fucking know that."

I inched closer. "Yeah. I do. You're not going to do anything to break parole. You have nothing to worry about."

His head snapped up, incredulous bewilderment carved into his features. "You think I really have to *do* something to get sent back? With Caskey roaming around, waiting for his moment to fuck me over, we'll be lucky if I make it another six months."

Panic pooled in my stomach, but I shook my head vehemently. "No. I won't let that happen."

He settled on his ass, propping his back against the entryway wall, his knees bent and his hands hanging between them. "If I've learned anything over the years, Thea, it's that anything is possible. And after today, it's not just possible, it's likely." And then Ramsey tried to break my heart all over again. His eyes sparked like the boy I'd once known. "I never wanted you to be a part of this, Sparrow. I tried to let you go so I didn't drag this kind of filth into your life. But you just wouldn't listen. Fuck. Why won't you ever listen to me?"

"I do listen, but sometimes I just don't care."

He barked a humorless laugh. "Now that's the damn truth."

I lowered myself to the carpet within arm's reach, but I was careful not to touch him. "Ramsey, you aren't dragging filth into my life. *You* aren't filth."

He thrust a hand into the top of his hair. "No. But I'm not the man you deserve, either. You should be sitting on a porch swing, carefree with your hair blowing in the wind right now, not cleaning up your house after the cops stormed in and tore the place apart searching for drugs. You deserve better than this, but from the day I took that plea bargain, I knew trouble and disgrace was all I'd ever be able to give you. And let me tell you, that is a hard fucking pill to swallow when you're in love with a woman. But it's the truth. You deserve better than me. I knew it then. I know it even more after today. You gotta let me go, Thea. You just have to."

A mixture of panic and anger rolled through me like a chill. "Don't start this shit again. It didn't work out for you when you got locked up and it's sure as hell not going to work out after what we did this morning."

"I can't take care of you. If you stay with me, you'll always be one step away from going back to that prison too. Whether I do three more years and finish my sentence or if Caskey manages to pin something on me and I go back for another decade, either way you'll be alone all over again. I can't be responsible for that." He pounded the spot over his heart. "You gotta help me out here. I barely lived through it the first time. I need you to hate me. I need you to leave and never look back."

My head snapped to the side as if he'd slapped me. And in a way, he had. Over and over and over again for twelve fucking *years*. But for once, I was starting to understand why.

Ramsey was a caretaker. He'd done it for his mom when she'd been married to his abusive father. He'd done it for Nora when they were growing up. And he'd done it for me, on and off throughout our entire relationship.

And when he'd left, I'd been alone. So tragically alone.

But that wasn't the way my life stayed forever. After Ramsey was arrested my dad stepped up and resumed his role in my life. Girls like Tiffany came out of the woodwork after they found out what Josh had done to me, leaving me with more friends than I knew what to do with. Then Nora moved in and we shared a room, which sometimes made me wish like hell I could have been alone again.

Because being alone wasn't my deepest darkest fear.

It was his.

"*There was never a day when I didn't want you to be mine, Sparrow. I just loved you enough to hope you wouldn't have to be.*"

Have to be.

Have to be.

Like being his was a chore or an option.

Nora had been right for all those years. Ramsey was still very much in love with me. Time had changed a lot of things, but that was not one of them. Convicted felon or not, he was a good man. With good intentions. And a good heart.

Unfortunately, he was so damn *stupid*.

"You're right," I whispered, crawling over to him.

He sucked in a sharp breath. "I am?"

I swung a leg over his hips to straddle his lap and wrapped my hands around either side of his neck. "Yeah. My life would be easier without you."

His forehead wrinkled, and his brow furrowed. "I'm sorry, Thea. I'm so damn sorry. I never should have left you that night."

I had no idea if he was referring to when he'd left me in the tent or when he'd left me to run over Josh with his car. It didn't matter. Regret was nothing but a chain tethering you in the past.

I rested my forehead on his and rubbed my thumbs over the stubble on his jaw. "So, when are we going to do it?"

"Do what?"

"Ride a time machine into the past and make it so we never met at all."

He leaned away and curled his lip. "What?"

I feigned confusion. "That's what you're proposing, right? We go back in time and when my mother dies, I go to my room and lock the door instead of going to the Wynns' tree. You jump out, break your own damn leg. Boom. My life is all rainbows and unicorns." I tilted my head to the side and tapped my lips. "No, wait. Josh would still be alive, and now, he'd be sitting next to me in fifth grade. I'm not sure that would have ended any differently. Okay, what about—"

"Thea," he warned.

But he needed to hear how fantastically ridiculous it sounded when he tried to tell me I should let him go. And as far as I was concerned, that ludicrousness was up there with time machines and the ripple effect.

"We go back to when Josh was born. I know what you're thinking. We can't exact revenge on a baby." I dramatically lifted my finger in the air. "But! We can kidnap him and send him to the rainforest to be raised by wolves. I won't have that scar on my leg from when he tripped me in kindergarten, but you could learn to love me without it, right?"

Glowering, he shifted me off his lap and stood up. "Stop joking around."

"Who's joking?"

Even with his temper slipping, he extended a hand to help me up. "Maybe we should just send me to the rainforest instead."

I took his hand. "Oh, I know. What could—"

"Jesus, woman. *Enough.*"

Crossing my arms over my chest, I matched his glower with a death stare. "Sounds stupid, huh? Kinda like you telling me to just unfall in love with you, unkiss you, untouch you, undo my entire freaking life because it would be *easier.*" I swung my arms out to my sides, slapping them against my thighs when I dropped them. "It's impossible, Ramsey. Easy or not, letting go of you is not an option."

He clenched his teeth. "You don't have to undo anything, you just have to let go of the life we planned together because *that* is what's impossible. I fucking wish I could give that to you. Trust me, I will be hanging on this cross every damn day, knowing you're out there with someone else, but—"

I stormed toward him. "Then get off the fucking cross! No one asked you to be there!"

"I did," Nora said, suddenly appearing at the mouth of the hallway.

"No!" Ramsey shouted. "Nora, no."

Buckets of tears ran down her face, dripping off her chin. "Something good has to come from all of this. I've told you that a million times. And I genuinely think that thing is you and Thea finally getting the life you were meant to have."

Suffocating urgency blanketed the room.

"Don't do this," Ramsey begged.

She shook her head. "You'll never stop pushing her away. You want her. You love her. And if you can't have her, you will spend the rest of your life alone. I can't let you do that, Ramsey." When her eyes flicked to me, her heart-stopping devastation hit me like a sledgehammer.

Twelve years, nine months, six days, eight hours, and forty-four minutes. That was how long it took for my life to explode all over again.

Obliterating me in its wake.

"I killed Josh, Thea."

TWENTY-TWO

Ramsey

Twelve years earlier...

"WHAT ARE YOU DOING?" NORA WHISPERED, SITTING up in bed.

Tucking my head, I snuck in through her window. I was trying to avoid my dad. He'd been a fucking dick when I'd snagged the condoms from his room. After seeing what Josh had done to Thea, knowing that I would have been there to stop it if my dad could have put the fucking tequila bottle down for once, I wanted to kill him that much more. But I did not have time to worry about the bastard who had raised me.

"My window was locked," I told her, stomping through her room to mine across the hall.

She followed after me. "Are you okay?"

The bite marks on Thea's naked body flashed on the backs of my lids, causing a deadly combination of adrenaline and failure to burn my skin.

"Not even close," I muttered, snagging my keys off my dresser.

"What happened? Are you still pissed at Dad?"

"Fuck Dad," I bit out, going right back through her room to the window.

She caught my arm before I had the chance to leave. "What is going on with you? Where's Thea?"

In bed, asleep, broken and battered because I couldn't take care of her.

I yanked my arm away and climbed outside.

"Ramsey," she hissed, following me out, because crawling up my ass was Nora's favorite pastime.

I usually didn't mind though. At least I knew she wasn't catching the brunt of my father's bullshit. But that night I did not have the time nor desire for an interrogation.

I had to find Caskey and beat him senseless.

I marched to my car and snatched the door open. It wasn't locked. Nobody wanted to steal that piece of shit.

My ass had barely hit the seat when my sister slid into the passenger side.

"Get out," I barked, stabbing my key at the ignition. My aim was shit thanks to the fire raging in my veins.

"No. There's something going on, and if you're not going to tell me what, I'm going with you."

I finally got the key in place and gave it a twist. The engine sputtered, not catching, so I gave it another try. "You cannot come with me tonight, Nora."

"Too bad. Looks like I already am." She grinned and buckled her seat belt.

When Nora got her mind set on something, there was no changing it. I would have had to physically carry her out of that car in order to make her stay home. And even then, she would have woken up the whole damn neighborhood, including Thea, if I tried to force the issue.

"Suit yourself," I said, snatching the car into reverse once it had finally rumbled to life.

We hadn't made it more than a few miles when I realized I had no fucking idea where I was going. Caskey lived in the mayor mansion downtown, surrounded by a tall iron fence. I could have been fucking Spiderman and I would not have been able to get to him.

But it was a Saturday night; there was no way that asshole was at home already.

Nora was only a freshman, but the school was small and she knew enough of my friends to stay in the know.

"Where are the parties at tonight?" I growled.

"Uh," she drawled. "Since when are you up for partying? Oh my God, did Thea break up with you?"

"No." Though, after the shit that had gone down, she should have. I white-knuckled the steering wheel. "Just tell me where the hell everyone is hanging out tonight."

She motioned a hand over her basketball shorts and oversized T-shirt. "I'm hardly dressed for a party."

"Nora!" I boomed, my voice echoing around the car. "Tell me where."

"Jesus, cranky much?" she mumbled. "Fine. Avery Johnson invited all the seniors over for a field party, but I heard a lot of the juniors were planning to crash."

I slowed at the stop sign and hung a hard right onto the long dirt road that led to the Johnsons' farm.

"You gonna tell me what's going on now or should I start guessing?"

I shook my head. No fucking way was I telling her what Josh had done to my Sparrow. Thea didn't want to call the cops or tell her dad. She and Nora were close, but I was reasonably sure she did not want my blabbermouth sister to know about it, either.

Dirt flew up as I sped down the road, my car making a hell of a racket each time I hit one of the bumps in the uneven road.

She braced one hand on the dash and the other on the handle above her hand. "Right. Yeah. This totally seems like nothing. We're just out for a late-night drive, huh?"

"Shut up," I rumbled.

We were still at least a mile away from the Johnsons' driveway, but cars lined both sides of the road. Squinting and searching for Josh's black pickup, I flipped on my brights, but they were useless against the dry cloud of dust.

And then, out of nowhere, God delivered me both a miracle and a tragedy.

"Watch out!" Nora screamed as a shadowy figure staggered down the center of the road.

I stomped on the brakes, skidding to a stop inches away from him.

Josh.

Drunk as a fucking skunk.

Alone on a dark road.

After he'd put his hands on my Sparrow.

I smiled from ear to ear. Come on. If there was ever a sign that this asshole needed to pay, that was it.

"Stay in the car," I ordered.

"Oh, God, why? What are you doing?" Nora asked, panic clear in her voice as she suddenly read my intentions.

I got out without replying.

"Ramsey," she hissed, rolling the window down.

Ignoring her, I rounded the front of the car.

Using his hand to block the headlights, Josh swayed on his feet and slurred, "What the hell, dude? You almost hit me."

There was no *almost* about it. I gave him no warning as I

wrapped my hand in the front of his shirt and then buried my fist in his face. Blood exploded from his mouth. But all I saw was Thea, naked and cowering in a tent.

"You motherfucker!" I roared, hitting him again. "You think it's okay to fucking touch a girl." My fist landed in his eye and he stumbled back, but I yanked him toward me again, my face vibrating as I roared in his face, "My girl!"

He shoved at my shoulders. "Get the fuck off me. I didn't do shit to Thea that she didn't want."

He could have dumped a gallon of gas on me and flicked a match at my feet and it still would have enraged me less. My vision flashed red and rational thought left me.

I hit him. And hit him. And when my hand was aching to the point I was positive it was broken, I hit him even harder. I held him by his throat, only his tiptoes scraping the dirt road as I walked him backward, unable to punch him hard enough to give myself any kind of satisfaction.

Finally, when I couldn't hit him anymore, I threw him to the ground and kicked him in the stomach. "Stay the fuck away from her."

He rolled to the side, coughing and spitting out blood.

And then Josh Caskey sealed his own fate.

He laughed, pushing up onto all fours. "If it's any consolation, she wasn't nearly as good as your sister."

It was a verbal knockout punch. A wave of nausea threatened to take me to my knees and I stumbled backward, barely able to stay on my feet.

I couldn't process anything.

The crunch of tires on the dirt road.

The roar of the engine.

The headlights getting brighter.

Everything moved in slow motion.

By the time I realized what was happening, it was too late.

For him.

For her.

For me.

"No!" I screamed as Nora ran over Josh.

TWENTY-THREE

Thea

BETRAYAL, THE LIKES OF A KNIFE, PLUNGED INTO MY chest. My whole body jerked and the room tilted as though the Earth had suddenly fallen out of orbit.

I flicked my gaze between Ramsey and Nora, the same desolation showing on both of their faces. "What are you talking about? That's not possible. You weren't even there." Tears started to fill my eyes. "You told me you were at home asleep that night."

"Thea," Ramsey rasped, attempting to pull me into a hug.

Confused and becoming angrier by the second, I ducked out of his reach. "Don't you touch me." I swung my irate gaze back to Nora, not giving the first fuck that she was now trembling. "Explain."

Ramsey lifted his hands in surrender and stepped between me and his sister. "I'll tell you everything."

"I didn't ask you," I hissed while leaning around him to keep my gaze locked on my *best friend*.

"I never meant for this to happen," she croaked. "I never meant for any of this to happen."

With all patience exhausted, I yelled so loud that it shook the window. "What did you do!"

She swallowed hard, her breath shuddering. It might have made me a horrible human being, but I didn't feel a lick of guilt for forcing her to tell me how she had ruined my entire fucking life and then lied to me about it for half of hers.

"He raped me when I was twelve," she confessed.

My stomach soured, and Ramsey let out a pained groan.

She kept talking. "I thought I was cool because one of the ninth-grade boys wanted to hang out with me. He told me to keep it a secret because he was worried Ramsey would get pissed he wanted to date his little sister." She laughed and it was wholly sad. "Date. That was all he had to say. I was so desperate for someone to love me and he was this hot older guy. I thought he was my knight in shining armor."

Screwing his eyes shut, Ramsey pinched the bridge of his nose. "Stop. Please."

"I can't," she breathed. "He convinced me to sneak out and meet him at the high school baseball field one night. It started out sweet, with him saying he wanted a picture of me to put in his wallet. It didn't stay that way long."

"Jesus," I breathed. Bile burned the back of my throat as memories I'd long since packed away came clawing to the surface.

His heavy weight as he held me down.

The pain of his teeth sinking into my flesh.

The panic when I realized I wasn't strong enough to fight him off.

I slapped a hand over my mouth and tried not to gag.

She moved around Ramsey, getting closer with every word spoken. I was still raging with betrayal, but I didn't trust my legs enough to back away.

"He told me he'd show everyone the pictures if I told. I had no idea what images he'd captured, but I knew how filthy I felt on the inside, and I was mortified that someone might see that." Her breath lodged in her throat. "If I'd told somebody, I could have stopped him right then. But I was too scared. I didn't know there were other girls. I didn't know, Thea, I swear. Or I would have said something."

It wasn't her fault. At least not that part.

"What did you do?" I whispered, wishing like hell that the time machine I'd mocked Ramsey for was real.

"I was sitting in that car, watching Ramsey beat him up, and when I'd heard what he'd done to you, I broke. Shattered into a million pieces. But one of those pieces put the car in drive and stomped on the gas." A sob tore from her throat. "You and Ramsey were the only real family I'd ever had. And two years after I'd let Josh get away with what he'd done to me, I learned I'd all but *allowed* him to do it to you too."

My entire being from my heart to my soul, past and present, ached.

I hated that she'd had to survive Josh Caskey too.

I hated that she'd had to suffer in silence for so many years.

But most of all, I fucking hated that the woman I viewed as my sister and the man who I thought was my soul mate had lied to me over and over every goddamn day for almost thirteen fucking years while I'd drowned in an ocean of guilt.

Ramsey hadn't killed Josh for me.

Ramsey hadn't been forced to give up his entire life for me.

I hadn't fucking caused Ramsey to spend over twelve years behind bars.

She had.

And he'd chosen that when he'd taken that plea bargain, knowing good and damn well it should have been Nora.

"Fuck you," I spat. "Fuck both of you."

Nora looked surprised.

Ramsey looked almost relieved.

The constant sting of pain and anguish I'd lived with every minute of every day since Ramsey had been arrested surged through my veins, morphing into a sludge of deception. I was wearing pajama pants and one of Ramsey's hoodies, but I wouldn't have given a damn if I'd been naked.

I needed to get the hell out of that house.

Spinning on a toe, I stomped to the front door and snatched my keys off the hook. My wallet sat on top of the contents of my purse, which had been dumped out, all of my personal and private belongings scattered across the floor. And wasn't that just so damn symbolic of my life. I picked it up and tucked it under my arm.

"Thea, wait. Just listen."

"What for?" I snapped. "Nothing you have to say will change anything. Spin it whatever way you have to in order to sleep at night. But the facts are you killed Josh, Nora. Then you killed Ramsey by letting him take the blame. And *then* you sat around for twelve fucking years, holding me when I cried and filling my head with lies about how much he loved me, when you had the ability to stop it all." I watched with a sick pleasure as every word struck her like a bullet.

"That's not fair," Ramsey rumbled.

"None of this is fair!"

Nora folded her hands in front of her like she was saying a prayer. "Please listen to me. I tried to tell the cops. But he'd already signed a confession. They wouldn't even take a statement from me. They had their man. They didn't want to hear anything I had to say."

"So you quit? You just went home? And just thought, *Oh, well. I tried. Have a nice life, Ramsey.*"

"I...I..." she stammered without actually saying anything.

It was Ramsey who found his words first. "I told her to stop." He stabbed a finger at his chest. "*I* made the decision to take the fall. She didn't even know what was going on. And by the time she did, it was too late. For fuck's sake, I never expected it to get that far. I told them I hit a deer. I figured worst-case scenario, I'd get a ticket or a fine. But then—"

"Oh, so we're back to this being my fault? Because I told the cops about Josh and it gave you a motive to kill him? A motive to kill a person you didn't fucking kill!"

He shook his head adamantly. "No. Jesus Christ. It was never your fault. I did this. I did all of this. I was trying to fix the impossible. She was a fourteen-year-old girl who had lived through hell."

"I lived through hell!" I exploded. "I fucking needed you and you weren't there!"

With long strides, he closed the distance between us. Instinct told me to back away, but I wasn't afraid of Ramsey. There was nothing left of me for him to destroy.

He grabbed my hips, fisting his hands into the sides of his hoodie. "I know! And there has never been a part of this, including spending half my life in prison, that I hated more. I abandoned you. I ruined everything. But I tried to let you go because you deserved better than that. This is not Nora's fault. She wanted to tell you. So many damn times, she begged me. But she needed you. You needed each other. I couldn't be there, but dammit, I didn't want either of you to be alone."

I gritted my teeth and gave him a hard shove. "Always the martyr."

"Martyrs die, Thea. I'm not that fucking lucky."

"I hate you," I hissed into his face.

"Good. You should. I've been trying to make you see that all goddamn week."

I wanted to slap him. I wanted to punch him. I wanted to make him hurt the way their betrayal was destroying me.

But I didn't have another decade of my life to waste on Ramsey and Nora Stewart.

"You two deserve each other." With that, I marched out of their lives for what I hoped was forever.

Bypassing the 4Runner I'd bought for Ramsey, I went straight for my old Camry in the garage. I peeled off his hoodie and threw it on the ground, not giving a damn if anyone could "see my tits" through my tank top. I didn't want anything that reminded me of them.

If only the scars on my heart were so easy to get rid of.

As I pulled away, Ramsey was standing in the front yard, a storm in his eyes, and I didn't have to return his stare to feel the intensity creep across my skin. And despite being hurt beyond all reason, there was a part me that wanted to climb out of that car, dive into his arms, and never leave.

Numb and lost, I drove around for several hours, piecing together all the clues I'd missed over the years. I didn't have my cell phone, which was probably a blessing of sorts. I couldn't decide if I'd be more pissed that they had the balls to be blowing up my phone with calls and texts or if I'd be heartbroken that they weren't.

It didn't matter; I was already pissed and heartbroken enough to last a lifetime.

When I finally pulled into my dad's driveway, he was sitting out front, waiting on me. His face was gentle, but his shoulders sagged with relief.

Nora must have called. Fucking Nora. She was such a huge part of my life that there was no escaping her, not even at my own father's house.

I shuffled barefoot up the sidewalk.

He met me halfway. "I had to rearrange all of Misty's sewing supplies, but I made the bed up in your old room. You can stay here as long as you want."

My nose stung as I peered up at him. "Did you know?"

He didn't even look sheepish when he answered, "Yeah."

Of course he knew. I was the only fool in this equation.

Jesus, my own father. Just slather on another layer of deceit, why don't ya.

"How long have you known?"

He sucked in a deep breath. "Since Nora tried to kill herself while you were in Australia."

My whole body jerked and I felt like I'd been hit by a freight train. "What?"

He tossed an arm around my shoulders and attempted to pull me in for a hug, but I was in no mood for comfort. I didn't even recognize my own life anymore.

I'd spent two months in Australia when I was twenty. It was one of the countries Ramsey and I had made plans to visit, but they didn't allow felons. So I went without him, drinking in every morsel of culture and history so that I could one day share that with him.

And while I was there, Nora tried to kill herself, and apparently no one had thought it was necessary to tell me.

Lies. All the fucking lies.

I stumbled on the edge of the sidewalk as I tried to get away from him. "What the hell is happening right now? I mean, seriously, Dad. What the fuck?"

My father watched me closely. "Nora's always looked up to you, Thea. There was a lot she never wanted you to know."

"Fuck Nora. You are *my* father." I stabbed a finger in his direction. "You are supposed to look out for *me*!"

He shoved a hand into his pocket and showed exactly zero remorse. "That's exactly what I was doing."

I laughed without humor. "My entire life has been a lie. How is that looking out for me?"

He smiled. "Because lies or not, you *lived*. You smiled and laughed. You traveled the world. You created a successful business. And you were hell-bent on taking over the whole damn world that had wronged you. Those were all the things I did *not* do when I lost your mother. My job is not to be your friend. My job is not to make sure you have all the facts of a troubled girl's life. My job is to *protect you*. So I did whatever was necessary to shield you from the pain so that you could *live*. I have no regrets, Thea. None."

I bit my bottom lip when he flashed me a smile. I wanted to scream at the top of my lungs until it disappeared from his face.

But he had a point. And I *hated* that he had a point.

The hurt and betrayal were still a wildfire raging inside me, but when he wrapped his arms around me for a hug, I didn't back away.

"You are a fierce and passionate force of nature, just like your mother. And I'm so damn proud of you for everything you have accomplished in the face of adversity. I know you're going to be angry for a while, and I'll give you that time. But whenever you're ready, I'll tell you everything you want to know." He kissed me on the top of my head. "But I'm going to need you to get in my house and do your wallowing in Misty's sewing room. She decided to make another pot roast for dinner when I told her you were coming over and I cannot face that abomination alone."

I choked on a laugh as the tears fell from my eyes. "Does she know too?"

He shook his head. "No one else knows, baby. She thinks you and Ramsey got into a fight. It might be best if you ignore the mountain of relationship books she put on the nightstand for you."

"There probably isn't a section on how to handle it when your boyfriend gets out of prison for killing a man he didn't really kill and your entire family has spent the last twelve years lying to you about it."

He chuckled. "Probably not."

The afternoon sun was still high in the sky as we stood there, father and daughter, wrapped in each other's arms. It was the house I'd run away from when my mother had died. It was where Ramsey and I had spent countless days and endless summers growing up. We'd ridden our bikes in the streets, stolen kisses when my dad wasn't looking, and formed a bond that I was positive could never be broken.

Only now I wasn't so sure.

TWENTY-FOUR

Ramsey

I SNATCHED THE PHONE OFF THE KITCHEN COUNTER, answering it on the first ring. "Hello."

"She's here," Joe said.

A blast of relief ravaged my system. "Oh, thank God."

I'd spent the hours since she'd been gone pacing, cleaning the mess the cops had left, and cursing the universe's vendetta against me. I had no right to worry about Thea. I had no right to anything anymore. But she'd been upset when she'd stormed out and nobody had been able to reach her for hours.

"How is she?" I asked like a moron. She was wrecked and I'd caused it all over again.

Guilt churned in my stomach. How was it that I so desperately wanted the best for her, yet I slayed her at every turn?

"She's...understandably hurt," Joe replied. "But she just lied to Misty about being excited for pot roast, so I think she's going to pull through. And based on that mark on her neck, I'm guessing you two were starting to pull through too before shit hit the fan today?"

Jesus. What a clusterfuck. I rubbed my eyes with my thumb and forefinger. Only hours earlier, I was the happiest I'd been in years. I was making love to her. Promising her we'd figure it out. And now I was back to suffocating in a prison of my own making.

"Shit didn't hit the fan, Joe. It hit my entire life."

"I'll give you that one, son. Listen, how's Nora? She's not answering her phone."

I looked up to where she was sitting in the corner of the couch, her legs tucked beneath her and a mug of untouched coffee in her hand while she stared off into nothingness.

"She's, um...okay. I guess."

"That child has never been okay. She puts on a good smile. Nice show. But deep down, she's never stopped struggling. I'm worried this is going to hit her hard."

God, wasn't that the truth. Nora had definitely inherited the Stewart smile. You could never tell how bad things were with her. I'd learned that the day Joe had shown up at the prison to tell me that he'd found her unconscious with a bottle of pills at her side. He'd waited six months to tell me. Six months when I'd thought she was doing great. Six months that my baby sister was in a fight for her life and I had not the first clue.

While she had been in the hospital, she'd told Joe about the night Josh died. He'd said everything had come pouring out of her like a bucket with holes in it. He'd spent months trying to decide between what was right and what was wrong without ever coming up with an answer.

I'd never forget when he'd asked me what I wanted him to do with his newfound knowledge. There had been only one possible response: Nothing.

I'd already lost Thea. She was starting to move on, and flipping her world upside down again with the truth was only going to make it worse. And freeing myself by putting my sister in prison wasn't an option I was ever going to take.

I was a man chained in the middle of two women I loved with my whole heart. There was no such thing as winning in a situation like that.

When Joe had shaken my hand that day, he'd promised me he'd take care of Nora. I thanked him profusely, tears welling in my eyes. Then he'd shocked the hell out of me by pulling me in for a back pat, muttering, "Like it or not, one day you're going to be the man taking care of my daughter. You can thank me by doing it right."

I'd tried to argue, but he was having none of it and he left that day with a proud smile on his face.

Joe had kept his end of the bargain. He'd gotten Nora help. Boatloads of it. And little by little, the girl I'd once tickled until she peed her pants emerged from behind the façade.

But after today, I wasn't sure I was going to be able to follow through on what he'd asked from me.

I'd always known the day would come where Thea would learn the truth. As much as I was an integral part of the nightmare, it was Nora's story to tell.

I just wished like hell she hadn't blurted it out though.

There was so much I wanted Thea to understand. I'd wanted to explain why I'd made the decision I had. I'd never meant to hurt her, and with hindsight being twenty-twenty, there were so many things I would have done differently if I could have gone back in time.

All of them started with her.

All of them ended with there being an us.

Given the chance, I still would have covered for Nora. I wouldn't have been able to live if I hadn't. But I would have told Thea the truth. I would have let her make her own choices. I would have let her hate me. Or love me. Or whatever the hell she wanted from me. I'd have read every single one of her letters and replied with a million words of my own.

If I had known at seventeen years old that she was going to spend a lifetime loving me, I'd have given her a lifetime of me loving her too.

As if she felt me watching her, Nora lifted her haunted gaze to mine.

I shifted the phone to my other ear. "She's right here, Joe. You want to talk to her?"

Her eyes flared wide, and she waved me off.

"Nah. I'm going to come get some of Thea's things and I'll talk to her while I'm there."

"Actually, I was thinking Nora and I should get a hotel room until we can find a new place. This is Thea's house. I don't want to run her out of her own space."

"I thought one of the terms of your parole was that you had to keep a residence."

"It is, but I can call Lee and give him a heads-up. I'm sure he'll understand after Caskey showed up here today."

He let out a sigh. "How about you just stay put for a while? Thea's upset right now, but if anything were to happen with your parole, she'd never forgive herself."

"It's pointless to stay though. She's never going to forgive me, either."

"Son, you mind if I give you a piece of advice?"

"Please," I begged. "Anything."

"My daughter loves you. There is nothing, including this, that she wouldn't forgive you for. But you have to stop yanking her around. I commend you for trying to let her go when you were kids. A lesser man would have held on to anything and everything he could from the outside, not caring that he was dragging her through the mud in the process. But you aren't kids anymore. And she didn't let go. I know you're only trying to protect her, but at this point, your indecision is what's dragging her through the mud."

Guilt shredded me. "I just want her to be happy."

"You have to figure out what *you* want. Not what Thea wants.

Or Thea needs. Or what Nora wants. Or Nora needs. You, Ramsey. Look in the mirror and decide what you want out of the rest of your life. You might be surprised by how much that answer is exactly what they both need anyway."

My chest got tight, and I closed my eyes.

What did I want?

What did *I* want?

What did I *want*?

It wasn't a hard question. The answer hadn't changed since I was eleven years old.

"I want Thea."

"Smart man. Now, take my advice. Give it a day or so to draw up your battle plan. Your odds are better when she doesn't have lasers shooting out of her eyes."

I laughed, honest-to-God real laughter, because it felt like the weight of the world was lifted off my shoulders. The amount of groveling I had to do was colossal. And if she never forgave me, I wouldn't blame her one bit. But dammit, I was going to try.

Because deep down, I knew Thea was *it* for me.

And I'd known it long before I knew what *it* truly meant.

Thea had been right. I was hers.

Now, I just had to figure out how to make her mine again.

"Hey, Joe, does she still go out to the Wynns' tree?"

"Only when she's missing you. Which, assuming she survives Misty's pot roast, I'd give it about three days max."

Squaring my shoulders, I sucked in a hard breath, holding it until my lungs burned. Okay, so I had three days to figure out how to fix twelve years' worth of lies, mistakes, and heartache. Yeah. Sure. Easy enough.

Fuck. My. Life.

TWENTY-FIVE

Thea

I LIFTED A FINGER TO MY DAD WHEN HE APPEARED IN THE doorway. The tiny twin bed in my old bedroom had become my acting office over the last three days. Post-it notes lined the walls, and folders were strewn haphazardly around my laptop.

I pinned my cell phone between my ear and shoulder while typing out a reminder. "Oh, it's no problem, Mr. Lupica. Italy is beautiful this time of year. You definitely made the right choice. I'll let the hotel know about the peanut allergy and then you should be all set."

After a round of thanks on both sides, the world's easiest client hung up the phone.

Then I looked at my dad. "Hey. You're home early."

He shoved a hand into his pocket and leaned his shoulder against the doorjamb. "After the beating you gave me in Yahtzee last night, it's a wonder I was able to get to work at all."

I grinned. "Well, I hope you learned your lesson."

"Is the lesson that you used loaded dice?"

"Possibly."

He barked a laugh, but his eyes were serious. "We need to talk, Thea. You've been hiding for long enough. Nora's been calling the house nonstop."

I looked at my laptop and absently clicked through the

million tabs I had open. "Nope. Not happening. I have nothing to say to Nora yet."

"Thea, come on. She's your sister."

I leveled him with a glare. "She's not my sister. She's Ramsey's sister and we all see where their loyalties lie."

"Is that what this is about?" He stepped into the room, shutting the door. Misty must have come home with him. No use in dragging her into this mess, though over the last few days, she had been pretty skeptical about why Nora hadn't been around.

I curled my lip. "What the hell did you think it was about?"

Shoving the folders aside, he sat at the foot of the bed. "You're upset that Ramsey chose Nora over you?"

No. That was just the emotion of the hour.

Over the last three days, I'd been on a never-ending rollercoaster.

There was confusion and hurt, anger and bitterness, guilt and frustration.

I hated Ramsey and Nora.

I missed them.

I loved them.

I blocked their numbers.

I never wanted to see them again.

I went through old pictures.

I made my father tell me every single detail about what had happened when Nora tried to kill herself.

I cussed him out for not allowing me to be a part of her healing process.

I hated them some more.

I was too exhausted to hate them anymore.

I wanted to shake Nora.

I wanted to slap Ramsey.

I cried.

And cried.

And…*cried*.

Ramsey and Nora were my people. My family. My team. Even when Ramsey wanted nothing to do with me, because of Nora, he was still a huge part of my life.

Why hadn't they trusted me? They'd made decisions that had changed my life, so I should have gotten a say.

And yes, at the moment, I was pissed to all hell and back that Ramsey had essentially chosen Nora over me.

I shut my computer and set it aside. "If he loved me as much as he told me he did, he never would have taken that plea bargain. All he had to do was tell the truth. Nora probably wouldn't even have gotten in trouble after what Josh did to her."

He rested his hand on my foot and gave it a squeeze. "Nora tried to tell the truth. His dad was the mayor. The cops didn't care about the truth. They threatened to arrest her for obstruction of justice. We'd have ended up with both of them behind bars."

"She should have tried harder. I took out a billboard to make people see what Josh did to me. She could have gone to the police station at least twice."

He crossed and then uncrossed his legs. "Okay. Let's hypothetically say she did convince them to take her seriously and she was the one who ended up in prison. Do you really think Ramsey could have just gone on about his life, traveling the world, having a grand old time while his sister sat in prison?"

I clamped my mouth shut. No, Ramsey wouldn't have been able to do that at all. Stupid, loyal Stewarts.

"Exactly. He would have been a mess, and I'll be honest, I don't think you two would have been able to make it through that."

"You don't know that," I hissed. "And thanks to her, we never even got the chance to try."

"She was a kid, Thea. A troubled, terrified, naïve kid. Just like Ramsey. And just like you. I'm not saying it's okay. But this is what happens when dumb kids make grown-people decisions. I struggled like hell when I found out what happened. I was torn in half by my heart and my conscience. That poor kid sitting in a cell for something he didn't even do." He shook his head when emotion clogged his throat. "It was why I went to see Ramsey in prison. I needed to understand. And you want to know what he told me?"

I didn't want to care, but I was desperate to make sense of this mess. "What?"

"He told me he didn't know how else to fix it. Like any of this was ever his to fix. I swear that boy's heart is bigger than his brain, but that's not the worst quality a man could have." He blew out a ragged breath. "He didn't choose Nora over you, Thea. He chose the person he loved who needed him the most at the time. Trust me, Ramsey would have rather spent the last twelve years with you instead of showering with a bunch of naked men."

A laugh escaped my throat, but tears filled my eyes. "Why is everything so hard, Dad?"

His face got soft. "Now that I can't answer. But hard doesn't equal impossible, baby. You have to decide what you're willing to weather and what you're willing to quit."

Quit. That wasn't a random word choice. It was proof that my father knew me all too well.

The one thing I had never even considered quitting in my life was Ramsey Stewart.

"I need to think. Even if I do decide to weather this storm with him, there's no guarantee that he will too. He was already pushing me away again when Nora told me the truth."

He shrugged and shot me a knowing smile. "You would be amazed at what a clear conscience will do to a man."

I narrowed my eyes. "What do you know that I don't? And don't lie to me, old man. I know where you sleep."

His grin stretched as he lifted his hands in surrender. "I don't know anything. Though…have you been out to the Wynns' tree recently?"

Hope hit my veins like a drug and I scrambled from the bed, knocking over half a day's work in the process. I had no clue what I was even hoping for. It was just such a novelty for me to feel hopeful about anything anymore.

He sauntered toward the door, pausing before he walked out. "I'm sorry I checked out on you for so many years after your mother died. But thank you for allowing me back in and giving me the most incredible years of my life since."

My throat closed as I looked at him. God, time had changed us all so much.

And that's when it hit me.

That was what I was hoping for.

That maybe my archnemesis time would change us all again—for the better.

To steal the quote right out of Nora's mouth, there had to be something good that would come from all of this pain. There just had to be.

Maybe it would be that Nora could finally be free of all the guilt and pain.

Maybe I could let go of the past, forgiving and moving on, so it didn't follow us into the future.

Maybe Ramsey would see that he was worthy and allow himself to be happy—preferably with me.

Maybe time could release us all from our prisons.

That was the only good that we ever needed.

With renewed hope, the side of my mouth hiked. "Is that your final goodbye, Dad? You're worried I'm never going to speak to you again after I see what's at that tree, huh?"

He laughed and shook his head. "Go on. Get out of here."

He didn't have to tell me twice.

I felt like a kid again as I cut between houses and jumped over the big ditch. The path had grown over without Ramsey's and my constant traffic, but I had no problem finding my way.

The tall grass of the uncut hayfield rustled in the warm Georgia air. Time had even changed our old tree too. It was now the proud owner of a wooden rope swing.

Two years after Ramsey had gone to prison, I'd knocked on the Wynns' door in order to ask them if I could bury Sir Hairy Barkington under our tree. I was in a fit of hysterics after losing that dog to old age. I'd babbled my story with Ramsey and their tree from start to finish as fast as I could talk between the sobs. Honestly, I was shocked Lacey understood me. She hugged me no fewer than seven thousand times, and Mason broke out a shovel and dug Hairy's final resting place for me. Lacey told me I was welcome to come back any time I'd like. The very next day, that swing magically appeared along with a little wooden cross in the shape of two dog bones.

I'd gotten plenty of use out of that swing over the years. It was my escape when I needed to feel close to Ramsey.

It was where we'd met.

Where we'd fallen in love.

Where we'd spent the happiest days of our lives—and one truly unfortunate night.

Now, I hoped against hope that it was where we'd find our way back to each other.

Disappointment struck me when I reached the tree and found nothing but a dark-blue three-ring binder at the foot. I had no idea what I'd been planning to say to him, but it would have been nice to see him there again—waiting on me like he'd done so many times when we were younger.

I picked up the binder, smiling when I read the simple black sharpie strokes on the front: *Things Thea Wants.*

And then I gasped, feeling like time had started all over again.

There had to have been at least a hundred plastic page protectors inside that binder, and each one was filled with papers covered in my handwriting.

My letters.

Oh, God, he'd kept them.

I scanned the first one, tracing my fingers over the words. The rush of emotions I'd felt that day hitting me all over again. I'd mailed it as soon as Nora had gotten his address. It was only about three days before I'd received his one and only letter.

Between those lines, I was still so naïve and optimistic.

My gaze jumped down the page to a section that had been highlighted in yellow—and not by me.

I just want to leave, Ramsey. I'll buy a car and we can go, get the hell out of Clovert and never look back. Maybe by Christmas you'll be home and we can go to the mountains.

I turned the page and laughed as I skimmed over a dozen cuss words to the highlighted section.

We are not breaking up, you idiot. I love you and I still want you, so shut your stupid face.

Sinking into the swing, I settled the binder in my lap and continued to flip through the pages, each one inciting a different landslide of emotions. And surprisingly enough, not all of them were sad. There were stories about Nora's and my shenanigans and normal everyday stuff about trying heels and the big stuff like when I bought my first car.

There were jokes.

There was longing.

There was love.

Some of the letters I remembered like I'd written them only yesterday. Others, I had no recollection of at all. But each one had a highlighted line describing something I'd wanted.

I want you to come home.

I want you back.

Who the hell wants celery in their chicken soup? Not me!

I want you to know that I should hate you for everything you're doing to us. But I can't.

You should have seen Nora's face when I brought home that ceramic rooster. She might never speak to me again, but I wanted that damn thing more than anything in the world…except maybe you.

How long can you want somebody before you have to let go? It's been ten years and I still can't figure it out.

Page after page.

Want after want.

He'd highlighted them all.

My heart sank when I got to the letter I'd written the day Nora had told me he'd be coming home. Twelve long years and in my last letter, I was still begging him to let me back in.

I want us to be a family again, Ramsey. Please.

Tears dripped from my chin as I turned to the last page. This one was in *his* handwriting, and it hit so deep, stealing the air from my lungs, I wasn't sure I'd ever breathe again.

Things Ramsey wants.

And in big bold letters, with nothing else on the page, it read:

To be with Thea.

I slapped a hand over my mouth and read it over and over again.

To be with Thea.
To be with Thea.
To be with—

"Right after my twelfth birthday, you told me that we were best friends, and even if had a third nipple, I was required by best friend law to tell you about it."

Dropping the binder to the ground, I jumped at least ten feet in the air. Okay, slight exaggeration, but he'd scared the hell out of me.

"Dammit, Ramsey!" I yelled, craning my head back and finding him sitting on his usual branch in our tree.

And then all the fear and anger vanished when I realized *Ramsey* was sitting on his *usual* branch in *our* tree.

For some, it would have been a creepy man spying on an innocent woman. And yeah, it was kind of still that to me too. But mainly, it was too many years of dreams coming true. In clean sneakers and a fitted T-shirt that hugged his toned biceps, he was a far cry from the shaggy-haired boy I'd once known. But his eyes—those brown eyes that owned my soul—were exactly the same.

"I fucked up, Sparrow. I may not have broken the real law, but I committed some pretty heinous best friend crimes."

I sniffled. "Best friend law is the real law."

"I'm learning this. Oh, shit!" he exclaimed as the branch he was holding on to suddenly cracked.

"Jesus, Ramsey, be careful."

He blew out a hard breath. "Do you have any idea how hard it was to get up here? I'm old, Thea. I have no clue how I used to scale this thing every day. I've died almost eight times waiting on you to get here."

I shook my head and lifted the binder up in his direction. "You told me you didn't read these?"

He half shrugged. "I didn't."

"But you kept them?"

"As many as I was allowed. It was like a safety net for me, knowing they were there. I used to hold them a lot, flipping them between my fingers. It was crazy. Between the post office and the prison mail system, there were probably a dozen people who had handled those letters after you. But to me, the only thing that mattered was you'd touched them first. Having them was as much torture as it was reassurance. I never allowed myself to open them or read them." He smiled. "Until this week. I figured if I was ever going to get you back, I needed to get to know you a little better."

My stomach dipped. "You're trying to get me back?"

"Well, first, I tried to build that time machine, but that didn't work." His smile stretched, and his eyes twinkled. "Yeah, I'm trying to get you back."

God, how I'd waited to hear those words from him. Though they weren't exactly accurate.

"You can't get me back."

His smile fell. "Thea, please."

"I never really went anywhere."

His shoulders curled forward with defeat, and he hooked his arm around the tree for balance when the wind picked up. "I'm not sure that makes me feel better or worse."

"Worse. It should definitely make you feel worse. But it is what it is. You really messed up, Ramsey. You broke my heart every day for twelve years."

"I know. I know. But I swear to God I thought I was doing the right thing. All I've ever wanted was for you to be happy. And as I sat in jail in a set of cuffs and shackles, waiting to be transported to the prison, I knew the only thing I'd ever be able to give you was misery. I was terrified you were going to waste your life waiting for me. And guess what? I was right."

I shook my head. My father had been so right about him having more heart than brains. "You were wrong, Ramsey. Yes, I waited on you. But I didn't waste a single minute. I started my business so that we could afford the life we'd always dreamed of. I traveled to countries you'd never be able to visit. I built a relationship with my father again. I found a sister, who I am currently not speaking to and possibly won't for the next twelve years—or at the very least, twelve days. But we had some really great years. I discovered that I like going to the movies alone because I don't have to share the popcorn. I realize that I don't have to feel uncomfortable in heels and skirts. I made friends with women I used to make fun of. And yes, you are right—through it all, I was in love with a stupid, stupid boy. But I did not *waste* my life while I was doing it."

"Thea," he breathed, the apology crinkling his forehead.

I used the binder to shield the sun from my eyes and stared up at him. "Are we going to do this, Ramsey? I mean, really fucking do this? No more of your panic attacks where you tell me I deserve better or that you can't do this? I mean, life starts today, right now. I've spent twelve years choosing you. But dammit, this time, you have to choose me."

He shoved out of that tree so fast I didn't have the chance to move out of the way. Just like the day we'd met, he landed hard and bounced toward me.

Thankfully, when he crashed into me, he spun us so he hit the ground first, leaving my leg blissfully intact.

"I'm sorry. I'm so sorry. I choose you. I choose you, Thea. I choose us. I promise. I have absolutely nothing to offer you but headaches and stress, but if you keep me, I swear I'll spend the rest of my life providing you with love and Tylenol."

I smiled, his warmth blanketing me in a cocoon of security, the rest of the world fading away. Brushing his perfectly styled hair off his forehead, I mumbled, "Jeez, look who's desperate now."

He barked a laugh, but it did nothing to dissipate his panic. "Me. I am absolutely the desperate one. When I read through those letters, I felt so lost, remembering how amazing we were together. I want our life back too."

Lifting my head, I brushed my lips across his. "Sometimes you have to let go of the life you planned in order to live the one you're given. Things are going to be different, Ramsey. But different doesn't have to be bad. We have a lot of stuff to work out. A lot of hurt to work through. But if you're willing to take it slow and be patient while we do it together, I'm never going to tell you no."

He dipped and pressed his closed mouth to mine as he inhaled reverently. "I'll do whatever it takes, Sparrow."

"Then you should probably start by giving me a proper kiss, because when I get up from here, I'm going to yell at you a lot for almost breaking my leg again. Then I'm going to yell at you a lot for going to prison. And then I'm going to yell at you a lot for lying to me. But then, after I'm all yelled out, I might let you see my boobs again."

A Ramsey Stewart special appeared and it felt like he was fanning the fire in my soul that had only ever burned for him.

And then Ramsey kissed me, deep and frantic like a boy.

Gentle and skilled like a man.

All-consuming and claiming like my forever.

And he did it all tasting like watermelon gum.

TWENTY-SIX

Ramsey

AFTER THEA AND I LEFT OUR TREE THAT AFTERNOON, WE got a hotel and spent the rest of the night lying in the bed, talking, laughing, and making love like we were carefree kids on vacation from the real world. When our bodies were sated and our cheeks ached, the rising sun brought a whole new set of problems: the future.

That saying about the truth setting you free was bullshit. The truth was nothing more than a needle you could use to slowly chip away at the concrete walls of betrayal. It was going to take time for our hearts to stop hurting, the what-ifs to fade into what was, and the gaping wounds of regret to scab over.

But with Thea at my side, we made plans to do it together.

The first step in our future was getting the hell out of that town.

"I can't stay there, Lee. I'll end up going back. I know I will."

He rocked back in his chair and steepled his fingers under his chin. "Caskey's a good officer. He allowed his emotions to get the best of him when he showed up at your house. His captain has assured me—"

"And I'm assuring you his captain can't do shit to stop him. I'm not saying he's a bad cop. But he is a pissed off *officer of the law* who has the man who killed his brother working in his jurisdiction and living only minutes outside of it. That is not a safe environment—for either of us. Trust me, I've done a lot of shit to protect my family. I do not doubt that he will do the same to reap revenge." I leaned forward, resting my palms on the front of his desk. "I'm begging you. Let me take Thea and move to Savannah or Duluth. Or…anywhere that I'll get a fair shake at things. The sixty-mile radius the parole board has me on is not far enough away for me to have a fresh start."

His forehead crinkled with contemplation. He knew I was right. But I could only imagine the paperwork involved in getting me transferred, especially given that the request was made because of an upstanding cop.

"You can't leave Georgia."

"I understand that. But the state is two hundred and ninety-eight miles long and two hundred and thirty miles wide. That's a lot of space I could put between us."

"Okay. Let's say for a minute that I agree with you. You going to be able to find a steady residence, work, transportation?"

"Yeah." I cut my gaze over his shoulder and ground my teeth. I hated this part the most.

Well, that wasn't totally true. I hated the spending-almost-half-my-life-in-a-cell part the most. But the idea of Thea having to take care of me for the next few years came in a close second. However, if that was what it would take to get us out of Clovert and Thomaston, and away from the Caskeys, ending this entire fucking nightmare once and for all, then I was going to suck it up. For a while.

"I got a girl."

He rolled his eyes. "Everybody's got a girl, Stewart. Until your eye starts wandering, she kicks you out, you get fired, and have no place to go. Few nights and you get picked up by the local PD. Then this little transfer request I'm making on your behalf comes back and bites *me* in the ass. *Hard.*"

"My eye hasn't wandered in eighteen years. Thea's it for me. As soon as I can save up enough for a ring, I'm going to ask her to marry me. Start a life together. Maybe later, give her some babies. Give them all the things we didn't have growing up. That's the dream, right? Giving your wife and kids better than you had?"

His eyebrows shot up. "Marriage and babies isn't going to fix your problems. You been locked up for a long time. You sure you want to tie yourself down so soon?"

My lips hitched as I imagined my Sparrow's brown hair flowing in the breeze. "Yeah. That's exactly what I want. Since I was eleven years old and saw her running across a hayfield. Being tied down to her was my only dream. I spent every day while I was in prison trying to make her run the opposite direction, but not my girl. She's never stopped sprinting toward me. It's time for her to take a breather. I got a lot of time to make up for, but I can't do that staying here in town, where I'm constantly looking over my shoulder."

I inched to the edge of my seat, just short of dropping to my knees. "Look, I was a model inmate, never written up for behavior once. I don't drink or do drugs. My idea of a wild and crazy night is letting Thea pick the movie. I have plans. A woman. A sister. A life waiting for me. I don't want to go back. But I'm terrified if I stay here I'm going to lose everything all over again. I just need a transfer. Hell, you can even pick the place."

He stared at me for a long second. "And what about work? You've been working for her dad. It's not going to be as easy to find a job without connections."

"Thea owns a company and can work from anywhere. She'll put me to work. And let me tell you, Lee, she is pissed as all hell at me right now, so it's going to be serious shit-work for quite a while."

He barked a laugh. "You want me to sign this transfer, I'd keep your relationship problems to yourself."

"Oh, there's no problem. She'll enjoy watching me suffer. I'll enjoy that she'll enjoy it. And then late at night, when she crawls into my bed feeling a little guilty and a lot sweet, I'll enjoy it in different ways. But only if I can—"

He waved me off. "Get out of here."

"Exactly."

He clicked on the mouse of his computer, illuminating the screen. "No. I mean. Get out of my office. I've heard you, and I need to get some work done today that doesn't entail listening to you vomiting hearts and flowers."

My stomach sank, not knowing if he was going to look into my request or not. "Lee, I—"

"Out," he rumbled, staring at his computer screen.

Resigned for fear of pissing him off, I rose from my chair and started toward the door. He did, after all, have my future in the palm of his hand.

No sooner than I reached for the doorknob, he called, "When you were assigned to me, I went through your file. I saw the pictures of what he did to her."

I turned to look at him. "I see them every time I blink."

His face got soft. "I got four daughters, Ramsey. One of 'em came home looking like that…" He trailed off, shaking his head. "I got a buddy in Dahlonega. Nice little mountain town. You and Thea will have all the privacy you need to get to know each other again."

Relief tore from my lungs, stripping the emotion from my throat on the way out. I looked like a pussy, but I had not one fuck to give as I choked out, "Really?"

He nodded. "Give me a few days to get all the paperwork filed. I'll sign off on a travel pass so you two can start hunting for a house, but check back with me before putting down a deposit, okay?"

I nodded at least a dozen times, the constant pressure in my chest slowly deflating. "Thank you. Thank you so much."

He jerked his chin to the door. "Lead a good life. Be kind to people. Help your girl heal. Forgive yourself. Stay out of trouble. Make the world a better place. And raise those kids to be better people than any of us. That's how you thank me."

"I can do that," I rasped.

He didn't say anything else, and after a minute, I'd finally collected myself enough to walk out to Thea, who was waiting in the 4Runner.

"What'd he say?" she rushed out when I opened the door.

I slid into my seat, shut my door, and caught her at the back of her neck. Hauling her in, I pressed a hard kiss to her already tender lips.

"This is not an answer," she mumbled against my mouth.

Chuckling, I released her. "Dahlonega."

Her lips curled into a breathtaking smile. "That's like four hours away."

"We can get a little cabin in the mountains. Disappear for a few years until I finish my parole. Hopefully, if we really stick to a budget, I'll be able to save up enough money so we can travel when I'm done. It won't be Paris, but I should be able to afford Ohio."

"I have money," she whispered. "I have so much money, Ramsey."

I laughed and tugged on my seat belt. "So you've mentioned. But it's important to me that I can at least contribute to our lives together. It's not going to be nearly as much as you, Little Miss Money Bags, but I can try."

She kept grinning at me as she started the engine. "It's you and me. It's always *been* you and me. And it will always *be* you and me. Let's make a deal. This lifetime is on me. You can take the next."

Muscles I hadn't known I possessed sagged for the first time in over twelve years.

She wasn't wrong.

This lifetime.

The next.

And in all the ones that followed, Althea Floye Hull—soon-to-be Stewart, though she didn't know it yet—would always be mine.

Before she put the car into reverse, I leaned in for another kiss. I took this one deeper, opening my mouth and indecently dueling with her tongue in the middle of the parking lot.

I kissed her with a passion that burned in my soul.

I kissed her with apologies I'd never stop issuing.

But most of all, I kissed her with the promise of a future.

We'd eventually fight about the money.

We'd fight about Nora.

We'd fight about the lies.

Bitterness and guilt would rear their ugly heads more often than I ever would have imagined.

But through it all, we would be together. A team.

The way it was always supposed to be.

When she pulled away, I was breathless and smiling inside and out. Hope surged through my veins like the most potent drug I would ever need.

"Really?" She glared at me.

"What?"

She shot me an incredulous grin, revealing my secret gum trapped between her teeth.

"Hey! Give me that back, you little thief." I plucked it from her mouth and popped it right back into mine, tucking it under my tongue for safe keeping.

Her glare turned into a scowl. "It's strawberry."

"Yeah? So?"

"What happened to watermelon?"

I waved a hand out in a grand gesture. "I'm broadening my horizons. Trying new things. Experiencing life."

"Ah. That explains the porn."

"Oh my God! You did not just bring that up again. It was one time, Thea. One time. Let it go."

She started laughing. "Yeah, right. I'm not letting go of that kind of gold anytime soon."

Right. I'd be two hundred and seventy-five years old and she'd roll over in the grave to make fun of me for it.

And because it was her...

I'd love every damn second of it.

EPILOGUE

Thea

Six years later...

ALL NINE OF THE PEOPLE WHO HAD BEEN ON THE PUDDLE-jumper plane from Atlanta to Clovert milled around us as the drone of an unanswered phone played in my ear. I huffed and hit the end button only to call again.

"It's okay, babe," Ramsey rumbled. "I'm sure he just got stuck in traffic or something."

"Do you understand that Joe Hull does not do late? Like ever. Never ever."

His lips twitched as he threw his arm around my shoulders. "I know. It's always boggled my mind how he produced someone who is as habitually late as you are."

I craned my head back and glared at him.

His only response was to blind me with the Ramsey Stewart special.

After we'd sold the house in Thomaston and moved to the mountains of Dahlonega, my life with Ramsey slowed down. Just as we'd planned, we got a secluded cabin and spent our days cursing the shitty internet while trying to work and our nights cuddled around the fireplace, getting to know each other again. It was the craziest thing, considering we were teens the last time we'd spent any significant amount of time together, but within a matter of days, everything fell back into place—kinda.

It was like the bare bones of our relationship was still there—strong as ever—but our emotions were all over the place.

We'd bicker and relentlessly pick on each other.

But he'd watch me from across the room, his brows drawn and storms brewing in his eyes as if he were waiting for me to disappear.

He hated sitting around the house all the time, but he'd get overwhelmed when we spent too much time exploring our new town.

He was the first one in bed each night, naked with a sci-fi book cradled in his hand. But as he fell asleep, he'd toss and turn while becoming reacquainted with sleeping on a soft mattress. Much like everything in our lives, it was a process. One he seemed to finally master when he learned the fine art of sliding into me from behind when he'd wake up anxious in the middle of the night.

For those first few months, having him back was so surreal. And beautiful. And perfect. And everything I'd dreamed of. But most of all, it was terrifying, because as the days passed, I was more and more convinced I was going to lose him again.

This meant, when we'd bicker and relentlessly pick on each other, I'd laugh until I'd burst into gut-wrenching sobs. He'd hold me and kiss me and reassure me, but the fear never truly left.

Then it was me chewing on my nails and watching him playing solitaire on the coffee table as if *he* were going to vanish with my next blink.

And at night, when I'd wake up with nightmares that he was gone again, he'd wrap me in his arms, whispering how much he loved me and vowing that he'd never leave. This was how I learned the fine art of climbing on top of him and riding him hard and steady until my sated mind allowed me to rest.

Nine months, one week, and four days after Ramsey had come home, we got into a huge argument over absolutely nothing. What can I say? The man had no clue how to load the dishwasher, turn the damn lights off, or transfer clothes into the dryer. As most arguments do, it spiraled and zigzagged through petty annoyances that had nothing to do with the reason the fight had started. Shortly after he'd shouted at me that I always parked crooked in the driveway, I slammed the bedroom door and went to bed that night alone.

The smell of bacon and coffee as I exited my room the next morning melted any lingering frustration. And then the sight of Ramsey Stewart on one knee in the middle of our small kitchen, holding a diamond ring, melted me completely.

"It's over," he whispered. "We still have a long way to go, but I feel like the past might really be behind us. Last night, we argued. You slept in the bed. I slept on the couch. Neither of us disappeared. I didn't freak out. As far as I know, you didn't, either. I didn't go back to prison. The world didn't end. We were just two normal people fucked up and madly in love, arguing over meaningless bullshit. I want that forever, Sparrow."

I slapped a hand over my mouth. It wasn't at all the grand proposal women dreamed about, yet it was more romantic than anything I'd ever heard.

But Ramsey, being Ramsey, couldn't leave it at that. "Your hair looks like a family of birds took up residence in it overnight and you're not even wearing a tank top that shows your nipples, but I have never and will never in my entire life want to marry someone more."

My heart was so full I didn't even give him shit before diving into his arms and smothering him with kisses. Eventually, I said yes, and then we made love on the floor in our kitchen until the bacon burned and set off the smoke alarms. As we ran around the kitchen in various degrees of undress, laughing and opening the windows to air out the house, I realized just how right he was.

From the outside, no one would have guessed the heartbreak and drama that had tainted our lives. And for once, we didn't feel the all-consuming repercussions of it, either.

And that was when I finally forgave Nora.

I would love to say that, when things had worked out with me and Ramsey, I'd been able to immediately mend my relationship with her. It would be a lie though. I struggled for months trying to figure out why the betrayal burned so much hotter with her.

But that day, with a diamond on my finger, while I watched my future husband run around in a cloud of bacon smoke as a symphony of smoke detectors screamed all around us, I realized I loved my life.

And with that kind of freedom, the *coulda, shoulda, woulda* game didn't matter anymore.

It was hard to be bitter and angry when you had everything you ever wanted. And dammit, I wanted Nora to be a part of that. We did a lot of crying that first night on the phone. She apologized for not telling me the truth. I apologized for not being there when she'd needed someone. And Ramsey nervously paced, waiting to pick up the pieces.

She drove up the next day and spent the weekend with us. We did a lot of crying then too. Explaining, talking things through with and without Ramsey, and eventually burying it all in the past where it belonged.

RELEASE

Two weeks later, Ramsey got permission from his parole officer to drive back to Clovert. We'd sworn we wouldn't go back until his parole had ended, but when it came to having a wedding, there was only one place we wanted to be.

With only my father at my side and Nora at Ramsey's, we vowed forever in an intimate ceremony under our old tree. I wore a beautiful white dress and hired a photographer to document the occasion. But nothing made me happier than when we returned to the safety and security of our home the very next day.

We lived the next two years of our lives like most newlyweds. We made love. We watched movies and grilled out. We argued over more stupid crap. But unlike other couples, we woke up every morning marking off days on a calendar that counted down until our lives could truly begin again.

The day Ramsey was released from parole, it felt like we'd both been freed. We spent weeks moving all of our belongings into a storage unit so we could drive straight to the airport and buy two tickets on the next flight to Las Vegas as soon as we got the final paperwork. From there, we went to California and Arizona before hopping across the ocean to spend a week in Hawaii.

That was where Ramsey got his first tattoo. He'd been talking about it for years. I had to admit, being as fond as I was of his naked body, I was hesitant at first. But after the way his face lit when he showed me sketches of his ideas, there was no way I ever would have argued.

He'd chosen an Old Norse Valkyrie with her wings spread wide to cover the majority of his back. Her right side was young and angelic. There was no mistaking the playful tip of Nora's lips or the willowy shape of her body, but it was the left side of that tattoo that stole my breath. She was covered in armor with

271

a sword at her side. Her flowing, brown hair was mine. Her eyes too. And a sparrow sat proudly upon her shoulder.

There had been so many times when he'd been in prison that I'd questioned who I was. I felt weak and stupid for faithfully waiting on a man who had pushed me away. And sometimes, as I grew older, I questioned who I was as a woman for ravenously holding on to the dreams of a sixteen-year-old girl. But as I lay awake one night, tracing my fingers over the dark lines of that Valkyrie's armor, bits and pieces of me healed from knowing that, in his eyes, I'd always been a warrior.

After that, I'd learned to love his tattoos. They felt like sneak peeks into how he viewed the world. This was probably for the best, because hunting down tattoo shops everywhere we traveled had become something of an obsession for Ramsey.

It worked out. My obsession was watching him smile.

"Where could he be?" I whined as I hung up the phone, still no sign of my dad. "Misty said he and Nora left a half hour ago. It's only a twelve-minute drive to the airport from their house."

"Relax. They probably stopped for gas or to grab some coffee. He's eighteen minutes late. That's hardly reason to send out the bloodhounds." He curled me into his side and pressed a kiss to the top of my head.

All concern for my father's safety was momentarily forgotten as the wind shifted and I got slapped in the face with a stench that would haunt my dreams forever.

"Oh, God, not again," I groaned.

"What?"

I leaned forward, sniffing the butt of the baby strapped to his chest—because seriously, mom life was *glamorous*.

"Your son," was all I had to say.

"Shit," he breathed, speaking both figurative and literally.

RELEASE

The morning sun was peeking over the Georgia horizon, but my lids were heavy. It had been a long night, I felt like crap, and my patience was waning. Ramsey and I were skilled travelers. Together, we'd faced it all. Overnight flights squished in the middle seat rows apart. Exhausting layovers in miniscule airports without so much as a coffee shop. Delays. Cancellations. Spending hours on a runway just to be taken back to the gate.

But nothing, and I mean nothing, had prepared me for a flight from Seattle to Georgia with a seven-month-old.

We'd thought the red-eye would be best.

We'd thought he would sleep the whole way if we left in the middle of the night.

We'd *thought* leaving our house with four suitcases, a carseat, a travel crib, and a giant carry-on bag filled to the brim with diapers and formula was a solid plan.

We'd. Been. *Wrong.*

Apparently, Joseph James Stewart had a nervous travel tummy—or his father's sense of humor. One of the two.

The day I'd found out I was pregnant, Ramsey and I had been hiking the trails around Mount Rainier. One second, we'd been debating where we'd find the best view. The next, I was puking in the bushes.

We hadn't exactly been *trying* to get pregnant, but I'd forgotten to get my birth control prescription filled. We were nomads of sorts, so everyday tasks occasionally slipped my mind. Ramsey had known we weren't covered that month, and I'd reminded him repeatedly when he spent an entire rainy weekend in London between my legs. We were at a point in our marriage where we loved our lives touring the world, but secretly, we were both ready to settle down.

When I was done fertilizing the bushes that day, I found

Ramsey sitting on a rock, scrolling through his phone. He smiled at me, love and excitement blazing in his eyes, and said, "So I found a place we can rent in Spokane until we figure out where we want to live permanently. It doesn't have a room for a nursery, so we'll have to decide before he's born."

I sat on his lap and rested my head on his shoulder. "What makes you think it's a boy?"

He placed his hand on my stomach. "God knows I'd end up in prison again if He gave me a daughter."

I giggled, covering his hand with my own. "You know I might just have a stomach bug. I haven't taken a test or anything."

"Nah, he's in there, Sparrow. I can feel it. Life's about to change again."

"That's a good thing though, right?"

His eyes sparkled as he peered up at me. "He's a part of you and a part of me. It doesn't get any better than that."

Nine months later, our son was born looking just like his father—smile and all.

We never left Washington, though we did buy a house on ten acres. There had to have been a thousand trees on our heavily wooded property. But within two days of moving in, Ramsey had picked a favorite and dubbed it *ours*.

It wasn't the same. It didn't hold over twenty years of memories—good, bad, and ugly. But with Ramsey at my side, we made new memories—good, great, and amazing.

A red SUV pulled up in the passenger pickup lane just as I started to search through my bag for yet another diaper.

Nora rolled the window down and called, "Jeez, about time y'all showed up!"

Ramsey narrowed his eyes, but his scowl was watered down by a massive smile.

My father scrambled out of the passenger seat. "Sorry we're late, buttercup. They closed Wombly Road, so we had to take Juniper, but there was some kind of Christmas parade going on."

"Why weren't you answering the phone? You scared me to death."

He released me. "I left it at home, but I hope this gives you a little insight to how I feel when you don't pick up my calls during naptime."

I rolled my eyes, but he ignored me to pluck Joey out of the carrier on Ramsey's chest. "How's my big man doing?" he cooed.

Ramsey curled Nora into his side and teased, "I'm good, Joe. Thanks for asking."

"Oh my lord, what is that smell!" Dad exclaimed, holding my son out in front of him.

Nora swooped in and took Joey. "Don't be such a wimp. It's probably just a—dear God. What are you feeding this monster?"

I laughed and gave her a hug before taking the baby. "You guys load up the car. Ramsey, install the carseat. I'll use the back seat to change—" I abruptly stopped when a sparkle on Nora's finger caught my eye. Balancing Joey on my hip, I grabbed her wrist and yanked it toward me. "What the hell is that?"

She snatched it away. "You aren't supposed to see that yet."

My mouth fell open as Ramsey barged into the huddle to grab her hand too.

"He proposed?" he rumbled at his sister.

She plugged her ears like a very mature thirty-two-year-old woman and hummed, "La, la, la, la, la! I'm not talking about this yet."

All eyes turned to my dad, but he was busy staring at his shoes.

Of course he knew—he was the keeper of all secrets.

"You knew about this and didn't tell me?" I accused.

His head popped up and he shoved his hands into his pockets. "Yeah. And Thea's pregnant too. There. We're all even. Now, can we all get the hell out of here? Misty is alone with a cookbook. This isn't going to turn out well for any of us."

I swung my accusation to Ramsey. "You told him?"

My husband, who was still wearing an empty baby carrier, tipped his head back and stared up at the sky. "Come on, Joe. I told you that in confidence."

"Holy shit," Nora laughed. "You're pregnant again? Already?" She punched Ramsey on the shoulder. "Good work."

He shot her a sneaky grin and mouthed, "It's a boy."

"Seriously, Ramsey?" I scolded, but it only made him laugh.

Everyone broke out into congratulations, swapping hugs, admiring Nora's ring, and rubbing my belly. It didn't matter that Nora was parked illegally and we were standing on the sidewalk outside the airport.

We were all just so genuinely happy.

And when you lived a life like ours, you learned to embrace the good times whenever and wherever you found them.

Thrilled at the news of another grandson, my dad took Joey from me again, laughing and dancing him around, stinky diaper and all.

Ramsey sidled up beside me, grinning like the boy I'd fallen in love with. Dipping low, he put his lips to my ear and whispered, "I love you, Sparrow."

Twenty-four years, three months, one week, five days, eighteen hours, eleven minutes, and counting… "I love you too, Ramsey."

THE END

OTHER BOOKS

THE REGRET DUET

Written with Regret

Written with You

THE WRECKED AND RUINED SERIES

Changing Course

Stolen Course

Broken Course

Among the Echoes

ON THE ROPES

Fighting Silence

Fighting Shadows

Fighting Solutude

ABOUT THE AUTHOR

Originally from Savannah, Georgia, *USA Today* bestselling author Aly Martinez now lives in South Carolina with her husband and four young children.

Never one to take herself too seriously, she enjoys cheap wine, mystery leggings, and baked feta. It should be known, however, that she hates pizza and ice cream, almost as much as writing her bio in the third person.

She passes what little free time she has reading anything and everything she can get her hands on, preferably with a super-sized tumbler of wine by her side.

Facebook: www.facebook.com/AuthorAlyMartinez

Facebook Group: www.facebook.com/groups/TheWinery

Twitter: twitter.com/AlyMartinezAuth

Goodreads: www.goodreads.com/AlyMartinez

www.alymartinez.com